THE
BUCKSKIN
TRAIL

PRAISE FOR *THE BUCKSKIN TRAIL*

"I have been a fan of JoAnn Arnold for several years now. The locales and events in her stories are diverse and exciting. She has such a talent for bringing her characters to life. *The Buckskin Trail* is no exception. I found myself completely immersed in Kelzi's story. . . . These characters will hold your heart until long after the last page is turned."

— BARBARA BLUEMEL, editor

"In the tradition of Tony Hillerman or Louis L'Amour, JoAnn Arnold has created her own unique murder mystery, *The Buckskin Trail*. . . . The emergence of Kelzi from a seemingly insignificant girl into a beautiful, scholarly crime solver makes *The Buckskin Trail* an exciting read."

— LYMAN DAYTON, producer of *Where the Red Fern Grows*, *Against the Crooked Sky*, and *Seven Alone*

JOANN ARNOLD

THE
BUCKSKIN
TRAIL

SWEETWATER
BOOKS
AN IMPRINT OF CEDAR FORT, INC.
SPRINGVILLE, UTAH

ISBN 13: 978-1-4621-1822-9

Published by Sweetwater Books, an imprint of Cedar Fort, Inc.
2373 W. 700 S., Springville, UT 84663
Distributed by Cedar Fort, Inc. www.cedarfort.com

LIBRARY OF CONGRESS CATALOGING-IN-PUBLICATION DATA

Names: Arnold, JoAnn, author.
Title: The buckskin trail / JoAnn Arnold.
Description: Springville, Utah : Sweetwater Books, An Imprint of Cedar Fort,
Inc., [2016] | ©2016
Identifiers: LCCN 2015045655 (print) | LCCN 2015048373 (ebook) | ISBN
9781462118229 (perfect bound : alk. paper) | ISBN 9781462118229 ()
Subjects: LCSH: Cherokee Indians--Fiction. | LCGFT: Detective and mystery
fiction. | Thrillers (Fiction)
Classification: LCC PS3601.R585 B83 2016 (print) | LCC PS3601.R585 (ebook) |
DDC 813/.6--dc23
LC record available at http://lccn.loc.gov/2015045655

Cover design by Rebecca J. Greenwood
Cover design © 2016 Cedar Fort, Inc.
Edited and typeset by Melissa J. Caldwell

Printed in the United States of America

10 9 8 7 6 5 4 3 2 1

Printed on acid-free paper

I would like to especially thank my husband, Brent, for his dedication in helping me bring this book to life.

I also want to thank Lyman Dayton, Barbara Bluemel, and Georgia Carpenter for their willingness to read and share their ideas.

Also by JoAnn Arnold

Miracles for Michael
Journey of the Promise
Pages from the Past
The Silent Patriot
Prince Etcheon and the Secret of the Ancient

CONTENTS

CONTENTS

INTRODUCTION

INSIDE A BURNING HOUSE, A SOFT, GLOWING LIGHT APPEARED ABOVE A young girl huddled beside the lifeless bodies of her mother and father. In the light stood a Cherokee brave—a silver feather intertwined in his long dark hair, his deerskin clothing glistening in the light.

"Kelzi," the brave whispered, kneeling beside her.

Kelzi looked up into his eyes, the tears in her own seeming to fade. She handed him a piece of rolled buckskin. He placed the buckskin inside his shirt, gathered her in his arms, and disappeared into the light.

ONE

May 1995

THE INVESTIGATING OFFICER AMBLED THROUGH THE SMOLDERING ashes of what had been, several hours before, a beautiful brick home with a gabled roof, arched windows, and a walk-around, decorative porch that added a touch of another time. The home belonged to Amedohi and Katherine Tsali. The slightly scarred tree house, about fifteen feet to his right, belonged to their daughter, Kelzi.

The officer had been inside the home many times and noted that, though it did not appear lavish, it was tastefully decorated in a style that mirrored the individual heritages of the couple—Cherokee and Irish.

The officer's dark-blue uniform appeared more of a dusty gray, gathered from the ash residue that swirled around him. His eyes surveyed the devastation, his face showing little emotion. He checked the time on his watch. It was 3:23. The afternoon sun was now hidden behind a haze of smoke while the air carried its scent.

In the distance he heard the firemen discussing the fire while loading their equipment back onto the trucks. The remains of two vehicles they found partially buried in the rubble of the garage seemed to be the center of their conversation—suggesting that, for an unknown reason, the family who lived there was unable to escape before the fire entrapped them.

The muscles on the back of the officer's neck tightened, and he quickly turned away from the voices that seemed to entangle him. The officer found the chief on one knee—his elbow pressed against his thigh, his fist pressed against his mouth, and his eyes glued on something in the rubble.

Hearing the investigating officer approach, the fire chief glanced up with smoke-irritated, bloodshot eyes. "Is that what I think it is?"

Avoiding eye contact with the fire chief, the officer laid his metal case atop the rubble and ash and studied the charred human remains buried in the debris. Removing a pair of latex gloves from his case, he stretched them over his hands and carefully brushed away the ashes until the evidence spoke for itself.

The two men stood, their eyes locked on the remains, the officer's arms folded across his chest. The fire chief's hands pressed against his hips.

Finally the fire chief heaved a deep sigh. He took a step backward, mentally calculating something in his mind. He furrowed his brows, rubbing his fingers over his chin. "I've been in this home numerous times. As I recall, the front door was approximately fifteen feet straight ahead of me, and I ask myself, why were they unable to escape . . . unless the fire started where they stood." He paused, his eyes searching for something not visible. He shook his head. "Amedohi was a respected lawyer throughout the state of North Carolina. He and Kate made a handsome couple." A deep sadness revealed itself in his eyes as he cleared his throat. "I'll leave you to your work." He turned and walked away.

The investigating officer pulled the radio from his belt, pressing his thumb against the button while wiping away the perspiration that trickled down his face. "I need a forensics team at the core of the fire investigation," he said, his voice scratchy from the inhalation of smoke.

He lifted his eyes and quickly scanned the area around him.

Strapping a surgical mask over his nose and mouth to prevent any more of the gray residue from getting into his lungs, the officer brushed ash and debris from what remained of a rib cage. He removed long tweezers from inside his case and slipped them between the pallid bones, blindly searching through the rubble when his radio crackled and a voice informed him that the forensics team was two minutes out.

Time was short. Sweat stung his eyes. His throat felt dry. His heart pounded. Moving rapidly, he found what he was looking for. His work was finished and two objects were safely inside his pocket; he cautiously scattered ashes around the area.

He leaned back, letting the air flow through his lungs unhampered while his heart calmed to a steady beat. Still, his mouth felt like cotton, and he could taste the ash that had somehow found its way to his tongue. In fact, his clothes, hair, and skin were completely covered with the stuff.

As soon as forensics arrived, the officer directed them to the evidence and then stepped away, letting the three men do their job. A few minutes later, he heard their voices meticulously identify and label each piece of evidence.

When their work was done, the officer suggested that if the remains were those of Amedohi and Kate Tsali, it might be necessary to search for a third body . . . that of their eight-year-old daughter, Kelzi.

A thorough search managed to produce remnants of bone tissue as the ashes were raked—nothing more. It was determined, however, that they might not find more evidence since the bone tissue of young children is typically soft enough to be melted by the extreme heat of a fire.

Inside the lab, the DNA samples extracted from the unidentified bone fragments proved to be those of Amedohi and Kate. Further investigation indicated the deaths were accidental, although the cause of the fire was never determined. Two weeks later the case was stamped "Closed."

TWO

The Transformation

HER EYES CLOSED IN SLEEP AS THE LIGHT SLOWLY FADED INTO THE shadows and silence prevailed until another voice whispered her name. "Kelzi."

She opened her eyes, directing them to the gentle, dark-brown eyes looking down at her, aware of the tears that moistened them. "Grandfather?" she whispered back.

"Tell me what a Shaman is, Kelzi."

Without hesitation, she replied, "A Shaman is a spiritual person who knows lots of things and does lots of things to protect her tribe. A Shaman can heal someone who is sick or dying."

Kelzi felt the warmth of her grandfather's arms around her as his whispered voice reached inside her heart, telling her she would live with her Shaman Grandmother Ahyoka—on the Cherokee Reservation—for many years. He explained all that she would learn with her grandmother at her side. He promised Kelzi that Ahyoka would protect her with all the love she carried inside her.

No further words were spoken, and the warmth of Kelzi's grandfather's arms faded from her while all that he had said remained deep within her heart.

Yona had driven for nearly five hours when he exited the freeway and drove through a small town, turning onto a dirt road leading him to a vintage log cabin surrounded by trees. It was exactly as Ahyoka had described it. She had also made the point that he was to ask no questions and to only converse pleasantly with whoever opened the door.

With anticipation, Yona slowly walked up to the front door and knocked. Within seconds, a tall elderly man opened the door. His white hair that fell to his shoulders nearly glistened. The clothes he wore and his pleasant smile seemed almost angelic when he invited Yona into the cabin.

Yona couldn't help but notice the beautiful antique furniture that adorned the room as he stepped inside. A candle-lit lamp, sitting atop an elegant table, illuminated a stuffed settee. A beautiful curio cabinet, decorated with antiques, stood against another wall. Everything in the room had to have been designed and created in the late 1700s or early 1800s.

His eyes were drawn to a four-poster bed in the darkest corner of the room where a child lay, a blanket folded in her arms. The old man carefully lifted the child from the bed and gently kissed her forehead as he walked towards Yona.

"The lass has eaten an'll yet sleep a while," the elderly man explained, lightly touching her eyelids with his fingers.

Yona wanted so badly to ask a question that flooded his thoughts, but the only words that escaped his mouth were a soft "Thank you" as the kind man placed the child into his arms before guiding him back through the front door.

"'Tis I ta' be thankin' ye, lad," the man said quietly.

The two nodded to each other and Yona walked to his car. When he had Kelzi settled in the backseat, he turned back to the house, wanting to ask a question. However, the man was no longer standing at the door. Yona walked back to the cabin and knocked and waited. No one answered. Confused, he carefully opened the door and stepped inside. To his shock, the room was dark. The furniture, which had minutes ago been shining in candlelight, was covered with dust and the room smelled as if it had been vacant for years.

It only took a few minutes for Yona's mind to process the fact this man was much more than he appeared to be. Yona's unasked question had been answered. His heart fell silent. Tears began to fill his eyes as he realized that he had talked with an angel.

Yona walked slowly back to his car. Once inside, he turned and looked into the backseat where the young girl, wrapped in a blanket, slept peacefully. This would be the first of many miracles to come.

Three hours later, Kelzi opened her eyes, finding herself in the backseat of a Jeep Cherokee. The person at the wheel was wearing a cowboy hat over long black hair that fell over a tan western shirt. She quietly sat up, her long black hair hanging loose around her face, her jeans and shirt carrying a slight hint of smoke. Tucking her hair over her shoulder and behind her ears, she found her attention drawn to a pair of dark, friendly eyes beneath heavy eyebrows peering back at her through the rearview mirror.

The man's deep voice gave away his identity. "*Osdasunalei, a-yo-li. Ho-hi-tas?*" [Good morning, child. How are you?]

"*Osdasunalei*, Uncle," Kelzi responded bravely, before adding, "I'm not afraid because I know why I'm in your car and why we are going to the reservation." Saying no more, she leaned against the backseat, quietly wrapping the long, loose locks of hair around her fingers. Her brows now furrowed, she began to focus on the farmland that stretched on for miles. Fruit trees, hay, cornstalks, garden vegetables, and tomato vines all separated into their own space, giving the land a calm, almost hypnotic, appearance. The western music coming from the car radio added a touch of rhythm to the setting.

Yona glanced into the rearview mirror, struggling to restrain the tears that filled his eyes, reflecting on all his mother had told him before she explained where he would find Kelzi.

"Are you tired, Uncle?" Kelzi asked, mistaking the moisture in his eyes for fatigue.

"You could say that," he replied with a chuckle.

"We can play a game called 'Did You Know?' to help you stay awake."

Yona knew the game well. He and Kelzi's father had played it often when they were children.

"Did you know," Kelzi began, "that many artifacts found in America today tell us the Cherokee tribe have lived in America for more than eleven thousand years?"

"Did you know," Yona replied, "of the ancient Cherokee tales that describe hunts of the mastodon—a large, ancient animal that looks very much like the elephants of today—at the end of the Ice Age?"

They took turns in naming the Seven Clans: Bird, Paint, Deer, Wolf, Blue, Long Hair, and Wild Potato before Yona asked, "Do you know why the number seven is so important to the Cherokee?"

Kelzi nodded. "Because it counts the north and the south—the east and the west. It counts above and below—and here in the center. The center is the place of the sacred fire."

Yona smiled. "I find you very knowledgeable for such a young person."

"My poppy taught me many things about his people. The Cherokee people used nature to make art. They hunted from nature and gathered from nature and gave back to nature." There was silence for a moment before Kelzi added, "Did you know, Uncle, that my poppy was building me a tree house and it was almost finished? But now it won't ever be finished, Uncle. It won't ever be finished and Poppy will never sit with me in my tree house."

Yona glanced into the review mirror to see a delicate, calm face, but the deep, brown eyes now seemed to tell a different story. He paid close attention as Kelzi leaned forward, placing her elbows on the top of the front seat before resting her right cheek on her arm.

With her tearful eyes focused on her uncle's face, she asked, "Are my mommy and poppy happy without me, Uncle?"

Not certain how to answer her question, Yona could only go with his own feelings. "I believe they are happy that you are here on Earth and safe. They are happy you will be living on the reservation, where your grandmother will be your teacher for many years." He paused and wiped away the tears that had formed in his eyes. "They want you to be happy for them now that they are in heaven. They want you to listen and learn from your grandmother. They want you to be strong and have much courage—for it was born inside you."

It was as if his next words had been whispered in his ear. "They love you more than I know how to tell you."

Yona checked his watch as they entered the reservation. The round-trip had taken just over nine hours. His fatigue matched that of the little girl in the backseat, who kept yawning.

"We're almost there, Uncle." Kelzi's face was pressed against the window as she gazed at the beautiful farmland with horses, cows, and sheep (all grazing at their leisure), the homes built with a touch of the past, and the school that spread itself over a full block. She counted two grocery stores and a post office. The streets were lined with trees and plants, adding beauty to the sun's labors. "I love the reservation, Uncle," she sighed.

"It appears that the people of this reservation love you, as well." Yona chuckled. "Look ahead. Little Wolf is especially happy that you'll be living on the reservation."

People of all ages, dressed in decorative costumes, were waving their arms in greeting. Kelzi was enchanted by the beaded deerskin dresses with handwoven waist belts, fringed underskirts, deerskin shirts, breech cloths, and knee-length beaded moccasins.

When the car stopped, Kelzi could see her grandmother approaching. Her eyes filled with tears when Ahyoka opened the back door and helped her out of the car. Kneeling in front of Kelzi, Ahyoka took her in her arms, holding her close.

Tears fell from Kelzi's eyes as she felt the comfort of her

grandmother's embrace, and her arms instantly wrapped themselves around Ahyoka's neck.

When Ahyoka stood once again, Kelzi took a moment to admire her grandmother, noting she was tall and thin with long black hair that glistened in the sun. Her eyes were the color of midnight, and though wrinkles appeared on her face, they hardly disturbed its beauty.

Harmonious voices began to flow to the rhythm of the drums, bringing her attention back to all those around her. A boy and a girl who looked around Kelzi's age walked toward her, carrying a stuffed Yogi Bear, just like the one she had before . . . before . . . she refused to let herself think about it.

When they presented their gift to her, she hugged the bear tightly and cried, "Aren't the Cherokee people beautiful, Yogi? Aren't they all so beautiful?"

Within a short time, the children had her playing their games, eating their food, and singing their songs. But she already knew the games, the songs, and the food because her poppy had taught her before . . . that day.

Kelzi spent her first week inside her grandmother's library—a room pulsating with color and energy that took the reader into another realm of learning. Bookshelves lined every wall. Books of every kind filled the shelves. A sofa, a recliner, a coffee table, and two lamps occupied the center of the library. A flute, a shamanic drum, and a grinding stone held their places of honor on the coffee table.

Monday of the second week just happened to be Kelzi's ninth birthday. Ahyoka had her put on a deerskin dress. She braided Kelzi's hair, took her hand, and guided her to a small river, explaining there was a new adventure ahead of her.

It was a beautiful day as Kelzi and Ahyoka walked through the woods. The birds were singing. The air was fresh and smelled of summer. She could hear children laughing in the distance.

When they reached the river, Ahyoka picked up a small drum lying against a tree and began to stroke it. Two boys and two girls, who had befriended Kelzi the day she entered the reservation, stepped from behind the trees with painted faces and began dancing to the beat of the drum. Kelzi felt the excitement that surrounded her. Another girl holding a small bowl of paint stepped beside Kelzi, dipped her finger in the paint, and wiped it across Kelzi's forehead and each cheek. "You are our family and our friend, Kelzi Tsali," she whispered, "from this day and through the eternities to come." She stepped back. "My name is Adsila."

A boy stepped forward holding a baby parrot in his hand. "I'm your cousin, Honia Haka. That means Little Wolf." He placed the parrot on Kelzi's shoulder. "For your birthday, your friends want to give you new life. He will watch over you and you will watch over him for many years to come. Happy Birthday, Kelzi."

Kelzi's eyes lit up and she squealed with delight while removing the baby parrot from her shoulder and placing him on her finger. She gave him a thoughtful look, tilting her head to the left then to the right. "I will call you Chekee."

THREE

The Revelation

THAT NIGHT, AFTER AHYOKA TUCKED KELZI IN BED, SHE TOOK HER granddaughter's hands and held them in the warmth of her own, looking deep into her eyes. "Tell me, young one. Tell me what is locked inside of you."

For a moment, chills ran down Kelzi's back, leaving her without speech, thought, or sound. Though her eyes were open, the room and her grandmother's face seemed to fade away. In their place, a lock appeared with a key inside it.

"Turn the key," a voice whispered. "Turn the key."

Kelzi pressed her eyelids together, the words echoing in her head. She begged the key to turn, unlocking what was hidden inside. Suddenly, the key did turn, allowing the memory that had been buried so deep to resurface.

"Every night after Poppy tucked the covers around me," she began, "and before he kissed me good night, he would whisper in my ear, 'Always listen to your dreams, for they will tell you many things.' Last night, Grandmother, I dreamed that I told you . . ." Kelzi shuddered and her voice became a whisper. ". . . I told you what I don't want to remember." Suddenly her teeth began to chatter and her body began to shake. Words became knotted inside her head, making it impossible for her to speak.

Ahyoka carefully wiped away the tears that fell down Kelzi's cheeks, then kissed her forehead. "Wait for me," she said softly, "and I'll bring you something that will take your fear away." Ahyoka hurried from the room, returning a few minutes later with a cup half full of a dark, smelly liquid.

The smell reached Kelzi's nose, and she wanted to gag. "What is that awful stuff?" she cried, pressing the blanket to her nose.

"If I told you that the liquid in this cup would take away the fear that hides in your mind and your heart, would you drink it?"

Kelzi swallowed hard. "You promise?"

Ahyoka set the cup in Kelzi's hands and knelt in front of her. "That is my promise."

Reluctantly, Kelzi took the cup and plugged her nose with her fingers. With all the courage she could muster, she lifted the cup to her lips and drank. "Yuck," she shouted when it was all gone and she could take in air once again. Before she could comment any further, however, a soft melody touched her ears, whispering the words, "Tell their story."

Kelzi looked up at her grandmother and the memory of that day began to tumble from her lips as if she was watching it in progress. "Someone, outside our house, was calling to Poppy. Poppy put the leather bag in my arms and hid me inside the big vent. He told me that no matter what happened, I wasn't to leave my hiding place."

Kelzi pushed the tears from her eyes. "They didn't even knock on the front door. They just pushed it open and walked into our house. They had sacks over their heads with holes in them so they could see. One shouted at Poppy, telling him to give them the deed. Poppy said he wouldn't give them anything. He shot Poppy and another man shot my mommy. I didn't help my mommy and poppy because I was too afraid."

"Kelzi," Ahyoka said, pressing her cheek to her granddaughter's forehead, "you helped them because you weren't supposed to help them. You were brave to do all that your father asked of you."

Kelzi looked into her grandmother's eyes. "Thank you for

thinking I'm brave because I wanted to be brave for Poppy. One day he told me that it's not wrong to be afraid; it's how brave you are when you're afraid that matters."

Ahyoka drew Kelzi close and kissed her forehead, easing the pain she felt in Kelzi's heart. "And your father was right. One day you'll realize how brave you really are, Kelzi."

Kelzi nodded, her heart feeling as if it was struggling to beat, but she still had something to tell her grandmother. "The men took the sacks off their heads and I saw their faces and I know who they are, Grandmother. I know who they are and I don't know why they wanted to kill my parents. They said something about destroying a deed and the only way they could do it was to destroy everything around it.

"They walked out of the house and that's when I could smell smoke. I got out of the vent and crawled to Mommy and Poppy. I put my arms around them. I told them I needed them to wake up because the house was on fire. But they couldn't hear me. The smoke got thicker and the fire came closer and closer but I didn't want to leave them. I could only watch the flames."

Kelzi hardly paused to breath. "Then I saw a light and inside the light I saw an Indian brave. His clothes were made of deerskin, and a silver feather hung from his long black hair. He knelt beside me and spoke to me in Cherokee, because he was Cherokee, like my poppy. He told me to not be afraid. He told me that Mommy and Poppy were safe in the spirit world. He told me that he was taking me away from the smoke and flames and away from the eyes of the men who killed my parents.

"He picked me up and took me into the woods where no one could see me. He whispered, 'If you listen to the rhythm of Mother Earth, you will never be alone. Never turn away from her and you will always know where to place your feet.' Then he touched my eyelids with his fingers and whispered, *'Aga-si-nu.'* He told me to sleep." Kelzi's voice fell silent.

"I love you, Kelzi," Ahyoka spoke softly, allowing her fingers to smooth her granddaughter's long dark hair and wipe the tears from the beautiful dark eyes that looked up at her, shadowed in sadness.

"I love you too, Grandmother." Fresh tears surfaced in Kelzi's eyes as she reached out her arms, wrapping them around Ahyoka. "I miss my mommy and poppy until it hurts my heart. How can I make it stop hurting so much, Grandmother?"

"You will always carry your parents in your heart, and because of that there will be times, as long as you live, when your heart will sense the tenderness of your love, and you will feel the pain."

In the quiet that followed, Ahyoka began to sing. The rhythm was hypnotic, causing the lyrics, filled with wisdom and comfort, to reach into Kelzi's heart. Within minutes, she was asleep. There were no nightmares. There were no dreams—only a gentle sleep that wiped away the fear.

Though the memory of her parents' terrible deaths remained inside her, Kelzi was able to slumber, allowing her the freedom to become a happy child—filling her grandmother's house with laughter and mischief. She was quick to learn and quick to speak out. She made many friends and, yes, even an enemy or two—but that's the way it is when one stands up for what they believe, she decided.

A picture of her mother and father sat on the night table beside her bed. Her father's tender smile and dark eyes were filled with kindness, and her mother's pretty face and soft green eyes always seemed to be looking directly at her, and Kelzi knew they were looking down at her from heaven. Each night, before going to sleep, she would kiss the silent faces smiling up at her. Even Chekee gave them a parrot kiss . . . when he felt like it. Yogi Bear simply sat on the bed and smiled.

FOUR

The Tree House

A FINELY CRAFTED TREE HOUSE, BUILT MANY YEARS, BEFORE BECAME Kelzi's captivation. Her grandmother gave her permission to do with it as she pleased, and Kelzi began her restoration and re-modeling—with the help of Little Wolf and Adsila.

The dust and clutter were soon removed. The wood floor was washed and polished. The rough wooden walls they painted green. Then, when the tree house was finally in order, they began to search in Grandmother's attic, where they found a small wooden rocking chair, about as old as their grandmother, which added even move value to it. Next they found a colorful woven basket and a skinny, three-shelved bookcase filled with storybooks.

With the help of Uncle Yona, the rocking chair found its place in one corner of the tree house, the woven basket in another corner, and the bookcase against the wall in between. Yona added one more attraction to the room—a colorful rug he claimed he had woven when he was just a year older than Kelzi.

When all was in place, the three of them sat inside the small doorway proudly surveying their work. (There wasn't room enough for Yona, so he sat on the tree limb closest to the door of the tree house.)

For a time they simply whiffed the smell of summer as it filled the room. They listened to the birds fluttering their wings around the tree, chirping their approval. There was even a discussion concerning the possibility of Yona and his son, Little Wolf, building an addition to the room, which pleased Kelzi immensely—knowing that in a few years she would begin to outgrow her tree house.

In school, Kelzi focused on academic study. She was quick to comprehend everything she read. She had a photographic memory and an incisive desire to learn.

By the time she was ten, Kelzi's determination and intellectual spirit began to show themselves. Her desire to learn not only inside the schoolroom but outside as well gave her an education well beyond her dreams. She called it the first chapter. Of what? She wasn't sure. She would wait and let the future decide that for her.

Inside the tree house, she let her imagination flow. Her basket held water and snacks while storybooks and Yogi Bear adorned her bookcase.

Kelzi would take Chekee on early morning walks through the trees, around the vegetable gardens, and along the bank of the river. She would tell her parrot her thoughts about family, friends, and heaven.

Chekee would listen intently—now and then inserting his opinion with a chirp—or he would flutter his wing against her hair, which meant that he totally agreed with her.

That year, Little Wolf and Adsila taught her a new skill. Every afternoon after school they took Kelzi into the fields or the woods for target practice. Her weapons? The bow and arrow. Her target? Whatever looked close enough to hit.

In between collecting the arrows and returning them to Kelzi, her two mentors corrected her flaws in the handling of the bow and arrow. Their patience and Kelzi's determination to learn enabled her to hit the target more often than miss it—after a full month of daily practice . . . to be truthful.

When Kelzi turned twelve, Yona added another room to the tree house, giving room for a growing young lady. It was during that year that Kelzi exchanged the storybooks for mystery and history books. She added a beautiful Indian doll that stood on the floor beside the chest. Colored pencils replaced the lead ones so she could sketch the world as she saw it from her lookout tower.

She had also become a competitive archer thanks to the patience of Little Wolf.

On her thirteen birthday, Kelzi added a colorful Indian blanket that hung over her rocking chair inside the tree house, and curtains that hung from the two windows.

This was the year her second chapter introduced itself in two lessons. Lesson 1: Learn to silence your footsteps. Lesson 2: Listen to the silent voice of Mother Earth.

She found herself in a wooded area close to her uncle's house where, every day for the first three months, her focus was on one thing: walking through the woods, one step following another without revealing where she was. After those three months, she could sneak up on any one of her friends. However, her uncle was a master at what she had yet to learn.

Because Kelzi's father had taught her many ways to listen to the voice of Mother Earth, her grandmother only had to add to her knowledge.

It was a year of intriguing observation and education meant only for reasons yet unknown to her.

During Kelzi's fourteenth year, the games were replaced by law books her grandmother had given her. A journal and pen sat neatly in the basket, which still held snacks and drinks.

It was also during this year Kelzi learned something about

herself that was almost creepy and needed to be discussed with her grandmother. Finding Ahyoka working in her garden, Kelzi asked if they could talk, to which her grandmother kindly agreed.

It took a few minutes before Kelzi could actually begin, not knowing just where to begin. "It seems," she sighed with uncertainty before clearing her throat. "No, I get the impression that when I . . . when I . . ." She shook her head in skepticism of what she was about to say.

"Whatever is it you have to tell me, Kelzi, just let it come out," Ahyoka said gently while touching her granddaughter's hand.

Kelzi took a deep breath and let the words fly. "I think I can read eyes. . . . I mean, I think I can tell what some people are thinking when I look in their eyes." By this time, Kelzi was quivering. "Tell me, Grandmother, is it true?"

"It is true," Ahyoka replied, taking Kelzi's hands in her own. "You are blessed to have this gift. Let no one else know that it lives within you, for it will be a weapon as well as a shield."

"Where does this gift come from, grandmother?" Kelzi asked, needing to know, needing to understand.

"It is a gift of your spirit, Kelzi, a gift that will be yours throughout your life, one you must always protect."

Ahyoka's words brought tears to Kelzi's eyes, tears that witnessed her humility . . . her understanding . . . her responsibility.

It was also an education Kelzi could only imagine. She was suddenly seeing everything and everyone from a different point of view. She became aware that the reservation was a place of peace and harmony, and her friends were true friends.

The gift, however, could also be annoying, at times and Kelzi had to teach herself how to operate the "on" and "off" button, so to speak.

At age fifteen, Kelzi had reached the height of 5 feet 6 inches. Her tree house now seemed a little smaller, which was to be expected. Still, she managed to fit quite comfortably inside its walls.

New curtains hung from the windows. Three Cherokee paintings decorated the walls, adding brilliant color to the rooms.

In spite of that, Kelzi now spent most of her free time inside her grandmother's library, studying law books, many identical to the law books her father had inside his library. His memories had inspired Kelzi to become a lawyer, standing up for what is right— standing beside and protecting the innocent

In her seventeenth year, Kelzi had outgrown her tree house. She was now a very striking young woman. She carried the physical genes of her grandmother. Her height was close to six feet. Her skin was a natural tan. She wore her black hair long and straight or rolled in a bun on the back of her head. Her stunning, dark eyes sparkled with confidence and boldness. Her face, however, belonged to her Irish mother—delicate and beautiful. She had her mother's tenacity as well, which was just fine with her, thank you very much.

The years had passed quickly. Inside the schoolroom, her education had been one of amazing adventure. Outside the schoolroom, her education was one of another kind. She had learned to walk silently through the woods. She loved the bow and arrow. Nature became her friend. Her gift of reading others' thoughts— when necessary—was something she had never imagined. In retrospect, she had, indeed, received an education she longed for.

At the age of seventeen, Kelzi graduated from high school and was accepted to Harvard, where her focus would be law. She was determined to follow in her father's footsteps.

Three days before Kelzi left the reservation, she braided her long black hair, put on her favorite Cherokee dress, and gathered together her bow and arrows along with a small blanket. Today, she would take a walk along her favorite path leading to the large oak

tree that had given her shade from the day she spotted it, almost eight years ago. Today, she would hit every target with her arrows. Today, she would sit beneath her tree and listen to the harmony of the river. Today, she would talk to Mother Earth, telling her of the sadness she felt. She thought about her years on the reservation—filled with love, laughter, and excitement—and of an education she could have only have received living there.

When she reached her destination, she spread the blanket beneath the tree and began her target practice, using a small tree next to the edge of the river, approximately sixty feet away. "Life is much like target practice," she whispered to herself when not every arrow hit its mark. "I only pray that I will not miss the target when it comes to protecting my people."

All that has been given to you here, all that you have learned, will be your guide in your future. . . . You will not disappoint your people. You are not alone.

Kelzi blinked, her eyes darting to the left, then to the right. Had she heard what she thought she'd heard? "Let me hear the words again," she whispered in the breeze

Once again she heard the words, and she seemed to feel the comfort of knowing that she, indeed, had communicated with Mother Earth. "Thank you," she whispered. "Thank you for believing in me."

"Kelzi," Ahyoka's voice called from a distance.

Kelzi looked up to see her grandmother walking toward her. She quickly wiped away the tears and silenced the sniffles that had appeared out of nowhere. "I'm here," she said, waving.

Ahyoka sat down beside Kelzi, holding something in her hand—something Kelzi hadn't seen in years—a bloodstained buckskin, rolled and tied with a leather cord. Though the buckskin appeared battered and knotted, she could see that it was still resilient enough to protect what it sheltered inside.

She cringed when Ahyoka placed the buckskin on her lap and said, "There is something we need to discuss before you leave."

Kelzi looked down, feeling her nerves shatter. She wanted to turn her eyes away but it was impossible to do so. It was as if the buckskin was drawing her to it. She touched it with her fingers. She untied the strings that kept the buckskin bound. What Kelzi saw sent chills through her. "This is what my parents died for?" she whispered, unable to conceive the authenticity of it all.

Ahyoka nodded. "And now you must take it with you and protect it just as your father did. It is time for that which is written inside to be seen and read so all will know of its contents—so there will be no doubt of its purpose."

Kelzi let her fingers outline the words on the parchment that lay inside the buckskin, reading them in silence.

"Always remember what you've learned at my side, for you have a great responsibility ahead of you," Ahyoka explained, taking Kelzi's hands into her own. "You have been given the gift to see what once was—but is no longer. You have a gift of the spirit, for you see the truth in the face of those who lie. Never let this gift pass from you." Taking her granddaughter's finger, she traced it over the small X beside each signature. "The X you see represents a stipulation to the deed that was added when your grandfather Tsali signed his name. The stipulation states that because many of the Cherokee clan of Chief Tsali no longer worked the land, the document was to be presented to the state every twenty years, showing it was still in the possession of a chieftain."

Ahyoka touched her granddaughter's cheek. "This is what I have been preparing you for . . . to face those who wish to take away our land. You are now that chieftain, Kelzi. What you see there represents a twenty-year period of time. Watch for the time when you must take your stand. The stipulation that was meant to be a curse was, instead, a blessing. Those who covet the land knew nothing of it until they attempted to take control of it."

Kelzi trembled, feeling the responsibility weigh her down. Her heart pounded. Tears filled her eyes. "Am I ready, Grandmother?"

Ahyoka took Kelzi in her arms. "You are ready, Granddaughter. Have faith. Let your body and your mind be filled with the strength that lies within you."

For several minutes, the two of them sat quietly beside the river, listening to the calming sound of the water as it flowed downstream—reflecting on memories of the past.

Three days later, with the help of her grandmother and uncle, Kelzi packed all that was hers into and on top of the vehicle Yona had given her. Included were Chekee, Yogi Bear, and everything in her tree house.

When everything was tucked inside, Ahyoka placed an envelope in Kelzi's hand. "Inside, you'll find the information you will need for Harvard."

Taking the envelope, Kelzi embraced her grandmother. "I wish I could take you with me as well."

Yona directed Kelzi's eyes to two figures running toward them—their voices crying out, "Wait! Don't leave yet."

Kelzi waved and shouted back. "And I thought you had forgotten me."

Adsila and Little Wolf were taking great strides to reach Kelzi. As they got closer, Kelzi could see what looked like a bow in Little Wolf's hand. Whatever was in Adsila's hand was still a mystery. By the time the two of them reached her, they were both out of breath.

"I just finished making this bow for you," Little Wolf sputtered, from lack of air. "It's in perfect alignment with your aim." Holding it horizontal in his hands, he presented it to her.

Kelzi was almost at a loss for words when she touched the bow. "It's amazing" was all she could think to say, aware of the work that had given it perfection. Those words brought a deep smile to Little Wolf's face.

Adsila placed seven arrows, one by one, across the bow—each arrow engraved with a name representing the seven clans. "Remember us, forever," she wept, tears falling down her cheeks.

Tears moistened Kelzi's eyes, as well. She carefully handed the bow and arrows to her uncle and then threw her arms around her two best friends, capturing them in a bear hug. "Thank you, thank you, thank you!" she sobbed.

"Promise to keep in touch with us," Adsila cried.

"You have my promise," Kelzi answered, adding, "You have my love. You have my appreciation, but you can't have my parrot."

With a burst of laughter and tearful eyes, the three parted, allowing Kelzi to get into her car. She started the engine while tears fell down her cheeks. She rolled down the window and waved until everyone disappeared in the background. When she got to the fence where the reservation ended and the rest of the world began, she stopped and stepped outside the car to take one more look at the home of her people. "Help me to hear Mother Earth when she speaks to me so I can prepare myself for whatever stands before me," she whispered softly.

Just then, a breeze stirred about her, echoing in her ear. *You will know when to listen.*

Kelzi registered for Harvard using her full name—Ahyoka K. Tsali. Everyone at Harvard knew her as Ahyoka K., and for the next three years, she seemed unaware of the beautiful woman she had become. She focused, instead, on her education, refusing to take summer breaks. Her determination and gift of intellect allowed her to graduate in the top five percent in her class, at the age of twenty-one.

Ahyoka, Yona, Adsila, Little Wolf, and all the friends she had to leave behind sat in the audience when Kelzi received her diploma. It had been a glorious day, and though they brought her priceless, handmade gifts from the reservation, Kelzi realized the gift of love they brought with them was the greatest gift she received.

FIVE

The Lawyer

AFTER ENDURING SEVERAL INTERVIEWS, KELZI ACCEPTED A JOB OFFER from her ideal choice law firm in upstate New York. She moved into a small apartment with front room windows that overlooked a small part of the city lights and close to her office. It was perfect for her needs.

One of the rooms became storage of all that had been inside her tree house: The rocking chair with a Cherokee blanket. The skinny bookcase filled with law books and a scatter of mysteries. The small chair and the Cherokee dolls. The wooden chest. The woven rugs. The handwoven basket still containing a few bottled waters and tasty snacks. The five Cherokee paintings. The blanket and pillow, folded up inside the chest.

The bow and arrows, now encased inside a wood frame, hung on the wall between two of the paintings. The leather satchel she personally ordered to protect the bow and arrows while at college now dangled from a nail next to the wood frame.

When everything was in its place, the tree room—as she referred to it—became her sanctuary and Chekee became her consultant while Yogi Bear became a decoration. When she had to think through all the possibilities of a case or simply get away from thinking altogether, she would slip into her tree room with her parrot on her shoulder and focus on law-intended ideas, possibilities, conclusions, and many other inspirations . . . or she would shut out the real world completely, letting her memories drift back to life on the reservation.

Becoming a lawyer wasn't without its struggles. Kelzi simply had to prove herself before being accepted into the world of law. The stress of competing for recognition and respect was something Kelzi had expected, but the challenge seemed overwhelming at times. It was with time and sheer determination that she began to gain the respect that opened up the doors for her, allowing her to prove herself.

By the time Kelzi reached the age of twenty-four, she was recognized as a brilliant lawyer. Knowing that each time she stood in front of a judge and a jury that she was preparing for the day she would defend her people, she became more and more aware of what she had yet to learn.

Kelzi's most recent case had been a tough one, filled with loopholes and political intervention, but her client, A. C. Vennerson, was innocent and the prosecuting attorney knew it.

Mr. Vennerson had been charged with murder in the first degree after a colleague who Vennerson had a high-ranking disagreement with—the prosecuting attorney claimed—was found with a bullet in the back of his head inside Vennerson's garage, rolled up in a rug as if ready for transport to an unknown area.

In her interrogation of the "proposed" witnesses, she used the guilt that flooded their eyes as a guide to plug the loopholes and crush the political intrusion of their testimonies . . . leaving them caught in the web of lies.

When it was time for the closing arguments, Mr. Stilman, the prosecuting attorney, tore at her web and actually succeeded in slashing a hole or two. Nonetheless, when it was her turn, Kelzi argued the distinct possibility and most likely probability was the fact that the evidence had been transported from elsewhere along with the body.

"Anyone who would leave a dead body wrapped in a rug inside their own garage for two warm summer days would be a fool—let alone ten days," she argued. "Anyone with an ounce of common sense would know the odor just might begin to extend beyond the garage. Dogs in the area would be barking. People passing by would soon get a whiff." Kelzi paused and looked directly at the jurors. "And that's just what happened."

She paused to give the jury time to ponder her words before continuing. "Why would Mr. Vennerson murder someone—roll the body in a rug—and leave behind obvious bits of evidence lying around in his garage for anyone to find . . . just before he and his family leave for a seven-day vacation." She held her hands out to the jury and shrugged her shoulders, emphasizing her next words. "Why would he do that knowing all that happened would happen, making him look like the obvious criminal?"

Kelzi took a moment to study the prosecuting attorney, noting his left eye was twitching, which meant he was feeling the pressure of possibly losing this case. With a nod in his direction, she turned back to the jury and continued her defense. "It's obvious that the true criminal in this case was aware that the Vennersons were gone when the evidence was planted. However, he . . . or she . . . apparently hadn't considered one very important point . . . how long the Vennersons would be gone.

"It's very possible the one who committed the crime waited and watched, ready to call the police as soon as Mr. Vennerson arrived home—giving them a well-rehearsed rendition of a story so believable that no one would think otherwise. However, the timetable didn't accommodate the crime—leaving considerable doubt as to the truth of the story."

Kelzi turned away from those seated in the jury box, letting a moment pass, allowing the drama of her remarks to be felt by everyone inside the courtroom. Slowly, she turned back to face the twelve with words that fell from her lips using passionate inflection. "We've dissected the lies and half-truths. We left no stone unturned. I now leave the decision in your hands."

Once the jury left the room to discuss the case and come to a decision, Kelzi had the opportunity to watch the observers as they left the courtroom. Still sitting in a chair on the back row was a man who had occupied that same seat every day this case was in session. She couldn't help but wonder what his intention could be. He looked to be in his forties. His graying hair was rather ruffled. His clothes were simple but his face, she noted with disgust, was the face of a dishonest man.

She turned and began to walk in his direction, feeling the need to ask him a few questions. Needless to say, as soon as he saw her coming in his direction, he stood and quickly left the room. She would not forget his face.

It only took the members of the jury three hours to come to a decision. As in all trials, once the jurors were seated, the judge asked the question. "Have you come to a decision?"

The head juror answered, "We have, Your Honor. We, the jury, find Mr. A. C. Vennerson not guilty."

Cheers came from the audience and, for the first time in three months, A. C. Vennerson was able to breathe freely again. He stood and took Kelzi's hand in both of his, tears streaming down his face. "You truly are a brilliant lawyer," he said in all sincerity. "I hope you don't mind if I say I also believe you're psychic. It seemed as if you could separate the truth from the lies told by the witnesses who testified."

Kelzi smiled, giving A. C. a wink, making him promise to keep her psychic ability a secret. They both laughed before a quick hug was shared. He repeated his genuine 'thank you' three times before he turned to his wife, who was waiting to thank Kelzi as well.

The short, slightly overweight, bald prosecuting attorney,

Frank Stilman, seemed to be more than just a little miffed when the jury announced the verdict, although Kelzi knew he was as much aware of her client's innocence as she was. She could see it in his eyes. But then, Stilman was an arrogant man who liked to win at any cost. He made a scene of ignoring her as he snapped his briefcase shut, creating an echo that sounded through the all-but-empty courtroom. Then, as if she were an afterthought, he turned to her, grunted something distasteful about her pedigree, turned his steely eyes toward the door, stuck his stubby nose in the air, and pushed past her.

Kelzi considered shouting rude and demeaning remarks at the man, but thought better of it. Instead, she called out to him, "Thank you, Mr. Stilman. It was a well-fought battle on both sides."

She could hear the garbled sound of deep anger escaping Stilman's mouth as he disappeared down the hallway.

The dramatic exit brought a smile to Kelzi's face as she gathered up her papers and slipped them into her briefcase before leaving the courtroom. Her steps were light as she entered the parking lot and unlocked her car. Throwing her briefcase in the backseat, she took her place behind the steering wheel. The clock on her dash glowed 5:30 p.m., reminding her that she was hungry. She made one quick stop at a pizza take-out and headed for home.

Chekee was sitting on his perch helping himself to some birdseed when Kelzi stepped inside their apartment carrying the pizza box. She patted her left shoulder and immediately Chekee's wings tickled her cheek when he landed . . . the signal for "glad you're home."

"We're going into the tree room," she exclaimed while opening the fridge and removing a can of soda. "I've much to tell you about my day."

Inside the tree room, Kelzi changed from her business suit and heels into comfortable jeans, a tee shirt, and moccasins before sitting cross-legged on her thick, round, woven rug. She opened the soda and then the narrow square box that held two slices of fully loaded pizza. Making sure her parrot had enough pizza crust to make him happy, she told him about their win and the rudeness of the offensive lawyer.

With only two bites left, Kelzi dropped the pizza into the box and wiped her lips and fingers with a napkin. She closed the lid and held her finger out for the parrot to take his place.

When they were eye to eye, Kelzi stroked Chekee's feathers. "I think you would have enjoyed the moment," she laughed.

The parrot fluttered his wings, mocking Kelzi's laugh. Then, without warning, the room became silent with Chekee dropping his wings to his sides, his eyes staring into Kelzi's.

Get the buckskin. The words echoed in Kelzi's ears, causing her to catch her breath. Chekee pressed his head against the back of her neck. Get the buckskin, Kelzi. The words were louder this time—leaving no doubt in her mind that she was being prompted and should do as directed.

The buckskin was hidden inside an old woven basket, beneath three Indian dolls and two Indian blankets. In less than a minute, she was holding it in her hand.

As if guided, she returned to the rug and sat down cross-legged. She closed her eyes and brought the buckskin to her heart. A spiritual Cherokee chant, learned on the reservation, began to flow from her lips. It was as if she was moving through time—standing beside her mother and father, hearing their voices . . . seeing their faces . . . holding their hands.

The chant slowly softened into a quiet echo that disappeared into the air, bringing Kelzi back to the present while leaving her mother and father in the past.

Chekee flew to her shoulder and stroked her cheek with his feathers, his beak touching her ear. "Not cry. Not cry," he cooed.

"I'm trying not to cry, Chekee," Kelzi sobbed, brushing the tears from her face. She untied the strings, allowing the buckskin to unfold. Inside were the two pieces of parchment made from animal hide. This time she opened the first parchment, aware of the map showing a large portion of land behind the hills of North Carolina. The words beneath the map—written in the Cherokee language—explained the purpose of the map.

> *Two men—a clan Chieftain and a white man—sit near the warm fire. They face each other, and they talk of many things. Their friendship is strong. The white man gives to the Chieftain a piece of parchment made from the skin of the buffalo, and tells him it is a gift.*
>
> *A map is drawn on the parchment. It is a map showing a large piece of beautiful sacred land behind the hills of North Carolina. Written below the map are the words: This sacred land belongs to the Cherokee. For upon this land their burial ground lies hidden from the eyes of those who would destroy it. The land shall be handed down from Chieftain to Chieftain until the last of days, so that it might be protected from any who desire to make the Cherokee land their land.*

The second parchment was a document deeding the land described on the map to the Cherokee. Below the words of the deed were the signatures of four generations of Cherokee chieftains—the names written in the Cherokee language followed by the English translation. The last two chieftains, who signed the deed, were Kelzi's grandfather and her father. Beside their names, a small X had been pressed into the parchment with ink. Next to the X a date had been written.

"This is what the men where after, Chekee," Kelzi explained while plucking a tissue from its box next to her. "This is what Mommy and Poppy died for." She blew her nose and wiped her eyes.

Kelzi traced her father's signature with her finger, her attention drawn once again to the small X and date pressed into the parchment next to his name. Taking the deed in her hands, she pressed it against her heart. The parchment felt warm . . . almost soothing. "Poppy," she whispered, "I promise to do what whatever is needed to save this land."

Inhaling deeply, Kelzi closed her eyes, awaking memories of her childhood and letting them take her on a journey back in time. She was five years old. She was walking with her father through the woods and the meadows and along the streams. He had her touch a tree or put her hand in the stream and whispered, "Close your eyes, Kelzi, and listen to the sounds that are silent to the ears of man. Listen with your spirit."

Though it seemed like a game, it wasn't a game. Poppy was introducing Kelzi to Mother Earth. He was teaching her to listen to Mother Earth, who would protect her until she no longer needed protection. He was teaching her to sense the wisdom of Mother Earth and to be grateful for her beauty.

Kelzi opened her eyes and glanced up at her bookcase, letting her eyes drift from book to book. Though the books were filled with formulas, equations, solutions, directions, decisions, assessment of man's understanding of man, and the earth and the universe, there was nothing written that could explain the rhythm of Mother Earth.

No book of logic could explain how the spirit of a Cherokee could protect and watch over her. But because of what she had witnessed, she didn't need an explanation—and because of her knowledge, she would know where to place her feet. "I have a responsibility that I cannot turn away from, Chekee." A feeling of intense courage came alive inside of her as she spoke.

Just then, the doorbell rang. On the other side of the door stood an elderly yet stately woman. In her right hand was an envelope with Kelzi's name written on the front.

"Sorry to bother you, Chekee," she said to her parrot, with a chuckle before turning her attention to Kelzi. "And you, as well, my dear." She paused, giving Kelzi a wink. "But a very kind Native American gentleman stopped by before you got home from work and asked that I give this to you." She handed the envelope to Kelzi.

"Why, thank you, Mrs. McCormick." Kelzi chuckled while studying the envelope. "It's very kind of you to be my mail carrier as well as my landlady." She stepped back and motioned with her arm. "Won't you come in?"

"Oh, I'd love to, dear, but my grandson is picking me up in five minutes to take me to a movie." Mrs. McCormick glanced at the envelope. "I hope the envelope holds only good news." She turned, gave a friendly wave, and hurried down the hallway.

Kelzi closed the door and wasted no time slitting open the envelope. Inside, she found a sticky note attached to a flight confirmation. The sticky note read:

Kelzi,

Tomorrow, this flight confirmation will take you back to Lamont. Once you have landed, go to your father's law office, where his partner will be waiting for you. I will meet you there.

The address and directions to her father's office were written below her Uncle Yona's signature.

Kelzi read the note a second time, giving more attention to the meaning of the words than to the words themselves. "It's time!" she whispered, reaching out and stroking her parrot's feathers. Giving him no other explanation, she simply placed him on her shoulder and walked back into the tree room, explaining he would have to stay with Mrs. McCormick while she was gone.

Chekee's pleasant eyes seemed to sadden as he dropped his head in acceptance of the fact that Kelzi was going away.

Wasting no time, Kelzi called her boss and explained that she would have to quit her job immediately, because of a personal responsibility. Before he could reply, she hung up the phone.

While making the decision of what she needed to take with her, Kelzi's eyes ventured to the bow and arrows, as if she knew she would need such a weapon, although she couldn't imagine why. Following her intuition, however, she removed them from their case and placed them into the leather satchel. Knowing she could never take them on the flight, she quickly boxed them up and addressed the box to the law building in Lamont in care of a certain office number.

Next, she packed what she thought she would need. Then, after checking to make sure everything was in order inside the apartment, she placed her parrot on her shoulder, stepped into the hallway and locked the door.

Mrs. McCormick seemed very pleased to babysit Chekee, making it easier for Kelzi to leave him behind. Promising her parrot she would be back soon, Kelzi left the apartment building with a prayer in her heart that whatever happened, from this point, she would be prepared for.

SIX

The Unexpected

KELZI SAT NEXT TO THE SMALL, ROUND WINDOW, WATCHING THE AIRport runway disappear below her as the plane ascended. She was finding it difficult to categorize her emotions. She let her head fall back against the headrest of her seat while her brain revolved around the words, *You will know where to place your feet.* Walking into a situation armed only with words left her just a little concerned. "I only pray I'm ready to listen," she muttered to herself. Closing her eyes, she allowed the fatigue she felt from her late-night preparation to lull her to sleep.

The voice of the flight attendant reminding the passengers to return their seats to the original setting, fasten their seat belts, and turn off all electronic devices brought Kelzi out of her undisturbed slumber. Once the plane had landed and parked, it didn't take her long to have her carry-on hanging from her shoulder and her purse in hand, waiting impatiently to depart.

After getting her suitcase and satchel off the luggage carousel, she searched for the rental car on Row D, #8 parking space, which took all of ten minutes.

When the luggage was safely stored in the trunk and her seat belt was fastened, Kelzi took a moment to take a deep breath before starting the engine.

Pulling onto the freeway was a no-brainer, which was a good thing since her brain seemed too involved in self-evaluation mode. *I have never felt so unprepared—not knowing what it is I need to be prepared for. I can't help but ask myself if my lawyer's mind is resisting Mother Earth's assistance. But then, am I really so confident in the courtroom? With everything I've prepared for, do I know what the jury is thinking? Do I know what the judge is thinking?*

The last two sentences jarred her into reality. She had to admit that when looking into their faces she actually did know—and, at that moment, it dawned on her that she had one very valuable weapon against the enemy. *Thank you for your input, brain.* She laughed, feeling just a little more confident than she had been a few minutes ago. Taking the freeway exit that would lead her to Mr. Franklin's office, Kelzi began to focus on her purpose and not the possibilities of success or failure.

When she reached her destination, Kelzi pulled into the parking lot, finding a parking place next to the law building. "Ready or not," she sighed while checking her hair in the mirror before covering her eyes with dark glasses. Once outside the car, she straightened her leather jacket, brushed her fingers over her tan slacks, and made sure her western boots still had a shine to them.

She stepped onto the sidewalk, conscious of all the people passing by—smartphones pressed to their ears, completely oblivious to anyone else around them. It was as if they were wearing invisible blinders, their eyes seeing nothing other than what occupied their own minds.

Kelzi, on the other hand, was aware of everything and everyone around her, her instincts on overkill. It wasn't until she was standing in front of an impressive, red brick, three-story building with its four colossal stone pillars and ornate fourteen-foot archway that invited her to enter antique double doors that she let her guard down.

"It's beautiful," she exclaimed, her eyes bouncing from the door to the bricks to the pillars and then to the massive American flag that waved gracefully from atop the roof, giving the impression that it was free of restraints.

A large inscription near the entrance of the building read:

Offices of Freedom
Built in 1833
Restored in 1986

Stepping into the historical entrance hall took Kelzi's breath away. She felt as if she had stepped back in time. Removing her dark glasses and strolling to one of the large windows facing the front of the building, she ran her fingers over the thick, handcrafted glass, touched the adobe walls, and admired the plaques, paintings, and portraits that decorated them.

She inhaled deeply, taking in the scent of another era—thinking how incredible it would be to step back in time, for just a day, to see the history that echoed through these halls. And just for a moment Kelzi felt like a child: free to explore, to learn, and to absorb the history. She wanted to smell the scent of glory—to feel the magnitude of independence. Instead sadness spilled over her. There was no time for thinking at the moment, only action. She turned and walked to the elevator, bringing herself back to the present and the responsibility that went with it.

When the elevator doors opened, a man in a janitor suit stepped out. He gave her a quick glance and hurried on his way.

A man carrying a huge mailbag stepped into the elevator just behind her, and the doors closed. They exchanged polite greetings while waiting for the doors to open on the third floor, where Kelzi stepped out of the elevator and into a quiet hallway.

Kelzi studied the layout. It seemed rather odd to see all the secretarial offices windowed with glass instead of enclosed with private walls. Maybe it's so they can keep an eye on the comings and goings of the people who walk up and down their halls, she thought.

Just then, two women discussing something inside one of the offices glanced up, watching her as she walked by. One of them smiled, while the other had an unfriendly scowl that gave her thin, refined face a look of disdain.

"Hello." The voice calling out from behind her was obviously Southern.

Kelzi turned to see the woman who had smiled at her just seconds ago. She was an attractive woman, about five feet five inches tall. Light-brown hair fell around her face. Her friendly, blue eyes sparkled, and she walked with an air of confidence. Kelzi guessed her to be in her early fifties.

"I'm Monica," the woman asked, giving Kelzi a friendly smile. "And I'm assuming you are Kelzi."

"I am," Kelzi replied, returning Monica's smile.

Monica opened the door to her office "Please come in."

Kelzi was quickly ushered into Robert Franklin's office, where her uncle Yona sat, waiting for her arrival.

When the two men stood to greet her, Kelzi took time to appraise Mr. Franklin. His hair was nondescript brown, graying at the temples. His eyes were perceptive, yet kind, hidden behind rimmed glasses. The nature of his character was refined.

Mr. Franklin was approximately five feet ten, meaning he had to look up at her, which didn't seem to intimidate him. After a full evaluation, her instincts told her she could trust him.

Kelzi turned her attention to Yona, who was wearing a suit and tie. His hair was tied back. His appearance reminded her of her father. She walked to him and gave him a hug. "Thank you for standing with me today."

"I stand with you every day," Yona replied, pressing his cheek against Kelzi's forehead. "You just can't see me." He motioned to a cushioned chair next to his. "Let's sit."

When the four were seated, Robert Franklin studied Kelzi. "All these years I thought you were dead until I received a phone call from Yona telling me of the deed that needed your signature below that of your father's." He leaned back in his chair and removed a manila folder from the front drawer of his desk, placing it in front of him. "Yona tells me you have proof that your father's death was not accidental."

As he spoke, Kelzi could sense a deep sadness inside him. "Solid proof only a true witness can bring to the table, Mr. Franklin," she replied. "I am that witness."

"You can call me Robert," he said with a smile as he opened the folder and slid it in front of her. "I believe I have everything your uncle asked for. Inside you'll find the pictures and names of the men planning to purchase the land."

Carefully, Kelzi removed the photos and the list, laying them on the desk while studying each face—forcing herself to stay focused and keep her emotions in check.

One look at the first photo caused a quick breath to escape Kelzi's lips. She could feel the anger stirring inside of her as she looked at the face smiling up at her. She picked up the photo and handed it to Robert and asked, "Who is this man?"

Robert studied the photo of a man with a lean face, dark eyes, heavy brows, a full head of white hair, and a neatly trimmed, white mustache hovering over his upper lip. "This man is Obadiah Hatchett, a highly respected, though rather arrogant, successful real-estate agent."

Kelzi handed him the second photo.

Robert stared at the photo, shaking his head. The face staring back at him wasn't particularly handsome but presentable. The dark hair was thinning on top and the eyes were piercing blue. "Police Chief Cecil Rawling."

He cringed as Kelzi's fingers came to rest on yet another photo of a man with a round face, pale eyes, and gray hair. "This is a picture of R. P. Fowler—a lawyer, a fine judge, and an outstanding member of the community." Robert suddenly found himself struggling to keep his composure. The man in this picture was a good friend.

"Eighteen years ago, he was the leader of the pack." She announced, handing him the fourth photo.

"Sam O'Connor," Robert responded, and Kelzi could see that he was beginning to understand the implication of what he was seeing. "Sam died a few years ago, but his son, Brannon, took his place as the lawyer for the group of men you see on this list," he explained.

Yona watched Robert's pained reaction to each photo and had to ask, "Didn't you begin to suspect that some of these men might be involved once I asked you for this information?"

Robert glanced up at Yona then back at the photos in front of him. "Of course I did. It's just that I find it difficult to come to terms with the reality of it all." He rubbed his hands over his face. "When does greed replace honesty in a man? When does it steal his conscience?"

Robert turned his attention to Kelzi. "I promise you that I'll do everything in my power to bring these men to justice."

"Thank you, Mr. Franklin," Kelzi replied. "And thank you for being my father's friend." She removed the buckskin from her purse and handed it to him.

Robert accepted it, his eyes scanning the specks of dried blood that peppered it. His hands shook as he untied the strings, allowing it to unroll on its own. He studied the deed, motioning Monica closer so she could study the deed as well. "This woman is my second-in-command—my private investigator. I trust her with any and all secrets that materialize in this office."

Monica took the opportunity to speak. "With all that Robert and I have learned in the past few moments concerning the photos Kelzi has in front of her, I ask myself, 'Why am I not surprised?'"

Robert gave Monica a startled look. "Why are you not surprised, Monica?"

"Information I found, quite by accident, while preparing the file on your desk. At the time, it seemed rather useless. But now I can see where it was leading." Pointing to the deed, she suggested they prepare it with Kelzi's signature and get it to the Recorder's Office before she continued with what she had learned.

It was agreed. Robert handed Kelzi a pen while placing the

parchment and document in front of her. Monica observed as Kelzi placed her signature on the parchment—both in English and Cherokee—adding the X and the date after her name.

Monica took a picture of the document and sent it through the printer, after which she pressed her notary stamp and signed her name on the printed document before handing the pen to Yona, who placed his signature on the document.

"Explain to the recorder that under no circumstance is she to tell anyone, inside or outside the county building, of this deed and the signature now affixed to it," Robert warned her.

Monica placed the copy of the document in a folder, gave Robert an understanding nod, and left the room.

I knew I could trust that woman the minute I looked into her eyes, Kelzi acknowledged to herself with a feeling of relief.

SEVEN

The Plan of Escape

SUDDENLY THE OFFICE DOOR BURST OPEN. MONICA ENTERED, HER eyes filled with fear and her finger pressed tightly against her lips. In her hand she held a small piece of paper, flapping it up and down until she got close enough to Robert's desk to drop it in front of him.

All eyes fell on the scribbled note.

Something strange is going on in Sally's office. It's like she knows who Kelzi is. Two men are in her office and they keep looking this way.
It's possible this office has been bugged.

Mouths dropped and eyes stared up at Monica. She leaned in close and whispered, "I should have recognized it the minute Miss Tsali walked by Sally's office, and I heard Sally mumble something that sounded like 'right on time' while glancing at the clock on her wall. It was like she had been waiting for that moment. I was foolish enough to believe she was referring to the mail carrier who stepped off the elevator right behind Kelzi. Then I heard her punching the buttons on her smartphone as I stepped out of her office."

"That woman!" A snarl was evident in Robert's whisper. "I've never trusted her. She's always been a little . . . what would I say . . ."

"Arrogant? Unfeeling? Selfish? Blameworthy?" Monica mocked quietly. "Am I getting close?"

Robert nodded as he tiptoed to the office door and opened it just far enough to see the windows of Sally's office, where two men were stepping into the hallway. He motioned to the other three while quietly shutting the door.

Monica grabbed Kelzi's jacket and handed it to her.

Kelzi quickly put on the jacket, rolled and tied the buckskin, then slipped it back into a hidden pocket inside the jacket.

Robert hurried to the back wall of his office where a sculptured bust of his ancestor, Benjamin Franklin, rested on a pedestal. He pulled the sculpture slightly forward. Silently, a panel behind the pedestal slid two feet to the left. He motioned for Kelzi to step through.

Kelzi gave him a look of awe and a quick nod before stepping to the other side of the wall. Now in the dark but still able to hear what was going on inside Robert's office, Kelzi warned herself to be strong, recognizing the fear rising inside her just waiting to challenge her courage.

"Go to your desk and pretend to be busy," Robert whispered to Monica as he pulled a folder from the filing cabinet and tossed it onto the desk. "Yona and I will be deep in a discussion over a case."

"Excellent," Monica whispered back, her eyes revealing sheer determination, though her hands were slightly trembling as she opened the door, just wide enough to slip through and into her office.

Robert dropped to his seat, giving Yona a nod and handing him a manila folder. Next, he cleared his throat and, in his unique, professional voice, began his dialogue. "I think you'll agree with what I have here . . ."

The conversation between the two seemed natural enough to make a listener believe they were truly engrossed in a discussion of law.

Inside her office, Monica busied herself at her desk while keeping one eye on the two men walking toward her. They were tall and muscular, wearing dark suits and dark glasses. Yet, with all the drama, they still looked more like criminals just out of prison, uncomfortable in clothes that didn't quite match their personas. She looked up at them and smiled as they walked through the door. "Good afternoon, gentlemen. May I help you?"

One of the men flipped out an FBI badge. He didn't smile. He didn't say good afternoon. He just grunted, "FBI. We need to speak to Mr. Roberts."

"It's Mr. Franklin, and he's in a meeting, at this moment." Monica pressed the warning button beneath her desk with her foot—bringing to life a blinking lamp inside Robert's office—while drawing the eyes of the two fake agents to the clock on the wall. "Please have a seat and he'll be with you in approximately eight minutes."

"Sorry, lady," the man growled as he walked past her desk. "We'll see Mr. Franklin now."

"Wait!" she cried, pressing the button again. "You can't just walk in like that." She hoped she sounded convincing.

The two men pushed the door open and walked into the room with Monica at their heels. Their faces were scarred and rigid, giving away the fact that they were hardened criminals. Even the nicely trimmed hair and the suits couldn't conceal the reality.

"I'm sorry, Mr. Franklin. These men claim to be FBI agents who can't seem to wait five minutes before talking to you," Monica said in breathless frustration—her eyes shielding the apprehension that knotted her stomach.

Both Robert and Yona, thinking they were prepared for this intrusion, found their hearts skipping a few beats when they came face to face with the muscles in suits.

From behind the secret door, Kelzi could see the evil that marked the faces of the two men. Their eyes glowed dark as sin. These men are not FBI agents but agents of another form.

"It's all right, Monica," Robert said before focusing on the two fake FBI agents. "What can I do for you, gentlemen?"

The two men flexed their muscles simultaneously while the one assigned to do the talking replied. "We received information that a woman bearing the resemblance of a suspect wanted for questioning by the FBI came into your office at 11:08 a.m.

"Then I'm afraid you've been misinformed," Robert replied pushing his chair back and steadying himself in defense of the intrusion. "As you can see, the person sitting next to my desk is a fellow attorney. We were discussing a case"—he paused to add drama—". . . a case needing our utmost attention."

The two men glanced around the room, both unable to avoid Monica, who was standing in the doorway with her arms folded and a scowl on her face, her fingernails tapping against her elbow.

"Check the restroom and the storage room," the first one said to his partner.

It only took a few minutes for the two men to confirm that there was no one else inside the office. Slighting Yona, they gave a curt "thank you" to Robert and turned to walk out of the room, only to find Monica blocking their way, her arms still folded across her chest, her fingernails still tapping against her elbow.

"If you will follow me," she said, successfully hiding her fear while eyeing them with a condescending look of her own authority. "I will escort you out."

Though their muscles flexed and their jaws clenched, the two men backed away from any offensive remarks that may have been floating around in their heads and rigidly followed Monica out of the office.

"She's a fearless woman," Robert whispered when the lamp blinked, indicating the two men had left. "I have to admit I had the impression that when the two barged in unannounced, walking the walk and talking the talk, they already knew they weren't going to find Kelzi. The fact that they seemed to know where the bathroom and the storage room were located without asking tells me they've been in my office before."

It was decided, through hand signals, they would hunt for listening devices. They launched a thorough search through the office, rest room, and closet, finding nothing. They were about to accept the fact that their suspicions were unfounded when Robert walked over to the Ben Franklin sculpture and carefully ran his fingers over the entire head before moving to the nostrils—finding something just inside the left side.

Monica led the two men through her office and out of the door, closing it abruptly behind them. Her eyes trailed them as they walked by Sally's office, noting that one of them glanced at Sally and tilted his head. Monica didn't miss the unmistakable—though slight as it was—nod the woman gave in return.

In the fifteen years she had known Sally, this was the first time Monica suspected that the cool, sophisticated, curvy, unfeeling, pitiless bully was involved in something unscrupulously illegal and downright treacherous.

Monica peeked at Sally out of the corner of her eye, catching a glimpse of a smile that had a sly implication, and it made her skin crawl. Everything suddenly seemed out of place in their efforts to keep this meeting a needed secret. Instead, everything that had attached itself to Kelzi's unannounced meeting with Robert had become like a pond of muddled water. First, Sally knew who Kelzi was the minute she walked by her office. Second, she was the one who contacted the two supposed FBI agents—but for what reason? To drag Kelzi away while the rest of them stood by? It hardly made sense.

What kind of danger had Robert placed Kelzi in by having her come to his office? On another note, what kind of danger had they placed themselves in by having Kelzi come to their office? On a third note, was she reading too much into the whole situation? She let out a deep sigh and shook her head. Taking a chance, she snatched another look at Sally, hoping the woman wasn't doing the same thing to her. But all she could see was Sally's back and a phone pressed against her ear.

Leaving the woman to her phone call, Monica headed into her boss's office to do some reporting of her own. Once inside she joined the three in the darkness of the room beyond the sliding wall. Knowing the bug was on the other side, she told Robert and Yona everything she had seen.

Kelzi puckered her brow, allowing her mind to weave through all that had taken place over a period of twenty minutes. It didn't make sense. Why the FBI agent charade if they already knew she wasn't in the room . . . and how did they know she wasn't in the room? Suddenly the light came on inside her head. If Robert now knew she was still alive, who else knew? Someone who was using Sally as the snitch because she was part of the puzzle? It was a no-brainer to believe the men Kelzi recognized in the photos were the ones who wanted her out of the way. They just had to set up their monitors to be sure they had what they needed before they took the next step. So, at this moment, how many steps had they taken?

Still, the question of how they knew she was still alive had no answer. There were enough answers for her to be concerned for her life, however. If these people were so prepared for this performance, she had to believe this was only the first act of what was ahead of her.

After destroying the listening devices in the office, the four stepped inside the concealed room where Robert relayed his thoughts to Kelzi, Yona, and Monica. "I believe the two muscle men were here merely to warn me or threaten me to stay out of the way." The tension in Robert's voice indicated deep agitation while the expression on his face revealed fear. "Why didn't I consider this possibility? With everything I know about the deed and the twenty-year stipulation, I should have been more watchful.

I should have taken every precaution. I should have checked for monitors and listening devices. I should have—"

"No," Yona interrupted, placing his hand on Robert's shoulder. "You can't blame yourself. With what we now know, we have to believe that Kelzi's life is, indeed, in danger. We can't waste time on what we should have done. We must think through what we must do now."

"It's not your fault, Robert," Monica added. "It's the fault of the spies, bugs, and phony FBI agents. The whole thing makes you feel like you're a character inside a spy novel, being manipulated at will."

The dark room behind the wall became silent, with all four people thinking the same thing. What if those who bugged the office also knew about the room behind the wall? What if they were waiting for her to leave the office and walk right into their trap? "We've got to get Kelzi out of here now!" Monica whispered. She reached out and drew Kelzi to her. "I thought of suggesting that we simply call a cab and you leave in your disguise, taking the cab to Robert's home. But when I think of all those villains have gone through to create this nightmare, there's no doubt in my mind that they have a cab waiting, just in case. One slip and everything Amedohi lived and died for will be nothing but a memory attached to a time bomb."

Robert reached for a flashlight that hung from a hook to his left. When it was in his hand, he turned it on, lowering its light to the stairs in front of them. Turning back to Kelzi and Yona, he motioned them to follow.

Before Monica could let Kelzi go, she had to give her a comforting hug, a hug that was returned with deep affection. "The Lord be with you, dear Kelzi."

"And with you, Monica. I only pray I haven't put you in grave danger as well."

Monica smiled through her tears. "If it is to be, I'll know we are truly in this together." She stepped back, allowing Robert to lead the way down six rickety, dust-filled steps where spiders hid below their webs in wait for their prey. It was a creepy venture with the rotting wood crackling and splitting beneath their feet.

The thought that sustained Kelzi at that moment was that the Cherokee angel would not have saved her when she was a child only to allow her life to be taken on this day. She promised herself she wouldn't be distracted.

When the door that would lead them outside the building stood in front of them—light glowing through the cracks—sighs of relief muffled through the air.

Yona removed his hat, placing it on Kelzi's head and tucking the loose strands of her hair beneath it. Next he pulled a pair of sunglasses out of his shirt pocket and placed them over her eyes before placing his hunting knife, sheathed in its belt, in her hand. "You'll know what to do with this, if needed," he said in Cherokee. Then, stepping back, he appraised his work, checking to see if the deed was tucked safely away inside Kelzi's jacket before drawing her close to him. "Whatever happens, Kelzi, will be what is to happen. Wipe all fear from you. Let courage be your guide."

Yona's whispered voice reached into Kelzi's consciousness and she wrapped her arms around him. "Thank you, Uncle Yona. Thank you for all you have done for me." Her tears dampened her uncle's shirt while his tears moistened her hair. She didn't want to let go. She felt safe and protected. If only I could take you with me, Uncle Yona, she thought to herself, knowing it wasn't possible. She stepped back, thanking him one more time before turning to Robert.

Tears were evident in Robert's eyes when he gave Kelzi a warm embrace before giving her instructions on how to get around the building to a slit in the fence that would give her a hiding place, if necessary. Next he handed her a piece of paper with directions to his house.

Kelzi could only wish that Robert wouldn't be facing more danger for what he had done for her, yet there was a strong feeling inside her that made her suspect he would encounter unwanted attention from the thugs who had just invaded his office, hired by the men who had called him their friend for many years.

"I'll come out of the building and be in plain sight. Hopefully, I can draw the attention of those who might be watching long enough for you to get to your car," Yona whispered in Kelzi's ear.

Kelzi nodded and pulled Yona's hat low over her eyes.

EIGHT

The Reality

KELZI REACHED OUT AND TOUCHED THE KNOB OF THE DOOR WITH HER fingers, turning it ever so carefully in an attempt to silence the squeaking noise of the rusted hinges. Though the attempt was in vain, there was no one on the other side to hear the noise.

Once outside, she took a few minutes to acquaint herself with everything that surrounded her before reading Robert's note that gave her the address to his home and how to get there.

Kelzi adjusted the dark glasses that kept slipping down her nose due to the humidity and warm temperature that now had her sweating inside the jacket. The hat, sitting just a few inches above her eyebrows, cast the appropriate shadow over her face while allowing drops of perspiration to slide down the sides of her face.

Memories of shadow walking on the reservation guided Kelzi as she cautiously made her way through an alley cluttered with discarded garbage entangled in weeds. When she reached the end of the building, she could see the parking lot to the right. Parallel to the law building, a sidewalk and fence stretched close to fifteen feet before curving to the right at a forty-five degree angle. There it extended both sidewalk and fence another five feet.

Between the sidewalk and the fence, tall, thick shrubbery added color and life to an otherwise boring setting. However, it was what was behind the fence that captured Kelzi's attention . . . a secluded hiding place.

She strode silently down the alley sidewalk—unseen from the parking lot because of the shrubbery—until her eyes spotted the break in the fence. Checking for prying eyes, and finding none, she slipped through the break, breathing a sigh of relief to be completely hidden.

There she waited for her uncle to step out of the building. He was to walk across the road and into a store, hopefully drawing away any eyes that might be watching for her long enough for her to escape to her car. Their plan relied on total speculation. But if she could get to the car and slip away, speculation would be enough.

Trying to control her impatience for the drama to be over, Kelzi took a deep breath while relaying thoughts to herself. Remember, fear trembles and hides when faced with courage, Kelzi.

Letting those words be her solace, she waited for Yona to walk out of the building. When he did, she literally felt a pulsation in her head as her eyes searched for any signs of suspicious characters. At that moment, everyone she saw looked suspicious.

She urged herself to start walking—the smartphone against her ear—the hat low over her face—her eyes eager for the rented silver Buick to come into view. When it did, however, she saw a man leaning against the hood of a car adjacent to it. His cowboy hat was slid low over his forehead, shadowing his eyes. In his hands he held a magazine, giving the appearance that he was simply reading while waiting for someone. The problem was that she knew who he was waiting for. He was hiding himself in his disguise just as she was hiding in hers.

This is one well-organized game, she thought to herself as a chill trickled down her spine. Whoever's coaching has all the bases covered. Was she escaping one nightmare only to walk into another?

A thought came to her. Take your steps in another direction, Kelzi.

"Sometimes the most critical advice is not received inside a university," Kelzi muttered to herself, sucking in air while arranging, in order, the skills that suited the situation she now found herself in.

From that point, she continued to remind herself of all she had learned on the reservation. First, make yourself invisible by using the shadows to your advantage so that you too become a shadow. Kelzi quickly lost herself in the deep shadows behind the shrubbery.

Second, be aware of anything and everything. Let your ears be your eyes. Time is on your side. Kelzi positioned herself so everything she needed to see or hear was at least audible to her.

She determined time was definitely on her side as long as she stayed behind the shrubbery inside the narrow, shadowed perimeter.

She pulled her smartphone out of her pocket and sent a quick text message to her uncle.

Cowboy on adjacent car.

She waited. Her smartphone vibrated.

Listen and watch.

With trembling fingers she texted her reply.

hidden, watching, silent

She tucked her phone inside her pocket. Five minutes passed, then five more before the scene in front of her changed. The man was no longer leaning on the adjacent car. Now he was standing, his eyes turning in her direction, focusing on something . . . or someone. Her ears caught the sound of two male voices in the distance. As the voices came closer, she recognized them. They belonged to the two men who had walked into Robert's office.

At this moment, they were walking directly in front of her with only a few limbs of shrubbery protecting her from their eyes. They were so close, the slightest movement or noise would have drawn their attention . . . so close she could smell their expensive cologne and hear their conversation.

"Don't worry. Once we take care of the broad, we'll collect our money and get out of this state." The voice was quiet but not quiet enough.

"Okay, we heard everything said in that hidden room. We know she went out the back door and was supposed to head toward the car. So where is she?"

Kelzi could see the man who had just finished his remarks, looking around the parking lot. He suddenly stopped and turned around, his eyes all but meeting hers. "She's not ahead of us," he remarked with a touch a sarcasm, "and she's not behind us."

Relief flooded Kelzi. The guy might be looking at the shrubbery. She was invisible to him.

"We know where she's headed, stupid," the other guy snapped impatiently. "That's what matters."

Okay, a change of plans, Kelzi, she thought to herself, thankful she had been hiding in the right place to hear the conversations she had heard, missing nothing of their intent. As soon as the men were too far away to hear, she texted Yona.

> Enemy knows everything. Bug in back room. They knew where I was hiding. All this was a game to make us think I would be safe—thinking I had an escape route.

While waiting for his reply, her eyes remained fixed on the two men. She saw them nod to the man in the cowboy hat when they passed by him. She watched as they disappeared only to reappear again, inside a late model black Chevy two-ton pickup.

The pickup pulled out of the parking lot and made a right turn. Were they planting another seed? Kelzi immediately sent another text to her uncle, giving him the direction taken by the pickup when it left the parking lot.

Within a minute she received the text from Yona.

> Turn left. Three blocks you will see a large parking lot beside a mall. Turn there and wait for me. Text when you have parked.

Just then, the cowboy slipped into the vehicle parked two cars away from the one Kelzi was aiming for. He started his engine and pulled out of the parking lot—making a right turn.

Taking a deep breath, Kelzi remained behind the safety of the fence, her instinct warning her of possible danger. Five minutes passed—then ten. It was time to move. Her legs seemed all but motionless in her attempt to get to her car. When it was finally in front of her, she pressed her hands against it for confirmation that it was real. "Get a grip, Kelzi," she scolded, pressing the button on the key chain that unlocked the door. The second she heard the sound of locks being released, she jerked the door open and jumped inside. Her heart was pounding so hard she could hardly breathe. But she was free.

Kelzi checked inside her jacket to make sure the buckskin was safe and the knife was buckled to her belt before pulling out of the parking lot and merging with the traffic.

"Take a breath," her brain begged. "Take a breath." She obeyed, letting the air enter and exit the lungs once before she checked the rearview mirror, thankful there was nothing suspicious behind her. At that moment, something occurred to her and the words we know where she's going offered a different interpretation of its meaning. It didn't matter if they turned left or right after they left the parking lot. They knew where she was going and that's all they needed to know.

She could see the mall a block ahead of her. She could also see the cowboy's car parked just outside the parking lot. Her phone vibrated against her hip. In one move it was out of her pocket and pressed against her ear. "The cowboy's parked where he can see me when I drive into the parking lot of the mall."

"I'm right behind you now," she heard Yona's voice in her ear. "Turn right on the street before the mall."

Kelzi did as she was told. She looked in the rearview mirror to see if Yona's car was visible when, all of a sudden, a car came out of nowhere, hitting the front of her uncle's car, knocking it off the road and into a tree.

That was all she had time to witness before she had to focus on the road in front of her. She needed to turn around. She needed to know if he was all right, but something stopped her, a whisper telling her not to stop but to continue in the direction she was going. She pressed the call button on her smartphone, listening to it ring four times before she heard her uncle's strained voice telling her to keep going and to stay online with him.

Again the whisper: Keep going. You will soon understand.

I'll understand what? she cried out inside her head. And where am I going after I move over in the outside lane?

Kelzi took a second to check her rearview mirror before making the move. What she saw caused her throat to tighten to the point the air in her lungs struggled to escape. The black beast was staring at her, tailgating her. Her hands gripped the steering wheel. Her eyes searched for the street sign she was looking for.

The streetlight just ahead of Kelzi gave her the information she needed. The street sign stood out in big letters—easy to read. She gave her uncle the information he needed. He put her on hold long enough to call the police, then he was back, letting her know the cops were on their way.

Kelzi's eyes were attentive on the road ahead when a gray van ran a stop sign and swerved in front of her, causing her to slam on her brakes. "I think the black beast just got help, Uncle. They've got me pinned in." With everything she had been taught, with everything she knew, Kelzi had no way out of the situation she now found herself in.

"We played right into their hands, Uncle," she sighed, trying to make herself believe there was a reason for this chaotic danger that was determined to deprive her of her responsibility.

Trying to keep her mind on the moment, she spotted another intersection just ahead. The light was green. The gray van drove through. She made a quick right. The black beast followed.

She found herself on an old road that seemed to have no

intersecting streets. Few homes dotted the area—then no homes. She was heading up a canyon.

Was this planned? Kelzi asked herself. Are they manipulating my moves, controlling my mind with their fear tactics? "Mother Earth," she cried out. "Tell me where to step."

Suddenly, her eyes began to dart back and forth between the road and the black beast behind her forcing her deeper and deeper into the canyon while the road was becoming increasingly narrower. She tightened her fingers around the steering wheel and pushed down on the gas, forcing the car to climb at an unsafe speed. The black beast slowly faded in the background, the gray van now behind it. "Courage, Kelzi," she whispered. "Don't let fear consume you or you've lost the battle."

The road was beginning to curve, which was not a good thing, considering the speed she was going. However, much to her relief, she spotted a grove of trees, very possibly indicating a rest area. This could mean, if she was quick, she could pull off the road and into the tree area. Either she could hide until the two other vehicles passed by or she could hide among the trees if those chasing her hadn't been deceived.

Kelzi felt her heart rate level to a steady beat and the quaking of her nerves was stilled. In less than two minutes her car was parked. The thought that her weapon in the trunk just might come in handy, caused her to quickly retrieve it before sprinting through the trees.

The sound of squealing brakes told her the driver of the black beast had seen her car. Seconds later, a gruff voice echoed through the trees. "You can't hide, lady. Before you can count to twenty, we'll have you fenced in." The voice was that of the man who played the part of the FBI lead actor in Robert's office.

Kelzi could hear the two closing in on her left. Like a ghost, she moved to the right just in time to see the two moving past her without a glimpse in her direction. Suddenly, one of them stopped and put out his arm, forcing the other guy to stop as well. She held her breath, praying she hadn't been discovered.

Instead of turning in Kelzi's direction, however, he pulled a smartphone from his pocket and punched seven keys.

"We've got her cornered, Buddy," he whispered after the person on the other end picked up—after which he snapped the phone shut and put it back in his pocket, nodding to his partner. "He's on his way."

Kelzi watched as the egotistical guy wiped the sweat from his forehead and above his lips. "We've got to separate," he growled while his eyes darted in every direction. "You search on your way back to the truck just in case she has the idea of getting away while we stupidly continue to search through trees. I'll work my way through this clutter to make sure she doesn't try to escape the other way."

The other guy nodded and turned, heading back toward the parking area as the leader directed his next comment to Kelzi. "You won't get away, woman. I can see you." He didn't realize that he was looking the wrong way to see Kelzi, who was hidden on the other side of a tree behind him. However, she had to admit that the guy wasn't completely stupid. She had considered doing just as he said she might do—except now, she had a third person to consider. Where was he? Was he close by yet out of sight?

Before she could give any more time to these concerns, a second thought hurled itself into her brain. As crazy as it sounded, it had to work. It was probably her only way out. She certainly had the tools to make it work.

Kelzi's steps were silent as she shadowed the first guy until he had almost reached his destination. With her bow and arrow ready, she called out softly, "Are you looking for me?"

The man stopped immediately, turning in the direction where he thought he had heard the voice—a pistol in his hand. It was raised, just as Kelzi hoped it would be. His rugged-looking face was dark with anger. His huge muscles were pulsating through his shirt, muscles that had no use at the moment.

"Can't have you taking a shot at me, now can I?" Kelzi inquired, from behind the tree.

"I don't think you understand the consequences if I let you live," came the gruff reply.

That was all Kelzi needed to hear. She pulled back the bowstring, stepped out from behind the tree, and let the arrow fly.

Before the man could pull the trigger, an arrow penetrated just below his right shoulder. He lost control of the pistol and it fell to the ground. He staggered backward, grabbing his injury with his left hand, his eyes cutting through her like a knife before fading into a mixture of confusion, pain, and anger. A loud cry escaped his mouth, serving as a warning to his partner as much as an expression of the intense pain he was in. At that point, his body began to drag him into a semiconscious state. "You'll be dead before this day's gone. Grady'll find you," he groaned as his head hit the ground.

"You'll live," Kelzi promised him before picking up the gun and throwing it over the cliff, along with his smartphone that had fallen from his other hand. Leaving him, she retreated silently through the trees, anxious to be done with this self-appointed task . . . yet she felt the wisdom and supremacy of her ability. She removed another arrow from the tapered leather pack strapped over her shoulder and placed it in position.

When her car and the Black Beast became visible, Grady was nowhere to be seen—a sign that he had, indeed, been warned by Milt's cries.

Seconds ticked by as she scanned the shaded area cluttered with foliage and trees, her ears picking up the sound of footsteps. At last, her eyes caught sight of something to the right of her. She slipped silently behind the tree in front of her and prepared the bow and arrow.

Suddenly, Kelzi heard bullets fly in every direction. She could see him now. His dark hair hung loosely around a face that she would have considered rather nice looking had it not been twisted in rage and deception. She watched as Grady reloaded his gun while walking toward the cars. When the gun was ready, he fired it until it was empty, once again spraying bullets in every direction— actually hitting the tree she was hiding behind.

She stepped out from behind the tree and calmly announced, "I'm over here." Grady could see her with her bow and arrow as well as she could see him fumbling with his pistol, trying desperately to reload. She aimed the arrow at the man's thigh, pulled back the arrow, and let it go, hitting its mark.

Her second victim cried out in pain. His right hand held onto the gun while his left hand struggled to hold onto the bullets. His knees gave out beneath him and he stumbled against a tree stump.

Kelzi placed another arrow in the bow then silently moved toward the same tree, coming at her victim from behind. She could hear foul language coming from Grady's mouth while he was attempting to load his pistol.

"Sorry," she said when she was directly behind him.

Grady dropped his weapon and turned to her, his hands in the air and his face scrunched in fear and pain. "Don't!" he cried. "No more arr—" Before he could finish that last word, an arrow pierced his other thigh. He fell to the ground, crying out for mercy.

Kelzi quickly took his pistol and smartphone—which was about to fall from his shirt pocket—and reassured him that he would live. "I understand you have someone coming. They should be here soon." She reached down, wrapping her hand around one of the arrows. "Here," she smiled, "let me take those out for you."

Grady's screams of pain echoed through the trees as both arrows were removed.

Wasting no time in returning to the parking area, Kelzi hastily wiped the arrows through the grass to get rid of some of blood before removing the knife from its pouch on her belt and slicing all four tires of the Black Beast. Milt and Grady would just have to wait for the rescue squad—wherever he might be at that moment.

Returning the knife to its pouch, she threw the bow and arrows onto the front seat, jumped into her car, and pulled away from the parking area—her hands slightly shaking. Well, maybe a little more than slightly, but she had to be proud of herself. She was completely in control and without fear from the time she got out of her car until she once again sat behind the wheel. Now the slightly shaking hands were evolving into a body chill. It was time to get off the mountain road.

Kelzi left behind two men in a rather agonizing situation.

Milt was now conscious with blood dripping down the left side of his shirt. His anger was competing with his pain, neither one coming up a winner. He forced himself to get to his feet, not daring to try to pull the arrow out. He staggered to a tree, using the trunk for support before staggering to the next tree. He called out to Grady without a reply. "Where are you, pal? I've got an arrow sticking out of my shoulder and could use some help."

"Sorry," Grady cried out, his voice snagged with pain, "but I had an arrow sticking out of each thigh . . . before the stupid broad pulled them out, leaving me to bleed to death. Tell me Buddy's on his way."

"He is, but the woman will be his first concern," Milt replied. "Just keep talkin' till I find you." Milt staggered from tree to tree, gradually closing in on Grady's gravelly voice until, at last, he found his colleague lying on the ground, his face twisted in pain and his jeans bearing the bloody evidence of the two arrows no longer there.

"She took my phone and gun," Grady uttered when Milt dropped down beside him.

Milt knew his own gun was missing. But his phone? He grabbed his shirt pocket only to find it empty. He cringed. Then he used words unfit for the human language in relating his anger. However, nothing he could say would change the situation they found themselves in and both had to agree that Kelzi was a lot more to handle than they had anticipated.

NINE

A Different World

KELZI GRABBED HER SMARTPHONE FROM THE PASSENGER'S SEAT AND pressed the key. "Kelzi?" she heard her uncle's voice through the phone. "Where are you? Are you okay?"

"I'm fine, Uncle," Kelzi assured him. "But I have something I need to tell you." In the process of telling him about the two men who now had arrow wounds while attempting to take her life, Kelzi was continually checking her rearview mirror for anything suspicious. Just when she thought she was safe, a gray van appeared in the rearview mirror closing in behind her.

Her body began to tremble. Her heart thundered in her ears as she cried out, "There's another truck behind me, Uncle Yona!"

Before Yona could respond, the vehicle was beside her, nudging her car, pushing it closer to the edge of the road and the edge of the mountain.

The truck's driver rolled down his window so she could see him glaring at her while maneuvering his vehicle against hers, making it difficult for her to maintain control. He seemed to be enjoying the moment—the broad, malicious smile spread across his face told her as much. Seeing his face also told her that he was the same man who sat in the back of the courtroom during the murder trial of A. C. Vennerson. These people had known, even before today, that she was alive.

Suddenly, the truck swerved into Kelzi's car with a surge of speed. Everything seemed to move in slow motion. The car was sliding over the edge, taking her with it. Nothing could stop it. She felt the pressure of her head hitting against the window, causing the glass to shatter and leaving her semi-conscious. Still she could feel the car colliding with rocks and brush as it fell.

All of a sudden, it seemed she was witnessing a miracle. She saw a light. She felt the warmth of the light. She listened to a word. Then she slept.

Through the receiver of his smartphone, Yona could hear the sound of metal striking metal. Then Kelzi's frightened voice. "It's trying to force me over the edge. Uncle! I . . . I can't control the car."

The last sound that came through his phone was Kelzi's voice crying out—then silence. Yona hammered his hands against the steering wheel, shouting out his anger. As he turned into the curve of the mountain, he saw dust fill the air as her car plunged over the edge.

Though Yona had contacted the police immediately after Kelzi made him aware of the van, by the time the officers arrived and standing at the edge of the ravine, the dust cloud made it impossible to see anything beyond it. An eerie silence mingled with the dust. Then a ripping explosion forced flames up the ravine, filling the air with smoke as it swallowed the car in its inferno.

Yona turned his eyes away from the flames. But he couldn't force his mind away from the thought that Kelzi was down there.

He watched the fire truck pull off the road. The firemen unraveled the hose and carried it down the ravine as a team of forensic experts with their equipment followed. They seemed to be moving in slow motion while the flames were consuming the car at lightning speed.

Yona walked to the edge of the ravine, his eyes focused on the men below him spraying their foam while others set up equipment. He could hear them discussing the possibilities of what they might find. Finally, he had heard enough. He turned away and walked back to his car, his eyes filled with tears.

How long he stood there leaning against the hood of his car, Yona had no idea. Time seemed to drift in and out of his head, serving no purpose until he saw one of the forensic experts coming toward him. The white mask that once covered the man's mouth and the goggles that protected his eyes now hung from his neck. Dust and ashes covered his clothes, hair, and face except for where the goggles and mask had been.

"Sir?"

"Yes." Yona's throat was so dry; his voice carried little sound.

The man removed the glove from his right hand and reached out to shake hands. "My name is Carl. I thought you might want to know what we found." He handed Yona a bottle of water before opening one for himself. "I won't waste time on all the specifics except to say there's not much left of the car beyond the metal. The door of the driver's side was open and we found nothing to indicate that your niece was inside when it burned."

Carl took a quick drink of water then continued. "We searched the area surrounding the burn zone and we found no sign of a body or evidence of an escape." He adjusted his weight to the other foot and cleared his throat. "What I'm trying to say is there's a possibility that your niece was thrown out of the car when it rolled, and was somehow pinned beneath it when it went up in flames. I'm afraid it'll be a few days before we can deliver the evidence . . . one way or the other."

"I understand," Yona acknowledged, knowing there was nothing anyone could do that would make a difference in the end result. His eyes watered. He could taste smoke in his scorched throat but the bottle of water remained unopened in his hand. "If she was pinned beneath the car when it exploded, what are the chances of finding any remains?" he forced himself to ask.

"It will depend on . . ."

Yona tried to concentrate on Carl's explanation but it made him sick to his stomach to hear the words. He simply stood there, the color draining from his face his heart aching with such intensity that he could hardly breathe. He wanted to climb in his car and drive away. Yet he couldn't bear the thought of leaving whatever was left of Kelzi alone at the bottom of the ravine.

"Are you going to be all right?" Carl asked.

"I don't know if I'll ever be all right again."

Carl nodded, handing Yona his card. "I understand. If you have any questions, just call me."

Yona thanked the officer, noting the sympathy that filled Carl's eyes, before he turned and walked away.

When all the cars and equipment were gone, Yona opened the bottle of water and took a drink, wishing he could simply erase this day. However, there was no way to erase it. Instead it clung to him much like the smell of the smoke clung to his skin, his clothes, his hair. It caked his tongue. It lingered in his nostrils. It polluted the air around him.

Knowing he had to stay until he had seen real evidence of the car, Yona slowly made his way down the ravine.

His eyes were dry as he stood in front of the foam-soaked skeleton of the car. His head throbbed in an attempt to sort out the questions that continued to shoot through his brain. They had fooled no one with their escape attempt. The secret room behind the door panel was no secret after all. Planted bugs had to have picked up their conversation and every conversation that included Kelzi's name in the days before. He had to ask himself—over and over again—where they got the information that she was even alive? There were no answers.

Knowing he had no other option, Yona pressed the button on his smartphone that connected him with Ahyoka. "She's dead," he cried, unable to shadow his emotions. "Kelzi's dead." His attempt to tell his mother what had happened seemed to come out all mottled. In his frustration, he finally asked. "Why was this allowed to happen?"

"Come home, Yona," he heard his mother say.

Come home, Yona—that's all she has to say? Hasn't she been listening?

TEN

The Unseen

AMONG THE ROCKS, TWISTED LIMBS, AND UNKEMPT FOLIAGE OF THE mountainside, Shannon moved among the shadows. The sound of screeching tires and metal striking metal alerted him, and he looked up to see a car plummeting into the ravine. He could see a young woman's face filled with terror behind the wheel of the car, but he did nothing because it was not yet his turn. Instead, he waited as a soft glow of light entered the interior of the car and all seemed to be still—for just two seconds. Then the glow of light disappeared and it was dark again, allowing the car to continue to roll end over end, until it lay silent at the bottom of the ravine. Compressed against the rocks and trees, it eventually exploded.

Shannon heard a simple word whispered in Kelzi's ear just before the light disappeared, leaving her lying on the ground next to him—her bow and arrows in their satchel by her side.

Shannon knelt beside her. Blood covered her face, seeping into her hair. Her left arm was bruised and bleeding from glass piercing her skin.

The sound of screaming sirens was a warning that Shannon needed to be on his way. He threw the satchel over his shoulder, picked Kelzi up in his arms, and silently disappeared through the trees, beyond the eyes and ears of the men sliding their way down the ravine. He carried her more than a mile to an old log cabin hidden away from the world, leaving no evidence of his presence behind.

Once inside the cabin, Shannon laid Kelzi gently on a bed in a room that had been waiting for her. He placed the satchel of arrows and the bow at the foot of the bed. He heated water on the wood stove and proceeded to clean the blood from her face, carefully applying pressure and using enough of his herbal remedy to sterilize the wound—a cut that ran three inches from the top of her forehead to just above her left eye and deep enough to reveal her skull.

Once he had managed to slow the bleeding, he threaded a small needle with fine thread, tied a knot in one end, and began his work. Stitching a wound wasn't new to him. He had stitched many in his lifetime and had become rather expert at it. He hummed a gentle tune as he pressed the needle through the flesh, silently counting each stitch as he did so. It took fourteen stitches to close the wound.

Shannon examined his work as he cut the thread. "'Tis done," he said to the unconscious woman lying on the bed. "Thar'll nae be a scar if I've done me work well enough. Could have done it all anither way, but 'tis the habit of me nature ta stitch. Now ta see ta the arm."

He carefully cut away the sleeve of the jacket to not disturb the glass piercing her skin. It was inside a circular hole in the material near the elbow—penetrating the flesh as deep as a half inch. During the next hour, he removed pieces of glass and cleaned and wrapped the wound in an herbal dressing.

When Shannon was able to remove Kelzi's jacket, he found the rolled buckskin. He smiled to himself as he untied the leather strap and let the piece of parchment become visible. He studied it carefully, smoothing it with his fingers before rolling it again and placing it on the small table next to the bed. Then he removed the leather pouch holding the knife and laid it beside the parchment.

Shannon covered Kelzi with a warm blanket and placed a thin cloth over the incision. "'Tis a handsome stitch, I'll be thinkin'," he whispered, lowering the light of the lantern to a soft glow and settling himself in his old rocking chair. Though he let his eyelids fall over tired eyes, Shannon's sleep was light, his ears alert to any sound that might escape the lips of the young woman.

The morning came and still Kelzi slept, though her breathing had become labored as if she was experiencing pain. She groaned and muttered something incoherently. Then she was silent, and her breathing returned to the unconscious state.

Shannon examined her wounds, finding no sign of infection. "'Tis healin', lass. Now so must ye. I'll be talkin' ta ye fer 'tis good ta talk ta the unconscious. 'Tis a sure way ta help the healin', an' ta let ye become acquainted so when yer eyes open ye'll know 'tis me. The name's Shannon Ranny. 'Twas once told only a lass would be proud ta wear the name. But when the one 'oo used his tongue ta stomp upon me name had ta be stitched himself, not another bothered ta mention me name in a risky sentence. Me friends—had nae enemies after that—called me Shannon with proper respect.

"Lived on this land long afore ye 'ere born. Made a bonny place of it too—aboot as bonny as me father's home in Scotland."

Shannon heated more water and prepared a breakfast of hot mush and milk. While he ate, he continued to talk. He told her stories of his childhood, and how he missed his homeland. "Had a wee cottage in the gentle hills of Scotland, we did. Me mum an' father—an' a scatter of children, thar wer. Oh, 'twas a life of a king. But the soldiers came, an' life changed fer the gentle folk . . ." His voice trailed off as if the memory was still too painful to continue.

After several minutes of silence, his voice filled the room again, and he began to tell her of his one true love. "'Twas a fine, bonny lass in all of Scotland. Hers was a beauty born within, an' when it could nae longer be contained, it sprinkled itself on everythin' she touched. 'Twas in the words she spoke. It cast its glow in her delicate green eyes an' in the shine of her silky, red hair, an' that was the way of it."

He leaned forward and smiled. "Could take the whole day

tellin' ye of me angel, but if more be said, I'd be sobbin' like a wee child. So I'll be tellin' ye aboot the son born of that love." He leaned back in his chair and began to rock. "'Twas as handsome as the father 'oo gave him his name, an' the mother 'oo gave him his birth."

Shannon chuckled. "Nae that I'm braggin', mind ye, fer I'd nae be one ta brag or tell a lie."

He thought he saw a hint of a smile cross the young woman's face, and he leaned close to her. But the smile was gone, if it had been there at all. He sighed and looked at the clock on the wall. It was almost noon and he dared not let her go much longer without some form of nourishment. "'Tis time fer ye ta wake up, lass," he whispered, taking her hand and caressing it. "Try, little bairn. Try ta wake up."

She stirred. But nothing more came from her. He sighed and caressed the hand he held in his. "I'll be wipin' more of me brew on the wound. If ye'll be feelin' the pain of it, speak yer mind."

When he touched the cloth (drenched in his brew) against the wound, Kelzi's brows came together and she groaned, "It hurts."

"Ah, as it should, lass," he replied, continuing to disinfect the wound. "Simply means ye'll be knowin' that ye are alive."

Kelzi's right leg twitched. She moaned as her body began to stir—the pain of the awakening making itself known. "Ow!" she cried, opening her eyes and glaring at Shannon. Her vision was so blurred she could barely make out his face. "Do you really have to do that?" Her words were almost as blurred as her vision when she spoke; however, there was no doubt to the resonance of anger.

Shannon laughed. "Aye, an' a happy man I am ta do so." But he pulled the cloth away and sat back, looking at her. "Tell me, lass, how be the pain?"

"Bad enough that if you touch my head with that cloth again, I'll slug you," she scowled, attempting to arch her eyebrows. However, the pain from the newly stitched wound forced her brows back to a less painful position.

"Oh, 'tis a look that could fry a frog I see afore me." Shannon chuckled, patting her hand. "But I'll nae hold it against ye, lass, fer ye cannae be ta blame."

"Blame? For what?" Kelzi cringed, trying to raise her head and focus her eyes at the same time. Finding it too painful to do either, her head fell back onto the pillow. Her eyelids closed.

An hour later, her eyes opened to the shock of finding herself in unfamiliar surroundings. "Where am I, and why am I lying here on this bed?" she sputtered, grabbing the cloth wrapped around her arm. "Why is . . . ouch!"

"Best nae be grabbin' at the cloth protectin' the wound," Shannon warned.

"Why didn't you tell me that before I . . . ?" Her eyes opened wide. Her mouth followed "How did I get a wound?"

"Be glad ta tell ye, lass, if ye can stay awake to hear the answer." His words met heavy eyelids sliding down over glazed eyes.

Time passed. Kelzi drifted in and out of a painful consciousness, her eyes attempting to focus on what appeared to be a statue in the distance. Slowly, the pain began to subside, allowing her to focus more and more on the statue, only the statue now seemed to be moving. When at last her vision cleared, she realized that what she thought was a statue was actually a man standing over her, appearing as if he had just stepped out of the past. His voice seemed to echo through her head when he said, "Ye are safe. Ye have nae to fear."

His words radiated through Kelzi's brain, causing turbulence. Her lids fell, covering her eyes. Her body seemed disconnected from her brain. Her voice was nowhere to be found. Her eyelids quivered in an attempt to open. Her brain was fighting to get her head and her body in sync.

When, at last, her brain connected with her mouth and her eyes opened again, she asked a question she desperately needed an answer to. "Will you please tell me why my head feels like it's been split open and why I feel I need to throw up . . . while I feel like there's nothing in my stomach to throw up?" Her voice was scratchy and barely audible.

"Aye," Shannon replied sympathetically. "'Tis a fact that yer head's been split open. Fourteen stitches it took ta sew it back together." He leaned over her and gently pulled her eyelid upward to check the dilation of her eye. It had improved to the point that he felt he could ask a question that would give him a little more insight to her condition. "Can ye tell me yer name, lass?"

Kelzi frowned painfully, trying to keep the man's face in focus. "That . . . should be . . ." She closed her eyes in thought, which wasn't working. She sighed in frustration, finding herself unable to find the answer. She tried again. "It's . . . it's . . . it's . . ." Panic pierced her insides bringing her voice to a reasonable volume. "I know my name; I just can't seem to remember it . . . right now." She shrunk beneath the covers whispering the words. "What happened to me?"

"Nae ta fear, child," Shannon consoled her. "It'll be comin' back ta ye soon enough. Let yer mind be calm." He patted her shoulder and gave her one of his most tender smiles. "Are ye a wee bit hungry, now?"

"I'm . . . I'm thirsty," Kelzi admitted. "A drink of water?"

"An' a taste of soup, perhaps?"

Kelzi nodded slightly, closing her eyes as a wave of vertigo hit. "I think . . . I think I'm going to throw up."

An hour later, when what had been thrown up had been wiped away and what was taken in had settled, Kelzi felt better—physically. Mentally, however, there was nothing beyond the man (who was obviously Scottish), the four-poster bed she found herself in, two windows draped with delicate lace curtains and white shutters, and a room filled with beautiful antique furniture.

She found it difficult to look into the face of the man, who had taken such good care of her when she couldn't take care of herself. "I'm sorry," she apologized. "I . . ." She stopped in mid-sentence, too embarrassed to continue.

"Thar's no apologizin' fer what ye cannae be responsible fer," Shannon assured her. "Ye'll be learnin' ta take the bree wi' the barm."

"Excuse me," Kelzi exclaimed, fourteen stitches preventing a frown from materializing and giving her enough discomfort to forgo anything other than a twitch.

"'Tis a touch of blarney," Shannon replied with chuckle, "ta bring a smile ta yer lips, so ye'll nae be worryin' aboot what's long in the past."

"And translated, what does the blarney say?"

"'Tis sayin' that ye gotta take the rough wi' the smooth."

Just as Kelzi was about to comment, something swept through her brain. A voice—a voice clawing at her memory . . . Shannon's voice. "Why am I hearing the sound of your voice inside my head?" Panic was beginning to grow inside Kelzi. "What happened to me? How did I get here?"

"'Tis a long story an' 'twill be comin' back to ye, soon enough."

Kelzi blinked then closed her eyes tightly. "What was I saying?"

"That ye heard me voice in yer head."

After taking a moment to allow the pain to become subdued, Kelzi asked, "Please tell me why I heard your voice in my head?"

Shannon replied with a gentle smile and an explanation. "'Tis part of the healin' an' part of helpin' ye remember."

Kelzi opened her eyes—for the first time able to see the face, clearly. She studied the man who stood over her. He stood tall, well over six feet. He was agile and muscular from hard work. He wore the clothes of another era—clothes of a mountain man, she guessed. His white hair reached his shoulders. He had a well-trimmed mustache and beard. Wrinkles creased his rather fine-looking but weathered face. She would guess him to be around sixty. She would also have to admit that he did have an honest face. "Your name is Shannon Ranny," she said.

"'Tis a proper name."

"You have a beautiful wife, a handsome son, and you're from Scotland." Kelzi managed a hint of a smile. "Of course your accent needs no explanation of nationality."

"Ay, an' 'tis a happy man I be ta know ye were listenin'."

The stitches in Kelzi's forehead seemed intent on wakening the pain, once again causing her eyes to close. Still, there was something else she needed to tell Shannon before she forgot. "When I heard your voice, when I listened to your stories, I felt calm and safe. When I couldn't hear your voice, I felt frightened . . . alone . . . disconnected."

"Aye, ne'er doubt the healin' power of a gentle voice reachin' inside the soul. Helps ta clear the fuzz from the brain."

Kelzi pondered his words before replying. "I have no idea what my name is, yet I know yours. While I know all about you, I know nothing about myself. Pain shoots through my head when I try to remember something . . . anything . . . and I feel like . . . like I've been run over by a steamroller. Will you please tell me how I got here inside this room?" Her eyes were now glassy, her voice barely audible.

Shannon took a cloth from the night table and wiped away the perspiration that had formed on Kelzi's forehead. "Found ye flat on the ground, I did, blood flowin' from yer head." He sat on the bed next to her, patting her hand. "Not a time fer askin' 'oo ye were, was it?" He sighed. "So what was I ta do with ye?"

Before Kelzi could respond, he left the room only to return with a glass half full of a yellowish liquid. He placed the glass in her hand. "'Tis a concoct ta help the healin'."

Kelzi took one sniff of the liquid, wrinkled her nose, and inquired, "Does it taste as bad as it smells?"

"Hold yer nose an' ye'll be none the wiser."

She shook her head.

He persisted. "Git on with it, lass. Drink it down."

She looked down at the repulsive yellow liquid, smelling its sickening aroma. She looked up at Shannon. He tilted his head, patiently. She pinched her nose between her thumb and finger, lifted the glass to her lips, and gulped down whatever it was inside as fast as she could.

"Yuck," she cried out when the glass was empty and she had finally stopped gagging. "That is by far the most disgusting stuff I have ever tasted." Suddenly, her memory flashed. No, it wasn't. She had tasted something that disgusting once before. But where? No answer followed, leaving her annoyed, baffled, and . . . very sleepy. Slowly, the mountain man disappeared from her sight. In his place stood four figures—the sound of their voices nothing but echoes inside her head. Then silence whirled around her and she found herself standing beside a tree. In the top of the tree, an ugly creature stared down at her. She could hear its anger. It jumped from the limb, knocking her to the ground. The creature's paw reached out to grab her. Before the paw could reach her, the dream faded away and soft music of a gentle lullaby touched her ears and she slept.

While Kelzi slept, Shannon returned to his rocking chair, letting his own wondrous and nightmarish memories return. At first he hadn't wanted to return to this place where it had all began. But now he knew he had done the right thing. It was the only way to take everything back to where it should be.

He watched the time slowly tick away knowing that the drink he had given Kelzi Tsali was touching her mind—as it should—cutting away at the barrier that held her memory a prisoner. He lit the lanterns when the sun disappeared behind the mountain. He warmed up the soup and made flatbread while humming a tune he sang to his son when he rocked him to sleep at night, in a time when life was peaceful.

"I've heard that tune somewhere," Kelzi called out to him, interrupting his thoughts.

A smile crossed Shannon's face and he peaked inside her room. "Ah, so ye've opened yer eyes just in time fer supper, have ye?"

"Why do I know that tune?"

"'Tis a fine question ta be askin'," Shannon replied simply, bringing her a bowl full of soup. "I hope ye'll be fit fer warm soup an' flat bread."

"I think I love flatbread," Kelzi said curiously. "I haven't had any since . . . since . . ." She looked up at Shannon, who was watching her.

She pressed her fingers against her temples, letting them massage away the pain that seemed to pierce her brain whenever she tried to think.

Shannon fluffed a large pillow with his hands and gently placed it behind her head. "We'll be eatin' soup an' flatbread, an' I'll listen while ye talk. Then, when ye have said all 'tis on yer mind, I'll be talkin' while ye listen." He stepped back. "Thar's nothin' like stirrin' the memory. Fer when ye tell another, ye learn twice yerself."

Kelzi wrinkled her brow—though it hurt to do so. "Well said . . . I think."

With large, gentle hands, Shannon straightened the blanket and tucked it comfortably around her. Then he stepped back, giving her the look a physician gives his patient after he has done all he could do to make her comfortable. "Yer feelin' well enough?" he asked.

"I'm fine," Kelzi assured him. "Actually, quite a bit better since my nap, thank you."

Shannon set her bowl of soup on her lap and handed her some flatbread. "An' were thar a dream while ye napped?"

She stared up at him, surprised at his question. "How did you know?"

Setting his bowl of soup on his lap and dipping in his flatbread, Shannon explained with a grin, "Askin' is part of knowin', lass."

Kelzi turned her flatbread over in her hand and dipped it into her soup just as Shannon had done, savoring the taste as she chewed it slowly before swallowing. When her mouth was empty, she told him her dream just as she remembered it. When she finished, she gave him an impatient stare. "Now, I believe it's time for you to talk so that I can learn more."

"An' ye'd have me say?" he asked, his eyes wide with childish innocence and a sparkle that revealed otherwise.

"I would have you tell me the meaning of the dream because I think you know more than you are telling me," she replied with a touch of annoyance.

He touched her forehead with his finger. "Then I'll tell ye 'tis a storm made up of witches brew whirlin' in thar, as me granny would say. All ye need ta do is silence the wind an' bring calm ta the storm."

ELEVEN

The Unexplained

THAT NIGHT, AFTER DRINKING MORE OF THE AWFUL TEA SHANNON insisted she drink, Kelzi's eyelids dropped slowly over her eyes, and the room disappeared. In its place, a small, rippling stream appeared. Beyond the stream, she could see miles of beautiful, green land sprinkled with clusters of trees. A soft breeze seemed to flutter about her. *Watch and listen*, it whispered. *Watch and listen*.

She felt more than heard someone behind her. She turned to see a woman dressed in a white deerskin dress with deerskin moccasins that came up to her knees. Her long, black hair shimmered in the sunlight. Around her neck a beautiful necklace, tooled from silver and jade, glistened. Beside her stood a man wearing intricate beaded deerskin clothing. His hair—as black as hers—fell to his shoulders. They stood together in the field of trees where nothing stirred but their voices.

"I greet you, ancestor of my father." The young woman spoke in a language that flowed with melodious rhythm—a language Kelzi seemed to know as well as she knew her own.

"I greet you, daughter of the chieftain." The Indian brave's voice echoed through the trees. "Mother Earth calls to you this day. She speaks to your heart. Listen to her words." He reached out, placing an exceedingly large ear of corn in the woman's hand; the shucks, though dry with age, shielded the cob. Kelzi could feel its weight. "This will be your weapon as you protect the land."

Shadows began to separate them, and Kelzi slept.

The smell of bacon touched Kelzi's nostrils and her eyes opened to sunshine, her dream all but forgotten—for now. She blinked and sniffed while her stomach growled with hunger. "Do you think I could have some of that bacon?" she called out to Shannon.

"The sound of yer voice 'tis a joy ta me soul." Shannon laughed, appearing at the doorway of her bedroom. "A plateful be waitin' fer ye at the table so I'll be helpin' ye ta find yer feet." He threw the covers away from her. "I'll be holdin' ye careful. Ne'er ta fear."

"Ne'er ta fear?" Kelzi exclaimed. "You're twice my size. I'll not fear in the least." She wanted to laugh, but as soon as she was on her feet, everything around her seemed suddenly out of focus.

"Careful, lass," he said, holding her firmly against him.

"I think I need to sit down," she said, nausea gripping her empty stomach.

Guiding Kelzi away from the bed, Shannon eased her into the rocking chair. She could feel his hand supporting her head until it touched the high wooden back. She closed her eyes, and they remained closed until her head stopped spinning. When she felt as if she could stand, she asked if there was a bathroom close by.

Shannon nodded. "Aye, lass. Thar be one. Nae modern, but functions well enough." He helped her from the chair, supporting her. But once she got the hang of movement again, the nausea that accompanied it settled down, and she found herself sore but mobile.

The bathroom was not modern by any means, just as Shannon had said. In fact, Kelzi felt as if she had stepped back in time at least a hundred years. The walls were logs that had been stripped of their bark and rubbed down until they were smooth. The next best thing to a toilet had a silver lid. Tucked away in its own little corner sat a small bathtub—the same color as the toilet lid. In front of her stood a silver sink cradled inside an antique oak washstand. Beside the sink sat a large silver pitcher of water. Above the washstand, an oval mirror framed in oak hung on the wall.

When Kelzi finished with one of the necessities of life, she closed the toilet lid, poured water from the pitcher into her hands, picked up a brownish colored bar of soap, and washed her hands—drying them with a small, embroidered towel.

When that was done, she raised her head and looked into the mirror. But when her eyes caught the image staring back at her, an eerie sensation crept through her body. It was the face of the young woman in her dream only she looked as if she had been in an accident. The long coal-black hair fell in tousled strands on each side of her face. A thin, white cloth was taped above a badly bruised eye. There were scratches and bruises on her face and neck.

She touched her face and pulled the pins from her hair, allowing what had not already escaped, fall down her back. "Shannon!" she cried out.

"Aye?" he answered through the door.

"I'm Native American."

"I'm thinkin' only half of ye be Indian. 'Tis the Cherokee blood of the Qualla clan. Are ye nae happy aboot the fact?"

Kelzi stepped back away from the mirror, watching her reflection as she did. "I feel just fine, thank you. And the other half is . . . ?"

There was no response.

Along with an intense feeling of confusion, Kelzi was becoming more and more impatient. She opened the bathroom door and glared at Shannon. "And the other half is . . . ?"

Shannon scrunched his face in thought. "I'm thinkin' I see a wee bit of temper in the sparkle of yer eyes. Nae that I be a witness ta its sting, mind ye. But it's waitin' in the bin."

"Could you get to the answer, please?" Kelzi scowled impatiently, stepping out of the bathroom, throwing Shannon more than a wee bit of her temper.

"I'd be obliged ta say that ye carry a bit of the Irish in ye." He pulled out a chair and motioned. "'Tis time ta sit down ta breakfast afore it grows cold."

Kelzi's eyes narrowed at Shannon's conjecture, but she held her tongue and sat down on the antique chair he held out for her.

He filled their plates with eggs, toast, and bacon. He poured hot chocolate into their cups. Then he sat down opposite her and clasped his hands, leaning them against the edge of the table. "I'll be sayin' the blessin'." He bowed his head. Kelzi bowed hers and listened to one of the most thoughtful blessings she had ever heard.

"I'm impressed with your show of humbleness," she commented when he finished.

"Aye, nae like a big mountain man ta be humble, is it now?"

"That's not quite what I meant," she replied apologetically. "But since you brought up the subject, you are the first Scottish mountain man I've ever met, and you seem very sure of yourself . . . not to be critical . . . just an observation. Much like your observation of a temper you thought you saw in a pair of eyes you barely know."

Shannon slapped his thigh and let out a hearty laugh. "Aye, ye've done a turnabout." Without another word, he bit into a slice of bacon and cut into his eggs.

Kelzi did the same, feeling the satisfaction of her turnabout against the Scottish mountain man. But after a few bites, her sense of victory faded, and she set her fork down on her plate. "I had another dream," she said while her eyes lingered on her food.

Shannon stopped chewing and gave her one of his saintly smiles. "'Tis a good sign."

Kelzi folded her hands on her lap and captured Shannon's eyes. "I feel like I'm sitting inside a fog, and I don't know the way out. I have no idea what tomorrow will bring or take away from me. But I do know that I felt safe in the dream and I felt sad when it faded from me."

Shannon pushed his plate away from him. "Tell it ta me, lass. Tell it as ye saw it so ye'll know the purpose of it."

"It was as if the veil was lifted from my eyes, and I could see beyond it," Kelzi began cautiously. "It was more beautiful than I could have imagined. I watched and I listened." Her eyes filled with tears as she told him everything she had seen and heard. When she finished, she wiped the tears away, looked into the mountain man's all-knowing eyes, and sniffled. "Tell me, Shannon Ranny. Tell me what it all means. For after all I've told you, I don't know its purpose."

"I could," Shannon agreed. "But 'twould be of little use. What ye saw, ye'll be understandin' on yer own."

"You stubborn old man," she muttered, shooting him a suspicious glare. "I think you know things I should know but don't, and I can't understand why you won't tell me." She paused long enough to make sure she could see deep into his eyes. "I dare you to deny my accusation."

Shannon patted her hand as if she were a child. "Lat the kirk staun i' the kirk yaird."

The tone of his voice told her that he was denying nothing. But before she could chastise him, he hushed her, touching her lips with his finger.

"Listen careful, lass, fer what I'm sayin' 'tis this; let everythin' be in its proper place."

"Let everything be in its proper place?"

"Aye, lass. 'Tis what I already said."

"And you are trying to tell me?"

Shannon leaned his elbows on the table. "Let yer mind think. That which 'twas said in the dream 'twas a message ta ye."

His words took Kelzi aback. But Shannon was right. There was a message in the dream and the message was for her. She had looked into the Indian brave's eyes. She had felt the weight of the ear of corn. Her heart began to pound as the fog began to lift. "I was the woman in the dream, Shannon." She grabbed his arm in desperation. "Help me to understand . . . help me know who I am."

Shannon patted her hand gently. "I'm thinkin' I'll be takin' ye ta a small stream with a gentle flow an' soothin' water wher' ye can rid yerself of the dirt that hides yer beauty. Then yer mind'll be clear."

Kelzi looked down at her clothes. For the first time she became aware of their appearance, and it wasn't a pleasant sight. Dirty, wrinkled blouse and slacks—stained with grunge and blood. Her fingernails looked as they had been digging in the dirt. Her hair seemed to come alive with an odor of dirty oil. Her scalp commenced to itch as if it was crying for shampoo. Why hadn't she been aware of this before now? Was her brain still in freeze mode? She looked up at Shannon. "I think I'll take your advice. I'll . . ." Before she went any further, another thought struck her. "But I have nothing to change into."

The mountain man stood up from the table. "Aye, but ye have, lass, an' I'll be gittin' what ye need." He disappeared into the bedroom Kelzi now considered hers. While she waited, she found herself completely at a loss as to what to expect in the clothing Shannon would return with. Would they look like his? A fringed, leather, cream-colored jacket with long sleeves, perhaps. Maybe a skirt . . . or fringed leggings. Moccasins . . . or boots. Or would the clothes simply be from a pioneer wardrobe?

While she anxiously waited for him to return, Kelzi glanced around the kitchen admiring the hand-carved cupboards, the handmade table, chairs, and curtains, and the antique wood stove. Everything inside the room seemed to bring with it a sense of peace. Everything seemed to be in its proper place—even the sound of Shannon's voice when he walked back into the room carrying a fringed leather bag over his shoulder.

At that moment, however, the fact that Shannon failed to stop and show her what was in the bag truly annoyed her. He simply walked past her and out the door, an amused smile dotting his face.

"Ne'er to fear. Soon ye'll be knowin' everythin' inside," he called back to her as he stepped off the porch

Kelzi couldn't resist giving him a frosty glare that led to the abrupt comment. "I'll have to admit that I find you quite charming at times. However, this is not one of them."

"'Tis kind of ye ta say so." Shannon nodded, his eyes filled with humor. "'Tis nae wise ta always be charmin' but ta be true ta one's self—an' ta be true ta one's self cannae always be charmin' ta others."

Kelzi reflected upon Shannon's wisdom and, interestingly enough, found herself agreeing with him. Didn't she have the same philosophy? Taking a deep breath, she walked out behind him. The beauty of what she saw, beyond the cabin, was amazing. The cabin itself had been built inside a forest of trees. Something stirred inside her and a memory flashed through her head. As quickly as it appeared, however, the memory tucked itself away as if it didn't exist, leaving nothing more than a slight buzz in Kelzi's head.

"How far to the stream ye might be askin'," Shannon asked, mistaking the muddled look on her face for something it wasn't. "So I'll be tellin' ye. 'Tis beyond the grove of trees ye see in front of ye. It'll be a nice dip in the stream that'll set yer shoulders straight. It'll be as if ye are breakin' out of the cocoon an' becomin' a lovely butterfly."

A smile appeared on Kelzi's face. Shannon always had an un-rivaled way of expressing himself, whether it be an answer to a question or making a simple comment. And though she still had no idea why he came to her aid—why he had taken the responsibil-ity to see that she healed and regained her memory—she somehow knew that she could trust him . . . that she could rely on him for whatever it was that she needed.

She stepped off of porch and into the sunlight. Above her, the sun scattered its rays through the trees. All around her, the fra-grance of the woods filled the air. Walking beside Shannon, she paused and turned, facing the cabin where the sun had decorated the logs with its rays, giving them a magical, storybook appearance.

"'Tis beautiful, is it not?" Shannon whispered, standing beside her.

"It's magnificent," she whispered back.

Together, they resumed their walk through the forest, Shan-non leading the way and Kelzi feeling with the beauty of all that surrounded her.

When the stream came into view, three giant rocks portrayed themselves as waterfalls giving harmony to the cascade.

Shannon handed her the bag, adding a pleasant nod before turning away. "I'll be leavin' ye here till ye return. Then I'll be showin' ye somethin' that'll stir yer memory fer good or fer bad. 'Tis a chance we'll be takin', right enough. Still, we'll have a go at it."

Before Kelzi could respond, the mountain man had disappeared through the trees. With a deep, wistful sigh and a touch of frustration in what he had, once again, left unsaid in his explanation, Kelzi opened the leather bag, letting her frustration melt into a need to see what was inside.

A faded blue towel was the first revelation. Beneath the towel, she discovered a long skirt made from a material she didn't recognize. All she knew was that it had the feel of soft leather. Upon examining it, she found a leather string that weaved its way through small, round holes beginning three-fourths of the way up the flared skirt until it reach the waistband, where it was tied. She carefully laid the skirt over a small tree limb to the right of her.

Her hands went immediately back into the bag to find a tan cotton blouse. Next, came underclothing from another era, a pair of fringed deerskin boots, a gray bar of homemade soap, and a small jar containing bubbly pink liquid that hinted of shampoo. On the very bottom, she discovered a pair of deerskin trousers much like the ones Shannon wore.

Setting the boots beside her, she removed the rest of the items from the bag and studied them. Her head felt heavy with questions bearing undisclosed answers.

Question 1. Where did everything inside the bag come from?

Question 2. Why does everything around me look strangely familiar? The trees, the grass that's covering the dark brown earth, and the beautiful stream?

Question 3. Where am I? Am I alive or dead . . . or caught somewhere in between? Could everything around me be nothing but an illusion?"

The thought was unnerving, causing a chill to ripple down her spine. If she was somehow caught between life and death, what was she doing here? And who was Shannon? Her body began to tremble. "Pull yourself together," she breathed. "Take it one step at a time." She could do that . . . as soon as she was clean.

Kelzi hung the blouse next to the skirt, the worn towel on another limb. She removed the dirty, torn clothing she was wearing—clothing that didn't seem a part of her any more than the outfit in front of her. Lowering herself into the water, she began to hum one of Shannon's Scottish tunes as she soaped and shampooed.

From that point, she felt she could let the steps take care of themselves without further intervention.

While she was rinsing the shampoo from her hair, an image of two children—a boy and a girl—appeared in the stream. They were splashing their hands in the water and laughing. The little boy had dark blond hair and a grin as big as a bear's. The little girl had long black hair and mischievous eyes.

I bet I can stay under the water longer than you can, she heard the boy say as he sprayed water into the girl's face.

I bet you can't. The little girl laughed returning the favor before diving beneath the water.

It all seemed so familiar—the laughter . . . the voices . . . the little boy . . . the little girl. Her mind opened and then closed itself to what her eyes were seeing, to what her ears were hearing, to what her heart was feeling, and the children slowly began to fade.

"Don't go!" she whispered, reaching out to them. "Please don't go." But the children disappeared and she was, once again, alone—except for the familiar pain shooting through her head, proving that a memory had touched her.

Her body began to shake violently and she knew she had to get out of the water. She could see the faded, blue towel hanging on its limb. "Focus on the towel," she whispered, forcing her legs to move. "Just focus on the towel." At last, she felt the grass beneath her feet and the towel in her hand. With a grateful sigh, she wrapped the towel around her and dropped to the ground—begging the pain in her head to go away.

Though the pain lingered, it was stubborn determination that enabled her to stand and dress in the clothing given to her, beautiful clothing that fit quite nicely and felt unexpectedly comfortable to wear . . . though it wasn't what she was used to. "So what am I used to? Think, Kelzi, think," she said, pressing her fingers against her temples.

She froze. She had said a name. The name was Kelzi. Her pulse began to race. "Kelzi what?" she shouted. She knew the last name. It was sitting there on the edge of her tongue—waiting for her to say it. Tears started to form in the corners of her eyes. She swiftly wiped them away. She wasn't the sobbing type. She was . . . she was . . . What type was she?

Lowering herself once more to the grass, Kelzi leaned her head against the trunk of a small tree and closed her eyes, feeling as if the air had been sucked out of her.

"'Tis how it returns," a gentle voice assured her. "A spatter here, a spatter thar, until ye put it all together, ere it be good or bad."

Kelzi opened her eyes to find Shannon kneeling beside her. She grabbed his arm. "My first name is Kelzi but I can't remember my last name . . . yet."

"Ne'er ta fear. It'll come ta ye soon enough." Shannon assured her as he helped her to her feet. "An' know this old mountain man'll nae leave yer side till all ye must remember an' do is remembered an' done."

She tossed him a bewildered frown. "And that means?"

"What 'tis intended ta mean, lass," he answered, ignoring the expression on her face. "An' that's the way of it."

Kelzi shook her head in frustration. "I think I need a wee nap." Without another word, she stood and slowly stomped to the cabin and into her room where she fell onto the bed. Within seconds she was sound asleep.

"Yer becomin' yerself, lass," he chuckled. "'Tis aboot time ye did so."

Shannon let the clock tick away while he rocked back and forth in his favorite chair—his thoughts on the events of the morning.

When the clock chimed, telling him it was noon, he silenced the rocker and left the house, carrying a hand shovel. He walked to the old maple tree that had shaded the cabin each afternoon for hundreds of years. Kneeling beneath the tree, he dug into the ground. When what had been buried lay on the ground beside him, he leaned his back against the tree and picked up the small metal box, holding it to him. Though he wasn't a man for shedding tears, they fell unchecked.

A noise caught his attention. He immediately regained his composure, wiping the tears away before Kelzi could see them as she approached. In her right hand she held the buckskin—its strings untied so the information was visible. In her left hand, she carried the hunting knife and the bow. The look on her face told him she had something to say.

By the time she reached him, she was all but breathless. "My name is Kelzi Tsali, and I'm a lawyer from New York. I can shoot an arrow with the best of them and the hunting knife on the bed stand was given to me by my Uncle Yona."

"Of course, lass. 'Tis time ye remembered."

Kelzi's eyes narrowed. "You knew all along. Why didn't you simply tell me in the beginning? Why have you withheld this information from me?"

"I'll be answerin' one question at a time," he replied, giving her a look of complete and justified defense. "Yet I'll be askin' one of me own afore I begin."

Kelzi opened her mouth to object, but Shannon was already asking his question. "Do ye clothes fit like ye wish 'em ta?"

For a second, Kelzi found herself speechless. She hadn't thanked Shannon for the clothes he had given her nor had she asked him where they had come from. "I . . . I'm sorry to be so inconsiderate, Shannon. I love the clothes." She only hoped the embarrassment she felt didn't make itself evident in her face. "They fit nicely."

Shannon nodded his approval before touching his chin and squinting his eyes. "Yes, ta the first question. 'Cause, goes ta the second. The answer ta the third is: they wer thar fer ye ta find when ye was ready to find em. Ye chose nae ta, till yer brain woke up the lawyer. Now ye know 'oo ye are an' what ye are. Ye know all that's in yer head an' yer hand." He smiled with satisfaction. "An' that's the way of it."

He patted the ground beside him. "An' now, Kelzi Tsali, I'm thinkin' thar's a wee bit ta talk aboot."

TWELVE

The Sleuth

WITHIN HOURS AFTER THE CRIME, THE STORY SURROUNDING KEL-zi's tragic death had worked its way through the police departments and law offices along the county line. When the story reached Cassidy Ranny, through Robert Lincoln's office, the emotional pain he had suffered many years ago broke the surface once again, bringing tears to his eyes

Cassidy had been Kelzi's best friend from the first day of kindergarten until her death at the age of eight when a fire destroyed her home and the lives of her parents . . . at least that's what was recorded and exposed. So what really happened, so many years ago, if she was still alive until today? Where had she lived?

So many questions that needed answers and, being a lawyer himself, Cassidy decided to take the responsibility in finding and exposing the lies and crimes against the Tsali family.

Cassidy's friends knew him as a lawyer carrying on the family practice with his father. But no one beyond his parents, one colleague, and a lawyer named Robert Franklin knew he had a second job. His undercover life as a sleuth had brought many criminal secrets to the surface without anyone knowing he was the mastermind.

When Cassidy was growing up, Sherlock Holmes mysteries had been his favorite pastime reading. It was if each story took him on a real-live adventure with Mr. Holmes as his teacher and guide. As a matter of fact, as a boy, he studied the books over and over again—in much the same way as he studied the law books as a college student.

It was the flawless, though rather eccentric Mr. Holmes, who created in him the desire to solve mysteries of the more in-depth cases that crossed his desk, using the theoretical, intellectual—and yes, even theatrical—deductions used by the famous detective.

It took Cassidy exactly one day, eight hours, and fifty-five minutes to retrieve all the needed data from his secret emissaries; to organize everything according to logical and illogical perception; to call his father, explaining that he had a client that needed his attention, which meant he was checking out clues; and let his intuitive mind take over. At that point, he theorized the danger he would find himself in if the wrong people found out he was sticking his nose in their business. The slightest mistake could be his undoing. What were Sherlock's words? There is nothing more stimulating than a case where everything goes against you.

The next morning, Cassidy pulled the year-old, gray T-shirt over his head and tucked it in his faded jeans. The mountain boots came next and then the baseball cap. Leaving his new, deep-red Cadenza parked in the garage, he climbed into his 1998, dark-green Volkswagen. In his mind, he jotted down Wednesday, June 2, 4:45 a.m. Just over an hour later, the Volkswagen turned onto Canyon Road.

As Cassidy reached his destination, the sun began to paint daylight across the canyon, adding shadow and highlight to the mountains and scenery. However, its beauty only added to the anger building inside him. How could such beauty be a setting for murder?

With no answer forthcoming, Cassidy rolled down the window and let the morning breeze inside the car—in an attempt to cool the emotion. He needed to think clearly. He wouldn't allow his anger to get in the way of this investigation.

The spot where Kelzi's car had been forced over the edge was close to a mile from an old log cabin built over two hundred years ago. There was nothing left of the cabin now. Lightning struck it in 1990, burning the cabin and everything around it to the ground.

Just at that moment, an odd thought occurred to him. It wasn't a thought of logic, per se, but it still fluttered around in his head just the same. Kelzi's murder was close to the cabin that meant so much to him as a boy. Was there a clue in the thought?

Sherlock once said, In solving a problem of this sort, the grand thing is to be able to reason backwards.

Reason backwards. And what did those words have to do with what had happened here? It was then that the words Search backward erupted in his thoughts.

Perhaps his investigation would lead him somewhere not yet thought of—not considered because everyone was thinking forward . . . or was it simply wishful thinking? Still, what if—by some small chance—Kelzi had escaped the fire and was critically injured, lying somewhere dying? What if she had escaped and was only slightly injured with a broken leg, yet unable to climb out? What if she had escaped and was afraid to show herself?

The police watched the car burst into flames and saw nothing but fire and smoke. There had to be immediate doubt that Kelzi survived . . . a doubt ruling out a thorough search of the area. They had concluded there could be no way she would have survived. Yet the obvious is not always the fact.

The ledge Cassidy had been looking for came into view. He looked for any vehicles that might be parked near the area he would be investigating. Luckily there were none.

Once his car was parked behind enough shrubbery to hide it, Cassidy worked his way down the ravine to what was left of Kelzi's car. The rusting metal skeleton was almost too agonizing to look at. It made him visualize Kelzi's fear and excruciating pain—causing his heart to break and his head to reel. He closed his eyes and inhaled deeply. "Get on with it," he muttered. "Just get on with it."

Turning and walking away from the scene, Cassidy made a great effort to calm his nerves as his footprints added their impression to the many other footprints highlighting the black dirt. They led him from one end of the wreckage to the other while his eyes focused on anything that could lead him to evidence. Nothing was there. He turned away from the wreckage, changing his focus. The rocks—disturbed grass—tiny blood spots . . . anything that would give him a clue.

Two hours later, battling discouragement, Cassidy dropped to the grass beneath a tree. "Am I a fool to think I might find something the cops overlooked?" he mumbled to himself, closing his eyes and leaning his body against the tree trunk. He dropped his arms to his sides—his hands falling against the thickness of the grass.

Time drifted by without offering any hope until, at last, Cassidy resigned himself to the fact he wasn't going to find evidence of any kind. With a heavy sigh of frustration, he reached down, grabbed a handful of grass, ripped it out of the ground, and threw it in the air.

Something fell on his shoe. It appeared to be a piece of material approximately three inches in diameter . . . a material heavy enough to have been attached to a jacket. On the edge of the material he found dried blood. His heart skipped a beat as a ray of hope enveloped him only to be followed by doubt once again.

"Still," he said to himself, "there's a chance, no matter how slim." He studied the scrap of material while analyzing the possibility that this evidence hidden from the eyes of the cops now lay in the palm of his hand. He had to believe this piece of torn, bloodstained material had been waiting for him to find.

THIRTEEN

Trail of Truth

K ELZI SAT ON THE GROUND NEXT TO SHANNON, BENEATH THE OLD
shade tree in front of the cabin. "Okay. You talk. I'll listen," she
announced while making herself comfortable. "But when you're
through talking, I had better know a lot more than I do now." She
flipped her hair behind her shoulders with a hint of impatience and
folded her arms, giving Shannon a look that told him she expected
nothing less than the whole truth.

"I'll nae be talkin' ta ye, lass."

Kelzi jolted upright. "What did you just say?" She was beginning to, once again, feel the frustration that seemed to flare up
rather quickly the longer she conversed with Shannon. She turned
to glare at him, but what she saw in his eyes startled her. A look of
sadness seemed to come from somewhere inside—reaching out to
her. She quietly took her place against the tree and waited.

As if he hadn't even heard her outcry, Shannon continued.
"'Tis a story I'll be tellin'—the trail of truth."

Kelzi quietly folded her hands on her lap and waited, giving
Shannon her full attention.

"Thar are those 'oo have taken the liberty of writin' thar own
stories of the Cherokee that are more in keepin' ta thar line of
thinkin'—ta cover up thar own conscience. But from me, ye will be

94

hearin' the truth." He reached out and touched her eyelids with his fingers. "Ye'll be takin' a journey, lass."

Kelzi's eyelids became heavy and all the scenery in front of her began to disappear, leaving her in a strange but beautiful setting. She found herself walking across a narrow gorge and to a green meadow that appeared to stretch for miles into the distance.

While Shannon's voice told the story, it literally came alive in front of Kelzi. She could see two powerful Cherokee braves: one a tribal chief and protector of his people; the other a scribe and rebel, who would become one of the greatest defenders of the Cherokee way of life. She witnessed the strong religious beliefs they carried within them. She saw proof of their written language—of their government that was unknown and not understood by those who first landed on the shores of the Americas.

Shannon's voice became more dynamic as he introduced Kelzi to the last of a tribe, who emigrated from the Great Plains of the Southwest to their distant relatives in the mountains of the east. He made it possible for her to actually witness all that he was telling her.

As she watched and listened, Kelzi felt the tribe's unspeakable suffering and broken spirits from the famine that had cursed their land. She felt their joy when those who lived in the mountains of the east welcomed them. She stood among them when those of the southwest presented their relatives with a grand gift—the gift of their language written on thin gold plates. She listened as the children learned to read and write from those same plates.

Her journey slowly became her reality, reflecting a strong attachment to her Cherokee ancestors while she learned from them.

She witnessed those who came to settle the territory thinking the Indians to be heathens, who could neither read nor write. Preachers, thinking they were superior to the Cherokee, came to teach them God's true religion. They never suspected the Cherokee cared nothing for their preaching, only the opportunity to learn their language.

The scene of Kelzi's journey changed as Shannon's story took her on another path, and she found herself standing in front of an old fence. The sky behind it was dark and filled with sadness.

"What ye see afore ye is whar the life of the great scribe an' chieftain, Sogwili, began. This is whar he learned his skills when but a wee lad. Thar he learned from his father that the white man 'oo came into thar camp ta trade came more ta spy fer the purpose of kidnappin' an' forcin' the Cherokee people into slavery. 'Twas a fierce an' violent beginnin' ta a fierce an' violent end fer those 'oo were the first ta set foot on America's soil. Can ye see em, lass? Can ye see the shadows of many warriors against the flames of a campfire?"

"Yes," Kelzi whispered, "I can see them."

"See the war paint on thar faces. See the flame from the camp-fire that glows in thar eyes. See the bows an' arrows on thar backs. Feel the beat of the war drums. Hear the pulse of the war cry that falls from thar lips an' brings courage ta thar hearts. Understand that they give thar lives in battle so they'll nae become slaves ta the white man.

"Thar leader, Sogwili, was a scribe an' a rebel, 'oo was one of the greatest defenders of the Cherokee way of life. Yet, fer all that he did fer his people, he'd be hunted down by traitors of his own kind and given ta the white man 'oo tortured him. They war' a witness ta his courage fer he ne'er cried out. He did a turnabout. He recited his Idigawesdi.[1] His pride made him stronger than those 'oo tortured him an' left him ta die.

"Nay, but he lived, and fearin' fer the safety of his people, he led 'em ta the west. But the white man soon followed him, an' this brave Cherokee leader was killed with a white man's rifle.

"Died a martyr's death, he did, an' his name cannae ever be forgotten. What he did fer his people would ne'er be forgotten."

Shannon was standing in front of Kelzi, now. Her eyes followed his movement as he reached down, picked up a narrow stick,

---

1. *Idigawesdi* is a prayer in which all who belong to the Cherokee Nation become unified and spiritually at peace in the face of a force that threatens to take a Cherokee's life.

and used it to write, with the symbols, the names of the Cherokee braves who would never be forgotten. When the symbols had all been sketched into the ground, he laid the stick at his side, and just for one brief moment, Kelzi felt as if the earth was quiet and at rest.

Shannon studied the young woman beside him, then dropped his eyes to the symbols sketched in the dirt. "Yers is a strong spirit, Kelzi Tsali. Ye have been chosen well. But I'm askin' if ye understand the sacrifice."

For several minutes, Kelzi sat there reliving all that she had heard and seen and felt. "I witnessed Sogwili's torture—his pain—his courage, Shannon. I heard his Idigawesdi." She looked deep into the mountain man's eyes. "I watched him die, Shannon. How can I not understand?" She wiped the tears away that had fallen down her face. "Tell me how you did this, Shannon. Tell me how you were able to bring all this to life for me."

"'Tis a simple answer I'll be givin' ye, lass. 'Twas a miracle meant fer ye, so that ye be understandin' why yer father was willin' ta sacrifice his life fer his people. 'Twas meant ta give ye courage so that ye'll nae be afraid when ye do what ye must do in the face of danger."

Shannon reached into his pocket and removed something wrapped in leather. "A gift fer ye, lass." He took her hand and placed it on her palm, closing her fingers around it. "'Tis a necklace made by Sogwili."

She opened her fingers, and her breath caught in her throat. In her hand lay a delicate replica of a bird, cut in silver, its wings spread in flight. Flames of gold swept over the lower part of its body above logs of silver and turquoise.

"What ye have thar is the Phoenix, 'oo burns then rises from its own ashes ta live again. 'Tis a symbol of earth, life, death, an' resurrection."

Shannon took the necklace from Kelzi's hand and placed it around her neck. "'Twill always be a protection ta ye just as the Cherokee spirit was a protection ta ye that day ye wer ta burn ta ashes, ne'er ta rise again till the resurrection."

Kelzi caressed the necklace with her fingers then brought it to her lips. "I can testify to you, Shannon. I've seen their courage. I can feel their love for their people." She paused, grabbing the mountain man's arm, tears falling down her face. "Shannon, I can truly feel their pain. I understand. I promise you that I am ready."

The two sat there in silence for several minutes, listening to the all-encompassing melody of Cherokee bravery. "This melody comes to ye, Kelzi," Shannon explained as it faded in the distance. "'Tis time fer me ta give ye something ye'll soon be needin'." He held out the metal box and placed it on Kelzi's lap. "Open the lid, lass."

Kelzi did as she was advised. Inside was a very large and very old ear of corn. The shucks were dried and gray, hanging loose from the darkened corn that clung to the ancient cob. On the shucks was painted the Cherokee syllabary.

"Tell me what ye see, lass," Shannon said, watching Kelzi's eyes study the ear of corn in depth. She carefully removed it from the metal box and caressed the dry shucks with her fingers, electrified by what she saw. "I've seen this before . . . I've felt its weight before," she stammered.

"Aye, lass. That ye have."

"What does it represent, Shannon?"

Shannon patted her hand. "In time ye will understand. But fer now, I need ye ta put the corn back inside its protector. An' I'll be askin' ye ta keep it close by, fer soon ye'll be needin' it."

Kelzi let her fingers linger over the parched shucks, as if their secret and their purpose had somehow become a fragment of her, making it difficult for her to part with them. When she finally put the ear of corn back inside the metal box, she cradled it in her arms. "You'll forgive me if I need a moment or two to absorb all that you've told me without helping me understand all that you've told me. You say that I'm going to protect my people's land with this shuck of corn without explaining what it is the corn represents and why I feel so drawn to it. Why can't you just say what it is you need to say without making it so difficult for me to understand?"

Shannon placed his hat on his head and grinned. "Ye hae a quid Scots Tung in yer heid. And that's the way of it."

The glint in his eye gave nothing away. Kelzi wasn't sure if he was paying her a compliment or scolding her—or both. "Translation please," she groaned

"In simple English it might say, ye can speak up fer yerself."

Kelzi thought for a moment before replying, "I think I'll take that as a compliment."

"As ye should, lass," he replied. "Now I'll be takin' ye ta see the beauty of the land that ye are ta protect. Ye'll be makin' a wee bit of lunch while I'll be gettin' the horses, fer 'twill take what's left of the day ta see enough of her beauty."

Kelzi recognized Shannon's ability to switch from one subject to another in a blink of an eye—without a hitch. But horses? Was it a touch of blarney he was giving her?

A touch of blarney it was not. Even before Kelzi had a wee bit of lunch in the basket, Shannon returned with two striking Palominos. They wore no saddles, only bridles. All she could do was to settle herself on the back of the horse, trying hard to keep logic from breaking apart the dream she found herself in. She was actually delighted to feel the pain caused from pinching herself in an effort to prove that everything around her was real—or wasn't real but compatible with realism.

Kelzi's logical mind continued to debate the issue while the two of them rode in silence for close to thirty minutes. The rustling of the leaves and the rhythm of the horses' hooves were the only sounds that resonated through the air.

When they reached their destination, Shannon's voice broke the silence with an explanation that caused Kelzi to wonder if he could read her mind. "Logic cannae debate God's work. Let the beauty of the land take ye away from it. Listen ta the whispers of the breeze. It fills the air with the sorrow of its story. Can ye feel it, lass?"

Kelzi nodded, closing her mind to logic and allowing her eyes to view the beauty of the land that surrounded her, feeling its sadness as well.

Even Shannon's eyes began to mist as he pointed to a path that lay ahead of them, all but hidden beneath the overgrowth of field grass and wild flowers. "Do ye see it?" he asked.

In that instant, a flashback from another time jarred Kelzi's memory. She reined in her horse.

Shannon was immediately beside her. "Let yer brain take a spring on its own fiddle," he advised soothingly. "Tell me yer story, lass, as we walk the path ye walked as a child. Ye know it now. Yer memory's awake."

Kelzi climbed down from her horse and stood beside a path all but hidden from the human eye. She cleared away the weeds that cluttered it. She knelt beside the path and let her memory take her back to another time. She could see a four-year-old girl, her hand in her father's hand, walking along the path. The little girl was listening quietly while her father told her about her ancestors.

Kelzi stood and stepped onto the path, following it while brushing away leaves with her shoes. "This path was made by thousands of Cherokee moccasins," she said, her voice hushed in reverence. "It's the path that leads to their sacred burial grounds. My father would saddle his horse, set me in the saddle, climb on behind me, and bring me here. He would tell me stories of his people who now rest in the sacred ground. He told me there were many acres of land and many hundreds of graves that must be protected until the Great Spirit comes."

Kelzi's brows suddenly furrowed and her eyes seemed to focus on something other than the path. A moment later, she climbed back onto her horse and turned so she could look at Shannon and realize the gift she had been given. Everything was now perfectly clear.

All that had happened to her had happened for a reason. She needed to understand fear so she could escape its grasp. She needed to feel courage so she could think without fear's distraction. She needed to be strong in her conviction in order to thwart the danger that would surely surround her.

Kelzi let her eyes survey the land. She could feel the strength of Mother Earth. She was a symbol of the necklace she wore.

Shannon smiled, letting silence reign, allowing Kelzi's mind to dwell on what she had just witnessed so she would never doubt her calling.

As if her mouth wanted to refresh her memory, she talked about her childhood and her friend named Cassidy, explaining that some days they would swim in the stream not far from where she and Shannon stood. Other days they would catch tadpoles or Cassidy would go to her house, and her father would tell them stories of his ancestors while her mother made them cookies. She hesitated at that point, glancing at Shannon out of the corner of her eye. "Somehow, I think you already know everything I'm telling you."

"Aye, that I do, lass—just as ye do. Ye cannae know what a touch of the past can do ta help understand the future, and we've not much time afore yer path be set ta the future. Know that all that ye learned on the reservation will be the strength ye'll carry inside ye."

Kelzi let Shannon's words penetrate her reasoning, taking it back to the reservation and the lessons of life she had learned. Did she ever think, when she was learning how to use the bow and arrow, that one day she would use that ability to save her life?

Smiling, she brought her thoughts back to what Shannon had said and was now beginning to realize how much he had given her and how she had taken for granted all that he had done for her. He had given her more than she could compute in her brain at the moment. However, she was beginning to understand that he also had pledged himself to all that was ahead of them.

"As much as I have a purpose, you have a purpose as well, or you wouldn't be here," she stated, hoping he would come forward with a needed explanation. When none came, she knew she had to be patient for yet a little while. She gazed in his direction, noting the all-knowing expression on his face. "I want to thank you for everything you've done for me," she said at last.

"Yer welcome, lass. An' now I'm thinkin' 'tis time ta eat."

Shannon escorted Kelzi to a grassy spot beneath a willow tree. "'Tis a bit of Heaven felt here," he said, sitting down next to her, the basket in his hand. He removed four pieces of flatbread, a bowl filled with blueberries, three strips of dried beef, two cups, two plates, two forks, and a water bag. He laid Kelzi's plate in front of her, filled with food.

Kelzi thanked him, but she didn't touch the food. Instead, another question introduced itself to her—a question that demanded an answer now. Folding her hands on her lap, she requested Shannon's attention, telling him of her experience when her car went over the edge of the mountain. "I could see a soft glow of light. From inside the light, a Cherokee brave appeared. I reached out to him and suddenly I was outside the car, watching it roll down the mountain while he held me as easily as if I was a child . . . and I was that child again. Far away from the flames, he laid me on the ground, touched my eyelids with his fingers, and whispered, 'E-ga-si-nu.'

"He told me to sleep. What did he mean, Shannon? What did he mean when he told me to sleep? Am I . . . am I somewhere caught between life and death? Is that why I could see the Cherokee life pass before me? And what am I doing here . . . with you? And what are you doing here?" she pleaded. "Tell me, Shannon, please."

Shannon placed his hands on her shoulders so the two of them were face-to-face. "I'll be tellin' ye that ye are alive, lass. Ye are alive an' well. An' thar be much fer ye ta do in the next few days ta prove that ye are alive."

Kelzi could see deep into the mountain man's tender eyes, eyes that revealed wisdom . . . eyes that spoke the truth. "Who are you, Shannon?" she asked. "All I know is that you're from Scotland, you love your wife deeply, and you have two sons who are as handsome as you are."

Shannon chuckled as he heard her call him handsome. But then, he had always believed that he was just that. He also believed she was ready to know his purpose in her life. "It'll be a strange story fer yer ears," he began, "but I'll tell ye what ye'll be wantin' ta know."

She sat up straight, focusing her eyes directly on Shannon. "I'm alive . . . I'm alive, and I'm listening," she said, quietly, anxious for Shannon to share his story.

"That ye are," Shannon agreed, nodding his head. "Byde weill, betide weill."

"Excuse me?"

"Simply means everythin' comes ta him 'oo waits—an' I'll keep ye waitin' no longer." Shannon paused, leaning against the tree, allowing his legs to stretch into a comfortable position. Then, he began.

"Ta start, lass, I'll nae be the age I may appear. Neither are me customs an' clothes of this time. I'll be tellin' ye right out. Born in the year of 1700, in Scotland, I was. Come ta America at thirty-two—with me bonny wife an' two handsome sons." His face became reflective. "Many acres we had, an' we built our hoose here. Five years passed an' me wife died givin' birth ta a stillborn. Had I nae had the responsibility fer the carin' of me sons, I would've pined away into death meself. Instead, I went ta the mountains ta find solitude, takin' 'em with me."

He adjusted his hat and brushed his hand over his eyes. "'Twas a friend ta the Cherokee people an' lived among them fer many years. Me sons learned the Cherokee way, the language, an' the religion. Ye call me a mountain man an' that's what I was. 'Tis what I am still."

Kelzi had become so mesmerized with Shannon's story that she was beginning to envision it in her own mind. When he talked of the deceit of the white man, she could see their faces, etched with lies—the treaties worth nothing but the ink covering the paper with lies. She came to realize that what she had witnessed in her dream, he had witnessed in his life. She understood why his desire was to remain with the Cherokee . . . away from those who took from the Cherokee all that was theirs.

"When thar chief took his people west, me sons an' I watched over thar land. After I died, me descendants watched over the land as I had done. Then one day, one came down from the mountain an' fell in love with the valley an' a bonny lass. When the two wer' wed, his father-in-law gave him a hundred acres. The two made thar home in this valley."

Kelzi wanted to ask a question but Shannon touched her lips with his finger. His touch caused a stirring within her, allowing him to take her on a journey of true understanding. To do so, he continued his story in the Cherokee language.

> *Long ago, the white man saw the richness of the land and became greedy. But there was an old mountain man who had lived among the Cherokee for many years and owned much land. He took a piece of hide from the buffalo and worked it until it became parchment. On the parchment he drew a map of the land he would give to the Cherokee. Beneath the map he wrote the words of a deed, telling of his ownership of the land that once belonged to the Cherokee and the spiritual land where their dead lay buried. Before this old man withdrew back into the mountains, never to return again, he placed his sign upon the deed, giving back to the Cherokee what had once belonged to them. The deed had to be honored, and when the children of those who had traveled west returned, they built their homes and began to farm the land.*

Shannon pointed, turning Kelzi's attention to the east, and spoke in English once again. "Yer father's home was the beginnin' of the Cherokee land. He protected the rights of his people an' the land that are thars. Still, in all his wisdom, thar was no stoppin' the white man from tryin' ta rid themselves of yer father's people. Afore he died, he had a dream, an' in his dream, he saw his child save the land of his people. 'Twas a dream more priceless than a sea of diamonds."

Kelzi thought she saw a tear appear in the corner of Shannon's eye when he pointed to the tree behind her. "Do ye see the syllabary, lass?"

Kelzi stood and turned her eyes in the direction of a tree where something was carved in the trunk. She walked to the tree and studied it carefully, tracing her finger over the imprint. "What does it mean?"

"Pull the bark from the tree," Shannon instructed her.

Placing her fingers around the edges of the bark, she could see where it had been cut away. It didn't give way easily. But when it did, it fell into her hands, and she could see that the inside of the bark had been slivered and something written in Cherokee syllabary was carved into its smooth surface. She read, "Always listen to your dreams, for they will teach you many things."

"'Tis a message from yer father, lass."

Kelzi held the bark close to her, trying to comprehend it all. Then she looked down at Shannon, her eyes filled with wonder. "My father wrote this . . . to me?"

"Aye, lass. That he did."

Kelzi knelt beside Shannon so she could look directly into his face. "I feel like I'm walking inside a dream. Tell me, Shannon, am I dreaming? Are you a dream?"

"Nae. 'Tis like a dream, but ye are awake, an' that's the way of it."

"Help me understand," she pleaded. "Not my responsibility, nor that of my father. But why a Cherokee brave? Why you?"

"I'll do me best, lass," Shannon said, crossing his legs in front of him, placing his hands on his knees. "'Cause the brave was the great Cherokee Chieftain over the land, he was given the responsibility ta watch over ye when yer life was in danger. 'Cause the land was mine, God sent me ta walk with ye till the deed is safe again."

Kelzi touched his face. "This is why I wasn't afraid when I woke up with you standing over me. This is why your smile is so gentle. This is why you make me feel safe. You are a gentle man, Shannon. You are a special spirit . . . an angel."

"Aye. This rugged, old, Scottish mountain man ye see afore ye will be yer advocate—visible only ta ye, an' that'll be the way of it."

105

Kelzi shivered in the thrill of the miracle she had been given, yet she had to say, "You're not what I envisioned an angel to be. I thought they wore white and were . . . well, angelic." She paused, letting her mind go over what she had just said. "Oh! Not that I don't think you're angelic, because you are a beautiful, angelic . . . angel." She shook her head. "I'm not saying what I mean . . . but I mean what I'm trying to say. You're my angel, Shannon Ranny— my very own angel!"

"That I am, Kelzi Tsali. That I am, an' I feel the responsibility of it from cap ta buckle. God gave me this assignment 'cause I know the truth. He chose Sogwili cause he is the truth. He chose ye cause ye have the truth. The next few days we'll be puttin' a stop ta those 'oo have the silver tongues an' deceitful hearts. Our way will nae be understood by mortal man, fer they cannae see beyond thar own understanding, which will be thar undoin'. On that day, Miss Kelzi Tsali, ye'll be standin' fer the Cherokee nation an' fer those 'oo will be speakin' through ye."

Kelzi found herself completely mesmerized by all that Shannon told her—her lawyer mind left to fend for itself. Worldly logic has no license where angels abide, where God presides. Whatever Shannon had in store for her would be as it should be. "Thank you, Shannon, for being who you are," she whispered.

"'Tis an honor, lass. 'Tis truly an honor, an' I be tellin' ye that some answers wait till the end ta be answered. But when the time comes ta claim the deed, the crimes of those 'oo committed them will be painted so dark on thar faces fer all ta see, an' thar will be no doubt."

FOURTEEN

The Plan

THE SUN HAD SHIFTED TO THE WEST, CASTING SHADOWS IN FRONT OF the cabin. Shannon sat beneath the old tree—folding his legs in front of him. Kelzi sat across from him, studying the all-knowing eyes of her angel. "I'm listening. Tell me the plan."

"Oh, 'tis one ye'll be proud of," Shannon exclaimed. "Aw the wit i' the warld's no in ae pow, an' 'twill be a joy ta be seek hir saw whaur ye got yer sair." Shannon looked up toward heaven. "Not meanin' ta be disrespectful, sir, only satisfied." Then he smiled at Kelzi. "Sometimes I'm speakin' afore me brain has time ta consider what 'tis I'm sayin'. But God knows what's inside me, so He'll be forgivin' me fer the touch of reckonin' that hides in me heart."

Kelzi couldn't help but feel a deep curiosity concerning Shannon's Scottish sayings that made no sense to her. She simply had to ask for a translation.

There was no translation. Instead, Shannon's explanation took another route. "I'd be tellin' ye that all the wit in the world is not in one head—though the heads of the foe believe it ta be. An' it'll be a joy ta seek redress from the people 'oo wronged ye. Simple words. When all the wrong is righted, yer life will return ta what it was afore we wer' acquainted."

Shannon's last sentence hurled shock waves through Kelzi. She wasn't prepared for the truth in this matter. "We both know that my life will never be the same as it was because you have given me something . . ." Kelzi's words caught in her throat, and tears she hadn't planned on surfaced. With a stroke of a finger she caught them before they fell down her cheeks. "I can't explain what I feel right now. But I think you know what I feel."

"That I do, lass," Shannon assured her, tilting his head. "That I do."

They talked of other things then—of Shannon's life as a mountain man and of his blessed death, as he put it, so that he could return home to his bonny wife. He explained that Cassidy was his fifth-great-grandson. "The lad is much like me in many ways, as ye will learn in time."

The conversation shifted. "Ye wer' like yer great-grandfather, Kelzi. Ye have the Cherokee spirit in ye. Courage is powered within ye. 'Tis a delight ta tell ye of the gift locked inside ye. It glows in yer face. It dances inside yer heart. Ye cannae be tossed in fear nor can ye be driven from yer task."

Shannon's voice faded into the background and time seemed to stand still—just for a moment—as an undaunted feeling of peace flowed through Kelzi, allowing Shannon's words to reach inside her and unlock the gift he spoke of—an awakening to the knowledge that would be her strength, an awakening to the understanding that Shannon was sent to protect her.

Kelzi moved to Shannon's side and leaned against the tree, touching shoulders with her angel.

Shannon twisted the tip of his mustache with his fingers. "Yer ta be in the middle of many a miracle, as ye see it ta be, so nae ta fear, lass, just know all is well." He paused for a moment to let Kelzi digest what he had said. "What ye need ta know, lass, may nae sound like logic ta a lawyer like yerself. I'll nae be fillin' yer head with delusion. But I promise I'll be keepin' ye on the straight path. And now ta be explainin' the plan ta ye."

As he talked, Kelzi listened with uninterrupted interest—never questioning his bizarre ideas or theories of how they would all come together. When he finished, she just sat there, astonished at his mind's eye, and imagined how his plan would play out. Finally she said, "It all sounds so . . . so crazy, yet so incredible. I think it just might work."

Shannon raised an eyebrow. "It'll work, or I'd nae have thought of it." With that said, he stood up, then reached down and helped Kelzi to her feet. "'Tis time to take another path."

His words reminded Kelzi that with all she had seen and experienced during the morning hours of the day, there was one more thing she needed to do before it was too late. She needed to see the car she was driving when she was forced off the road and down the mountain. When she asked Shannon if it was possible, his reply surprised her.

"'Tis a request I'd hoped ye'd be askin', lass. We'll be needin' walking sticks." He led Kelzi to the cabin, where he retrieved the walking sticks, handing her the shortest one.

Kelzi threw on her jacket, accepted her walking stick, and followed her angel as he guided her down a narrow path, almost invisible in the shadows of the late afternoon. The only sounds that touched her ears were the rustling of the leaves beneath her feet and the voices of the breeze and the stream as they came together. Her angel was quiet.

After hiking through the ravine, Kelzi found herself staring at the car destroyed by fire, its skeleton covered in black soot, tree limbs, scattered rocks, and mountain clay. The sight sent a revolting chill through her. Her stomach felt as if it was going to rid itself of everything inside it. She closed her eyes, pressing the palms of her hands against them to shut out the image of the car remains.

When her eyes opened, she focused on the mountainside where the car left evidence of its demise.

She could see Shannon out of the corner of her eye. He was close by, if she needed him. She shuddered, blaming the coolness of the breeze. Her insides felt like the muscles were attacking the intestines. *Okay, tough girl. Pull yourself together,* her brain warned her. *It's only a car.*

"It's only a car . . . it's only a car," she repeated to herself as she reached out her hand and touched the damaged metal, letting her fingers follow its contour. Yes, but it was the car I was driving, and they destroyed it. She knelt and placed her head against what was left of a door. She closed her eyes in a prayer of gratitude for the Cherokee spirit and the protection of a guardian angel. After a moment of inner conversation with herself, she called out to Shannon, "I'm doing fine."

"I know, lass," he replied.

She pulled herself to a standing position. Taking a deep breath, she backed away from the car. Not that she needed another look at what had been taken from her. She just wanted to feel the anger for what had been taken. She wanted to feel the tenderness of the miracle for what had been given. And she needed to put everything in perspective.

"Kelzi?" a voice called from somewhere behind her, and she felt as if her heart stopped beating. Her eyes searched for the mountain man, but he was nowhere in sight. Though fear wanted its place inside her, she pushed it away, allowing her eyes to follow the outline of a man in the shadows. "Who are you?" she demanded, keeping her voice firm.

The man stepped away from the shadows so she could see him better. "I'm Cassidy."

"He's tellin' ye the truth, lass," she heard Shannon say from somewhere behind her. "Now I'd be askin' him what he's doin' here."

"How do you know it's him?" Kelzi uttered beneath her breath

"All the good looks of the Rannys, he has. Now ask him."

Kelzi turned her attention back to the man in front of her. She had to admit that he did bear a resemblance to Shannon. "You say your name is Cassidy. So tell me your last name and, for further information, explain why you are here—in this canyon—next to this car."

"'Tis the way to put it to him, lass," Shannon complimented her.

"Oh, shush," she growled.

Cassidy took a step closer, looking slightly confused. "You ask me a question then tell me to shush?"

Kelzi rolled her eyes and shook her head. "Please. Just answer the question."

"My name is Cassidy Ranny. Kelzi Tsali was my friend when I was a boy. I thought she died in the same fire that killed her parents." He took a step closer. His eyes focused on her face. "Kelzi, where have you been for the past eighteen years?"

Kelzi took a step closer to Cassidy in an effort to see his face more clearly and look into his eyes in order to determine his honesty. The moment their eyes connected, her heart told her she was standing in front of her childhood friend. Had another miracle just entered her life?

Her thoughts were so wrapped up with the fact that Cassidy was standing in front of her . . . all grown up . . . she forgot the question. "I'm sorry," she sputtered. "What was it you asked me?"

"Where have you been for the past eighteen years?" Cassidy repeated, his voice now carrying a sympathetic tone. "I don't mean to come across as an interrogator. It's just that I've missed you and I need to know."

Kelzi smiled. This handsome man was truly Cassidy Ranny. She didn't mind answering his question, though it took some time to explain, simply because she had to begin at the beginning. She told him of her years on the reservation and her years at Harvard, ending with her current position as a lawyer in upstate New York. Her story could have easily been mistaken for a fairy tale if she hadn't been so emotionally immersed in its telling.

Before Cassidy could respond, Kelzi inquired, "Can you tell me what brought you to this place?"

Cassidy thought for a minute before answering. "I believe . . ." A frown crossed his face and he took a deep breath. "I believe I was prompted." He glanced up at the cliff next to them. He glanced at the burned car beside them. "I came to this spot with the impression that I just might find something the officers missed while investigating." He walked to the spot where he found the piece of cloth. "Here's where I discovered proof that you weren't inside the car nor were you beneath the car when it exploded.

"About a half hour later, I heard the rustling of foliage and I saw two people coming toward me. I waited . . . and here we are, facing each other . . . and, right now, I feel like I'm dreaming."

Shannon smiled, revealing the pride in his heart for this young man. "I'm thinkin' he's answered yer question well enough. An' I'm thinkin' he'll be a help ta us when the time comes. So the next thin' I'd be askin'—if I wer' doin' the askin', mind ye—if he'd be willin' ta stand with us."

"Are you serious?" Kelzi gasped, turning and staring at Shannon in disbelief.

"Of course I'm serious!" Cassidy exclaimed. "Don't you believe in promptings of the Spirit?"

Realizing Cassidy had heard the question meant for Shannon's ears, Kelzi glanced at Shannon, rolling her eyes. She whispered, "So what do I tell him about you?"

"We'll wait a spell fer that one. Just keep yer wits about ye."

"Right!" Kelzi suddenly found herself strangely captivated by the circumstances she found herself in. First, an angel rescues her from those who wish her dead. Then, a handsome prince enters with a wish to save her from further danger. Sadly, the prince can't rescue her from the possible danger that surrounds her. However, the angel requests the help of the prince, and together they . . .

"I'm sorry, I didn't quite hear you," Cassidy said, cautiously taking a step back.

It suddenly dawned on Kelzi what her childhood friend must be seeing in front of him. "I do believe in the prompting of the Spirit," Kelzi uttered through trembling lips, "and I'm sorry I seem rather off the edge . . . but I've been through a rather strange and frightening ordeal, and now I find myself talking to someone I haven't seen in years at the bottom of a mountain where a truck purposely forced me over the edge."

Cassidy took a step closer to her.

"Where, because of a miracle, I was saved from burning to death inside a car that now looks like a skeleton . . . while I'm trying to understand why you're here and why I'm here and if what I'm now experiencing is a dream . . . or real . . . or . . ."

Without warning, she found Cassidy's arms around her. Without thinking, she wrapped her arms around his neck and—feeling his strength—began to sob. When she was finally able to get control of herself, she stepped back and asked, "It's really you, isn't it, Cassidy? I could feel your shoulder beneath my head. I could feel your arms around me. That means you're real, doesn't it?"

"Didn't I tell you a long time ago that I would protect you forever?" Cassidy reminded her, wiping away the remnants of tears that still dotted her chin. "I promise you that I'll do whatever it is I need to do to help you through whatever it is you have to go through."

Cassidy studied the striking young woman in front of him. She was taller than he thought she would be. She was more beautiful, as well, which he didn't mind at all. He actually pinched himself to make sure he wasn't dreaming—it all seemed so mystical. In his heart, he felt gratefulness for listening when he should have listened and for acting when it was time to act.

"Tell me what happened," he asked. "Tell me where you've been these past few days." He gently touched her face as he examined the wound. "Tell me who stitched up your forehead."

"It's a long story," Kelzi replied. "I promise to tell you everything. But first, if you've been investigating, I need to tell you that the deed is safe and ask you if you would be willing to help me see that it is delivered into the right hands.

"You know I will," Cassidy replied eagerly. "Let's turn and walk away from this . . . this nightmare. Then you must tell me what it is I need to know."

FIFTEEN

The Reunion

KELZI MEANT TO GIVE CASSIDY THE SLIGHTEST GLANCE AS THEY walked away from the car. But she found her eyes lingering almost a full minute as she studied the strong profile of his face, remembering the deep-set eyes that looked into hers just moments before—their color a brilliant blue. His hair was still a soft, golden brown. His frame was straight and lean. His stride was that of a man full of confidence. She had to force her eyes away, telling herself she was simply analyzing him as if he were a client or the prosecuting attorney.

"Is he nae a handsome man, lass?" Shannon quipped, not fooled by her pretense. "A true Ranny from cap ta buckle."

Cap to buckle? Indeed he was. A giggle escaped Kelzi's lips.

"What?" Cassidy asked, giving her a puzzled look.

"I'm sorry," she apologized. "I was just thinking how much you look like someone else I know. A very kind gentleman, actually." She paused and took a deep breath. "Not only a gentleman . . . but an angel. An angel named Shannon Ranny."

Cassidy stopped abruptly, throwing out his arm, prohibiting Kelzi from taking another step. His eyes probed deep into hers. "Excuse me, did you say Shannon Ranny?"

"It seems ye jumped right into the well like a slung-stane,"

Shannon said from behind her. "Me thinks ye've caught his attention."

"'Tis good ta' know, Shannon," Kelzi mimicked him, under her breath.

A deep frown appeared on Cassidy's face. "Don't get me wrong," he said with a hint of caution in his voice, "but I can't help but wonder if you have a slight concussion."

Reviewing her day of learning, understanding, and accepting, Kelzi realized that if things were in reverse, she would have come to the same conclusion. She looked into Cassidy's eyes assuring him that she didn't have a concussion, adding that things were not as they seemed at the moment.

Cassidy cautiously agreed just before his eyes shot up, focusing on Kelzi's face. "You said . . ." He swallowed hard. "You said that Shannon is an angel?"

"Yes," Kelzi replied. "And now we need to talk."

"Right!" Cassidy slowly rotated his eyes, first to the left and then to the right while trying to appear calm. Which he wasn't . . . but he wanted Kelzi to think that he was. "Okay . . . I can go with that. I mean, I believe in angels, although I didn't know they had last names . . . last names like my last name." His nerves seemed to fray. "And the same name as my ancestor." He narrowed his eyes suspiciously. "Answer this question before we go any further. If you can see him, why can't I?"

"Because he's not your angel."

Cassidy strained to rationally absorb this information. During that moment, however, something else caught his eye. He reached out his hand and touched the sleeve of Kelzi's jacket. "The clothes you're wearing. They appear authentic Cherokee."

"They are authentic Cherokee," Kelzi replied, realizing Cassidy was experiencing the same sensations she had while trying to remember everything she had forgotten. The difference was that it was all totally new to him.

By now, the sun was beginning to set, and there was still much to talk about. Kelzi suggested they sit by the river and watch the sun set, just as they did when they were children. "Though it's a different river, it's the same sun, and that's what matters at this point, right?"

Cassidy said nothing. He only nodded, running his hands over his eyes and down the sides of his face as Kelzi led the way to the river bank.

"Besides, you need to be sitting when I tell you everything," she explained once they had found the perfect spot on the grass. For a few minutes, silence ruled while they watched the sun move behind the horizon, allowing the shadows of night to appear, just like they did when they were six and seven and eight.

"Okay, I'm ready to hear what it is you need to tell me," Cassidy said with a touch of impatience that was steadily growing inside him.

"What I'm about to tell you will sound strange to you," she began. "Just know that it is the truth." A sigh escaped Kelzi's lips before her words came out, guarded yet dynamic. "Shannon Ranny is my guardian angel."

Cassidy's spine tingled. His eyes darted from left to right and back again. His next words came out in a whisper. "Where is he?"

Kelzi glanced to her right. "He's sitting beside me."

Cassidy's eyes bulged. "Right there?" He pointed to the grass next to Kelzi.

Kelzi nodded and smiled.

At that point, Cassidy went silent, listening intently to every word as Kelzi described her angel, the deerskin clothes he wore. His strong Scottish accent. His sense of humor and kindly manner. She told him all that Shannon had done for her and how he had taken care of her, helping her to regain her memory, giving her the clothes she now wore. She told him the stories Shannon told her of the Cherokee Indians, of his life and the lives of his sons, of the one who came to live in the valley, and the one who became Cassidy's great-grandfather.

Cassidy had to believe her. When she finished, there was nothing left to say. There were no questions to ask and no answers required. Cassidy simply reached out, took her hand, and pressed it against his lips.

The emotion of his actions caught Kelzi completely off guard. She wasn't sure how to react at first. Then, as if it were the most natural thing to do, she laid her head on Cassidy's shoulder. "When the memories of our friendship returned, I asked myself how I could have forgotten them," she said wistfully. "But I now know why I've never been able to replace that friendship."

"That makes two of us," Cassidy whispered, letting the silence of the sunset draw them in as they watched it slowly fade behind the mountain.

Cassidy's fingers caressed Kelzi's hand. She nestled her head a little deeper into his shoulder, wishing the night could just hold them and protect them from the world of danger. "Remember when we would pretend to make time stand still?" she asked.

He chuckled. "I was just thinking the same thing."

"Why did we have to grow up and leave our childhood behind, Cassidy? Why did we have to cross over into this adult world? I don't think it's all it's cracked up to be."

"It's what we make of it for the most part, I suppose," Cassidy suggested, "until someone steps in our path and stirs up the dust—"

"And before we can continue on that path," Kelzi interrupted, "we have to stop and clean up the mess in order to see it again. Then we are stronger . . . and wiser . . . and braver because of it, right?"

"I believe that's how my grandfather put it." Cassidy chuckled.

For the next twenty minutes they talked of many things: of the time they mixed some emerald paint and blessed it to be the paint of eternal friendship. "We stood facing each other, paint dripping from our fingers, and—" Kelzi began.

"And I said," Cassidy interrupted, "'Kelzi Tsali, I will protect you with my life because you are my friend in this life and through the life that is yet to come.' Then I took my finger and spread a line of emerald paint across your forehead, your nose, and on each side of your face."

"And I said, 'Cassidy Ranny, I will protect you with my life because you are my friend in this life and through the life that is yet to come.' Then I spread a line of emerald paint across your forehead, your nose, and on each side of your face."

"And remember how red our faces were after my dad cleaned the paint off with turpentine?" Cassidy laughed.

The world stood still for just that moment, and they were children again, facing each other, taking the oath of friendship, laughing and playing, catching tadpoles, swimming in the stream, eating freshly baked cookies, and listening to stories.

Their world rotated, and Kelzi talked of her years on the reservation before becoming a lawyer. Cassidy talked of his life working with his father and becoming a lawyer himself.

The peaceful setting seemed to be drawing the two of them into its realm, and Kelzi asked herself if this was simply the calm before the storm. She could hear the caring resonance in Cassidy's voice. She felt the strength of his soul, the tenderness of his heart, the unrelenting courage embedded in his intelligence.

His next comment, however, brought her back to reality. "I know of the stipulation on the deed—that it expires in a few days. I have my sources who have been quietly listening for clues pertaining to the plans of the men who want the land."

Cassidy's words alerted Kelzi to the fact that there was much they had to discuss. She listened with intent to what he had to say.

"I started doing a little detective work. But all that greeted me was silence. There were no clues. Everything was just too tidy. It was like they knew something no one else knew and had no reason to discuss their plans because the plans had already been set in place. It all seemed too polished . . . too perfect. There had to be something. They had to know that you were still alive." He paused, giving Kelzi one of his Sherlock looks. "That's when I began walking the thin line of the law."

"Explain," Kelzi instructed, her lawyer's mind now alert and intrusive.

"I can only say that what I was able to uncover prompted me to continue with my investigation. My heart kept telling me you were alive. I thought it was because I didn't want to believe that my best friend was dead. But this morning . . ." Cassidy paused to clear his throat. "I threw logic out the door. I listened to a higher voice."

He cleared his throat for the second time while running his fingers through his hair. "I've witnessed a miracle, Kelzi!" He reached out and wrapped his arms around her. "I found you . . . I really found you."

For a moment, the two simply let time pass without conversation. There were no words that could adequately express the emotions of the miracle they both had witnessed.

At least five minutes went by before Cassidy broke the silence with a question, a question that hardly synchronized with the previous conversation. "Tell me, what does Shannon think of today's world?"

"Ah! 'Tis good ta be back in the conversation," Shannon chuckled. "Tell the lad I'll be wyce ahint the haun."

Kelzi worked her tongue around the Scottish expression as best she could. "Shannon said that he'll be wyce ahint the haun."

Cassidy clapped his hands together and a big smile appeared on his face. "I agree, my ancestral grandfather. I'll be wise after the event."

"I'm thinkin' this young lad'll be settin' the heather afire," Shannon announced, extremely proud of the fact that Cassidy had taken the time to learn a little of the Scottish language. He had been paying close attention to the two—listening to all that had been said between them. He knew he had seen and heard enough during the last hour to tell him all he needed to know. So when Kelzi told Cassidy about the cabin she had been staying in and invited him to go with her to see it, he said not a word against it.

In great detail, Kelzi began to describe Shannon's cabin, a description that proved to be a replica of Cassidy's grandparents' cabin that burned to the ground many years ago.

Failing to notice the expression on Cassidy's face, Kelzi took his arm and led him along the path while giving him a little more detail of the past few days of her life. In her mind, he was simply listening with intent. She never thought that something else might be the reason for his silence.

The sun had almost set when they stood in front of the cabin, giving it a rather mystical appearance.

Totally unaware that what Cassidy was seeing in front of him was completely opposite of what she was seeing, Kelzi was shocked when his face paled and his body cringed. In front of him were burnt remains and ashes of a long-forgotten cabin. Beside it sat a rusted relic of a 1940s pickup, its tires flattened with dried mud still clinging to the rubber.

Cassidy turned, facing Kelzi, his eyes filled with deep sadness. "Describe to me again what you see," he pleaded, failing to shadow his emotions.

Kelzi stepped back. "Excuse me?"

"What do you see in front of you?"

The peculiar sound of Cassidy's voice alarmed Kelzi, causing her to pause and study the expression on his face. What she saw told her something was terribly wrong. She turned back to the cabin and described the skillfully crafted logs, the large pictorial windows, the quaint wraparound porch, and every little detail in between.

"You've never seen this cabin before," Cassidy explained, trying to keep his wits about him. "Yet you've described it precisely as it was before lightning set it on fire, burning it to the ground."

Lightning set it on fire, burning it to the ground. Is that what Cassidy said? Yet before her eyes stood the cabin just as she had described it. Her thought process became suddenly muddled, making it impossible for her to speak. She couldn't see the tears, yet she knew Cassidy was crying. She wanted to scream at Shannon, to demand that he explain this spine-chilling camouflage.

"Tell me what you see, Cassidy," Kelzi begged. "Please tell me what you see."

Cassidy didn't speak, his focus completely on the burnt rubble scattered over a fractured foundation. The look on his face, however, gave Kelzi her answer. She turned to Shannon, throwing him a suspicious glare. "What haven't you told me?" she whispered under her breath.

The mountain man took a deep breath while stroking his beard. "He cannae see what ye see, lass. His eyes see only ruins of a cabin burned ta the ground when he was but a lad."

"You knew this and you let me bring him here," she stammered. "You're supposed to be an angel. How could an angel do such a cruel thing?"

"'Tis not a cruel thing I've done to the lad," Shannon explained. "'Tis a miracle I've given him so he'll nay doubt yer angel's plan."

Kelzi took a moment to consider the depth of Shannon's wisdom before she realized she should never doubt him again. She apologized for the misunderstanding before suggesting that all would have been much less complicated if he had informed her of this situation.

"Some things are better left unsaid till the time comes for the tellin'," Shannon replied without further explanation. "Get on with yer conversation, lass, so all will be said an' left behind."

Kelzi sighed, shaking her head, and turned back to Cassidy. "Please tell me what you see."

"I see the remains of a once-beautiful cabin," Cassidy began. "But it's no longer what I see, Kelzi. It's as if everything inside me is twisted and turned, giving me a different point of view . . . a different take on what I know and what I've learned in the past few hours." He cleared his throat and his eyes connected with Kelzi's. "Tell me the plan."

Now, fully understanding Shannon's perception, Kelzi began to explain. As she got further into the tactics, Cassidy's face lost its hollowed look, and his eyes came alive.

When the plan was completely unfolded, Cassidy leaned over and picked up what remained of a burnt log. "We never know when a flash of lightning is going to change our lives. We can only give, protect, love, and honor until that time comes." He returned the remains of the log to its resting place. "I tell you this because your angel has just enlisted me in the most ingeniously crafted strategy I've ever been exposed to."

SIXTEEN

The Rescue

THE TIME WAS 7:15 A.M. INSIDE THE JUDGE'S PRIVATE OFFICE—A room void of all electronic devices, as per the judge's request (and he kept a security device in his pocket just to make sure his request was upheld)—seven wealthy men sat comfortably in their expensive suits, shiny black shoes, and well-groomed hair, at least those who still had their hair. Cigar and cigarette smoke swirled about the room while glasses of champagne were held in the air as a toast to the success of their venture.

On the table lay a legal document proclaiming the right and ownership of property located in a designated area of North Carolina for the suggested amount of fourteen million dollars. The signatures on the bottom of the document were as follows: R. P. Fowler, Mitchell Oliver, Theodore Angers, Cecil Rawling, Andrew Perkins, Brannon O'Connor, and Obadiah Hatchett.

"Well, gentlemen," Judge Fowler crooned. "With the woman dead and the deed, at last, nothing but ashes, there is little else that can stand in our way. Wednesday afternoon at one o'clock, we will be sitting in the courtroom waiting to have the property placed in our care—property we've been waiting for for eighteen years."

"Hear, hear!" shouted seven voices in unison.

"We've left no stone unturned, no evidence left behind." The judge raised his glass. "To our future!"

"To our future!" the other six responded, letting the ring of their glasses as they touched the others bind their commitment.

In the hallway, outside the judge's chambers, a custodian was pressing fresh caulking around a windowsill. His name was Mehia, though most of the people who worked in the building called him Mayhem, for no other reason than the fact that he was quite the opposite. He was a slim man who moved about the building in almost total silence, doing his work without causing any inconveniences. He wore his cap low over his forehead, keeping his eyes concealed from onlookers while giving the appearance that he might be just a little slow—and that was the intention of the fifty-year-old man, who wished to keep secrets of his own. No one gave it a second thought if he was close by when they discussed public or private matters.

Mehia had the eyes of a hawk and ears that missed nothing of every conversation that he wasn't part of—be it confidential or otherwise. Of all the business people inside the building, he was the most knowledgeable, and his knowledge made him superior. His gift of the language and the code of the Cherokee made him the perfect partner for Cassidy Ranny.

As the men walked out of the judge's chambers, the notes Mehia had written were hidden inside his pocket. The fingers of his right hand continued to smooth the white sticky stuff. None of the men seemed to notice him. They were too involved in a private conversation not meant for his ears.

As soon as the men left the building, Mehia made a quick phone call and unlocked the judge's office door. Knowing the judge kept his office free of electronic listening devices by carrying a detector in his pocket, Mehia had been able to set up his newest invention.

The judge's detector wouldn't pick up information being fed through a long, narrow, piece of rubber tubing carefully embedded between the floorboards and the carpet. Inside the tubing was inserted a minuscule receiver that would send the words spoken inside the room through to a white connector just outside the room on the window seal and into a small receiver-recorder. Mehia's newest invention was remarkable and the timing was perfect for it to be tested.

Working quickly, Mehia removed all the evidence and returned it to his locker, except for the receiver-recorder, feeling no guilt for what he had done. Some may call it breaking and entering, and, if he was caught, it would be typed as such on his rap sheet. However, he had a purpose for doing what he did. One who uses the weapon of electronics to spy with criminal intent simply asks—without knowing—for the same in return to prove his guilt. Mehia's conscious was clear. He pushed a button on his smartphone and spoke two words in Cherokee. Two minutes later a Cherokee boy entered the locker room from the back entrance. Mehia handed him the receiver-recorder and the boy left as quickly as he had come.

Cassidy waited, trying to be patient, trying to stay calm. Periodically, he would check his watch, praying all would go as planned. *The meeting should be over by now*, he thought to himself, just as his office door opened and Mehia's son walked in. Without a word, the boy handed the receiver-recorder to Cassidy, giving him a sly wink before disappearing out the door.

Following the instructions Mehia had given him, Cassidy placed the receiver in his ear. It only took a few seconds before he could hear voices. Mehia's brilliant mind had supplied him with vital evidence that gave his case precedence.

One of Sherlock's quotes entered his thoughts and brought a smile to his face. "When one thinks he is above all others, he is liable to fall below them all. The highest form of man reverts to the animal when he leaves the straight and narrow road of destiny."

125

After leaving his office, Cassidy pressed the seven keys on his smartphone that connected him to Robert Franklin's office. "Is Robert in?" he asked when Monica answered.

Without wasting time on pleasantries, Monica whispered, "Cassidy, I need you to come to the office, now!"

Knowing from the sound of her voice that something wasn't right, Cassidy refrained from asking for an explanation. He simply promised he would be there in ten minutes.

Ten minutes later, Cassidy walked passed Sally's office, his eyes shielded beneath his ball cap. He did a quick take of Sally sitting at her desk, giving him what appeared to be a disdainful glare.

Interesting, Cassidy thought, wondering if she was displeased to see him walking by or if disdain was simply part of her façade. He could feel her eyes fastened on him as he stepped inside Monica's office. "I think I have fallen victim to that woman's well-rehearsed, condescending glare," he said, tilting his head slightly in Sally's direction.

Monica rolled her eyes, giving Cassidy a nod. She flipped her pen through her fingers and scowled. "Only when she's spying for the enemy, which we have yet to discuss. Follow me into Robert's office. We'll talk there. The bugs have all been located and removed." She led the way, closing the door behind her once they were inside. "I have—"

Cassidy cut her off with a finger to his lips. He pulled a small metal detector from his pocket and began his search while watching the little green light on the small piece of equipment in his hands, waiting for it to turn red. The light, to his relief, remained green. "Just wanted to make sure. Now, what were you saying?" he asked, putting the detector back in his pocket.

Monica walked directly to Robert's desk, anxiously rubbing her hands together. "I have a strange feeling Sally knows something we don't, but that's only part of what I need to talk to you about." She leaned over the desk and pressed a button on the answering machine. "I want you to listen to this."

Monica, there has been a family emergency that needs my

attention. I will be gone for at least a couple of days. Robert's voice sounded almost forced, as if he was in pain. Call Mr. Sims as soon as you get in the office and apologize for the inconvenience, and tell him I'll call him as soon as I can. Immediately the phone went dead, which could be diagnosed as a hasty hang up triggered by someone other than Robert.

Monica pressed the 'off' button on the answering machine. "The message was left at 7:14 a.m. It is now 10:10 a.m. I've tried calling Robert's smartphone, but there's no answer."

Sitting down in Robert's chair, Monica leaned her elbows on the desk and clasped her hands together. Her chin quivered as her lips moved, but she refused to panic. "I'm worried, Cassidy. First clue. Robert told me to call Mr. Sims." She shook her head, her eyes piercing Cassidy's. "There's no Mr. Sims . . . at least, not a person. When a case is starting to unravel, Robert always says, 'It's time to bring in the genius, Mr. Sims.' That meant we would begin working overtime."

Her eyes narrowed and her lips tightened. "Help me get to the bottom of this, Cassidy. I have a gut feeling that Robert is in danger."

Cassidy agreed. His eyes began to canvass the room while Monica tapped her finger against her chin, her eyes fixed in concentration. With her other hand, she tapped her nails against the desk in rhythm with her voice. "Call Mr. Sims . . . call Mr. Sims . . . call Mr. Sims." Suddenly, her eyes darted around the room. "Yes!" she whispered, reaching out and grabbing Cassidy's arm. "Start searching for anything out of place."

Without further explanation, Monica knelt down behind the desk, took a small key from around her neck and inserted it into the lock of Robert's confidential file drawer. The key turned and the drawer opened to her touch. Four file folders lay inside, each one a different color—blue, green, yellow, and white.

"Just as I suspected. Those—" Monica caught herself before expressing her frustration with expressions better left unsaid. "The red folder is missing." She slammed the drawer shut and returned to a standing position only to find her body shaking frantically. Her stomach churned while perspiration formed across her forehead and anger filled her eyes. "We've got to find Robert," she cried, grabbing the edge of the desk to keep upright.

Cassidy hurried to her side and helped her into Robert's chair.

"The truth was in that file, Cassidy. Everything we researched once we found that Kelzi was still alive. The copy of the deed she had signed and I had endorsed was in there. Robert had talked to the county recorder and he had agreed to file the deed even though Kelzi is no longer alive, with the hope that it will be accepted in the courtroom."

Monica paused, letting her head fall against the back of the chair, locking eyes with Cassidy. "We found some very interesting bits of information that, when it was all put together, became evidence—became proof of foul play. No one knew where it was kept except Robert and myself." She shuddered. "I hate those stupid, intruding, evasive listening devices."

Monica continued. "When we planned Kelzi's escape, we were completely unaware of what we were facing. We thought we had it all figured out, and all the time they were one step ahead of us, listening to everything we said. We didn't find the second rotten little bug until several minutes after she walked out the back door.

"It was Robert's thought that the two thugs disguised in suits were there to make us think they were searching for Kelzi when, in fact, they already knew where to find her. All the time, we were none the wiser. We were fools."

Before Cassidy could even respond, Monica's eyes fell on the middle drawer of her boss's desk, noting it was slightly ajar. She touched the sides of the drawer with her fingers, opening it carefully. "That was quick," she stammered in utter disbelief, pointing to a row of pencils inside the drawer.

Following her finger, Cassidy stared down at the neatest desk drawer he had ever seen. "What are we looking at?" he frowned.

"See how they're lined up?"

"The pencils?"

"Yes. Mr. Franklin can't stand to have a drawer ajar, nor can he stand to have his pencils out of order. He keeps them in order of color and size. What do you see?"

Cassidy looked closely. There were six pencils. Two yellow. Two red. Two black. The yellow and red pencils lined up perfectly. However, one of the black pencils was lying at an angle on the top of the other five, the sharp edge pointing toward Monica.

"What does it tell you?" Cassidy questioned.

Monica stepped away from the desk and folded her arms once again, letting her eyes focus on the pencil. Her brows furrowed and her mouth pressed shut in her deliberation. After a few minutes, she spoke. "The way the pencil is positioned, I have to believe . . ." She paused, pressing her finger to her lips. "I have to believe it's telling me that it's pointing to something behind me." Shaking her head, she added, "I'm thinking it's possible that when he came in this morning someone was waiting for him or maybe followed him into his office or forced him to come to his office early. It doesn't matter. What matters is that his only recourse was to arrange the pencil and leave the drawer ajar before . . ." She forced herself to remain calm. "Before whatever happened to him . . . happened."

Turning her attention back to the pencil inside the desk drawer, Monica ruffled her hair with her fingers, squinting her eyes in perception. Suddenly, she jumped up from the chair, her face animated. "I know what the pencil is pointing to." She stood, walked vigilantly to the statue, and pulled it slightly forward.

Cassidy's eyes became fixed on the wall as a panel slid to the side, leaving a black hole in its place. "Incredible!" he exclaimed, stepping in front of the opening. He put his fingers to his lips to warn Monica that he was going to do another search before any more words were spoken.

When only residue showed up in the corner where the listening device had been hidden, he continued, "If only hindsight could change the present." His eyes dropped to the floor when three spots, slightly darker than the carpet, caught his eye. He didn't need an investigation to tell him he was looking at drops of blood.

Not wanting Monica to panic, he slowly slid the heel of his shoe over the stain until he could get a closer look at the supposed evidence.

Monica pulled a set of keys out of her slack's pocket and asked Cassidy to wait there while she locked the office doors. When she got to the door leading to her office, Monica got down on her hands and knees and crawled through the room until she reached the outside door. Carefully, she raised her hand just high enough to insert the key into the lock. Then she crawled back into Robert's office, closed the door, and locked it with a second key, after which she stood and brushed the dust from the knees of her slacks. "What?" She frowned, seeing the animated look on Cassidy's face.

"Nothing. It's just that . . ."

"That I seem a little too theatrical." She raised her eyebrows. "You think I should have allowed the spy next door to see something we didn't want her to see?"

"I think you misinterpreted my look," Cassidy stammered. "Actually I was thinking that you'd make an incredible sleuth." He tilted his head toward the gap in the wall. "Ready?"

"You're quick, you know that?" Monica quipped, grabbing a flashlight from inside the closet. "I'm ready. Shall we see where it takes us?"

Cassidy pulled a small pen-like flashlight from his pocket. "Would you like to take the lead or shall I?"

Monica turned on her flashlight, focusing its light on the musty-smelling, creepy, webbed corridor. Though her courage didn't really falter, she simply thought it wise to let Cassidy take the lead.

Cassidy nodded and stepped into the darkness with Monica right behind him, almost breathing down his neck. The brightness of her flashlight revealed nothing but dust. It looked as if it had been disrupted just enough to cover up something that might draw the attention of anyone stepping through the wall opening. However, one mistake had undone the effort.

"This is all wrong! Robert's, Yona's, Kelzi's, and my shoe prints should still be here!" Monica uttered, kneeling down to touch the floor, making sure more recent dust hadn't simply covered the foot-prints. That's when she found something else even more disturbing. Her hand flew to her mouth, drawing Cassidy's attention. He knelt beside her. With the blue, iridescent light in his hand, he focused on small balls of dust pressed together. He placed the light directly over one of them.

Monica leaned in close, her eyes fixed on Cassidy's work as he carefully unraveled the ball—already knowing what he was going to find. Her nerves began to prickle. "It's his blood, isn't it, Cassidy."

"It's blood, but that doesn't necessarily mean it belongs to Robert," Cassidy answered in an attempt to console her—for what good it did.

"Do you want to make a bet, Cassidy?" she demanded furi-ously. "Let's quit wasting time. His life may depend on it."

Cassidy took a second to evaluate the situation. "How much do you know, Monica?"

"Everything Robert knows . . . why?"

"Because I think the first thing we should do is get you out of—"

"Don't even think of finishing that sentence," she warned him with a defiant stare. "I'm not going anywhere except with you. Once we find Robert, or at least verify that the dried blood scat-tered on the floor doesn't belong to him, I'll do as you suggest." She paused for a short breath. "And now that that's out of the way, let's get on with the investigation." She handed him the flashlight. "I'm right behind you."

With caution, they followed the drops of blood meshed with dust, which led them to the ground floor. But the evidence didn't stop there. Instead, it continued down the next flight of stairs . . . stairs that appeared to be recently splintered.

"You stay here," Cassidy whispered.

"Not on your life," Monica whispered back. "Where you go, I go."

"How did I know you were going to say that?" Cassidy mut-tered, turning his attention and the flashlight back to the challenge ahead of them, asking himself how much weight the stairs could handle. He was about to find out.

Cassidy took a deep breath before placing his foot on the first step. It shuddered but held. The next step seemed a little stronger. But the wood on the third step shattered, sending him to the next step with enough force to break through two more steps before he finally got his grip.

"Don't even try it," he warned Monica.

This time she didn't argue.

Clinging to the flashlight, Cassidy tested the next step before putting his full weight on it. It held. With his next step he was on cement. "I've reached the bottom," he called out.

"Find him, Cassidy," Monica responded. Anger, mixed with fear, surged inside her, but all she could do—for now—was wait.

Beyond the limited light of the flashlight, everything was pitch black and ghostly. Nonetheless, the light picked up drops of dried, dusty blood along the recently cleaned floor of the hallway. He followed them into what appeared to be a large storage room—filled with layers of dust and webs. The air around him became thin, stale, and stifling from lack of ventilation.

A cord hanging from the ceiling grazed his forehead. He reached up, grabbed it, and pulled. The bulb's dim light cast an eerie shadow about the room, revealing empty wooden crates and old office furniture stacked on top of each other and pressed together leaving only a walk space that led to another door.

Cassidy's flashlight reached into the dark shadows, his breath now shallow for lack of fresh air. His heart pounded in fear of finding death. His nerves twitched and tingled as the dim light captured a narrow line of blood leading to the door at the end of the walk space.

Cassidy wiped the perspiration from his forehead and above his lips. Next, he drew in as much air as he could before opened the door that led him into a disgusting, forgotten room. The odor was almost overwhelming. Dead mice remains were scattered around while live mice skittered for safety in between dusty wooden crates.

He stood in the doorway studying the room, letting the flashlight be his guide. He could hear a strange scratching noise that seemed to be coming from the center and to the right of the room. He stepped into the room, his flashlight drawing his eyes to something rather odd. Several mice were eagerly working their way through what appeared to be layers of cardboard, behind bits and pieces of a wooden desk.

In a room filled with wood, what are layers of cardboard doing here? Cassidy thought to himself, raising his eyebrows. Cardboard just large enough to cover an accommodating hole, perhaps? Could it be proof of a crime?

Using a desk leg, he scattered the mice, praying he wouldn't be bitten in the process. When the little varmints were out of sight, he quickly removed five 3-foot square pieces of cardboard, exposing a dark hole. Directing the flashlight into the hole, he could see a large canvas covering something . . . A body, perhaps?

"Robert," he called out, working his way into the hole until he could touch a piece of the canvas. He pulled it toward him, uncovering what was beneath it. His flashlight caught what appeared to be the sole of a shoe. "Robert!" he shouted, working his way deeper into the hole to find Robert, lying lifeless on the cement floor.

Immediately, Cassidy searched for a pulse, noting that Robert's shirt was covered with blood from a bullet hole just below the collarbone. A weak pulse brought hope. "Robert, can you hear me?" he asked. Silence met his ears. He tried again. "Robert, talk to me."

There was a soft moan before silence reigned once more.

Cassidy managed to examine Robert's unconscious body for fractures—finding one more bullet hole instead. There was no time to waste. He carefully pulled Robert's body from the hole, lifted him into his arms, and carefully walked a thin line around all the clutter on the floor, finally finding his way back to the stairs.

"I found him, Monica!" he called up to her. "He's been shot but he's still breathing."

"A blessing in disguise," Monica whispered to herself reverently. To Cassidy, she called out, "Tell me what to do." Her emotions were battling shock. Her nerves were fighting shutdown.

"Talk to him while I get enough empty crates to use as stairs," he answered, gently laying Robert on the floor.

Monica had no trouble keeping her one-sided conversation going. She told him all the things she wished she would have told him yesterday, before all this happened—things she wished she had told him a year ago when she discovered she was falling in love with him. She let the tears fall down her cheeks, unchecked, as she talked of the feelings that stirred inside her each morning he walked into the office and smiled at her. When he asked for her opinion then listened quietly, without interruption, as she gave it, and, many times, taking her opinion as the answer he was looking for.

Monica continued to pour her heart out to Robert until Cassidy stood in front of her.

"Oh!" she cried, her hands flying to her mouth when she saw the blood that covered Robert's shirt. "We've got to get him to a doctor . . . but no hospital. No one must learn that he's still alive. You agree?"

Cassidy agreed without hesitation.

Monica touched Robert's face. "My uncle is a doctor, no longer practicing, but he's good and we can trust him."

Cassidy prepared Robert for transport after carefully wrapping the wounds, hoping the blood would begin to coagulate. When he had done all he could for Robert, he hurried back to the lawyer's office, where Monica had wet cloths and dry towels waiting.

"I called my uncle," she said, handing Cassidy the cloths and towels to rid himself of the blood on his hands and jacket. "He'll be watching for you."

Cassidy nodded and quickly finished with the towels. Monica insisted that she check his clothes for any sign of blood.

"You're clean," she confirmed after a quick yet thorough examination. She checked her watch. It had taken them less than ten minutes to get to this point. It would take Cassidy five more to get back to Robert, once he was in his car—then twenty minutes to Monica's uncle's home.

Before he left the office, Cassidy made Monica promise to lock the doors to the office and get out of the building. As he walked down the hallway, he gave Sally a nod and a smile as he passed her office. She gave him a snub.

Deciding it most likely that Sally had informed someone of his visit to Robert's office, Cassidy made himself aware of everyone who passed him on the street or who was leaning against a nearby building or who was sitting in their cars seemingly waiting for someone. They all looked suspicious and innocent at the same time.

Sherlock had made the point: "If criminals would always schedule their movements like railroad trains, it would certainly be more convenient for all of us."

Cassidy climbed into his car, taking a deep breath in an attempt to slow his heart rate. He knew what he was about to do could easily be observed. He also knew there were no other options—and very little time. All he could do was to be observant as he pulled away from the curb and into the narrow alley that took him behind the office building. When he was sure no one had followed him, Cassidy hurried to the back door.

Keeping watch out of the corner of his eye, Cassidy disappeared through the door, reappearing seconds later with Robert's unconscious body wrapped in the blanket Monica found inside the office closet. Once he had Robert in the backseat, he checked for any bleeding before covering the unconscious man with the blanket and getting into the driver's seat. Wasting no more time, he drove away.

As soon as Cassidy was outside the building, Monica locked the office. Sheer determination—in spite of the tingling nerves—made it possible for her to walk down the hall and step into Sally's office. Looking at Sally's surprised, suspicious face, Monica found it difficult to maintain her cool. However, she did manage. In fact, she was rather proud of her performance as she explained that she was taking a few days off because her boss had to be out of town. "If there is any pressing business, just give me a call," she added, "and I'll come in."

"Well, enjoy your time off, dear." Sally's voice was syrupy sweet while her eyes refused to meet Monica's, a sign she knew about Robert. In fact, Sally could be thinking Robert was dead. Monica had to restrain herself from punching the woman in the face while telling her to take good care of the office.

Cassidy checked his watch as he pulled into Dr. Martin's driveway. It had taken him just under twenty minutes. The garage door opened and a man he guessed to be around seventy years old waited inside. The doctor was tall and thin with thick gray hair and a heavy gray mustache that hid his mouth—looking more like a cowboy from the old west than a modern-day doctor.

As soon as the car was inside the garage, the door closed and the doctor nodded to Cassidy. "Everything's ready."

Together, the two men carried Robert into a room and laid him carefully on a bed next to a tray of surgical tools. "Remove his shirt while I prepare for surgery," Dr. Martin said, his deep voice mimicking Monica's southern drawl.

In less than two minutes, everything was in place. The doctor pulled his surgical gloves over his hands and carefully examined the wounds. "I'd have to say that whoever put the bullet in this man's body didn't expect someone like you to come along and find him before he bled to death." He glanced up at Cassidy. "Perhaps you should step into the living room and watch for Monica."

"I'll do that," Cassidy agreed, relieved to leave Robert in Dr. Martin's hands. "Thank you."

"You're welcome, young man. And know this. I will keep my niece here until this strange book of events has written its last page."

Strange book of events, Cassidy thought to himself as he closed the door to the doctor's makeshift surgery room. *It is, indeed, all of that.* He checked his watch, sat down in a comfortable chair, and mentally sorted out everything that had happened from the time he woke up this morning to this moment.

He didn't have long to ponder, however, before Monica came

running into the house, her nerves frazzled. In a panic she cried out, "Tell me he is going to live, Cassidy!"

Cassidy consoled her and led her to the sofa.

Monica's jaw was set. Her eyes were steaming with anger. "Whatever you plan to do to catch the people who did this, I'm a part of it. Just tell me what to do."

"Can you give me full access to Robert's office?"

"I can and I will."

"Next, I need you to make a phone call to Sally telling her I'll be stopping by to pick up some specific files that I'm working on with Robert and she will need to let me in his office."

Monica scrunched her face. "But I'm giving you keys. Why—"

Cassidy interrupted. "She doesn't know that."

"Ah." Monica nodded—beginning to put the pieces of the puzzle together. "I understand. However, I must tell you that Sally's a pro. Nothing gets by her. That's what makes her such an impressive secretary. It's like she has an invisible antenna protruding out of her head. On the other hand, she's vindictive, callous, selfish, and calculating." She paused. "Maybe I should have left that last part out."

"It will be our secret," Cassidy promised. "Could her boss be involved?"

Monica squashed that idea with a look of outrage that ignited her face, letting him know that he shouldn't have even considered the idea. "Just delete those words from your brain," she scowled. "Mr. Peterson's a man of high integrity."

Monica checked the time on her watch. "My uncle is a good doctor, Cassidy. A man of faith, who has performed surgical miracles. If he said Robert will live—"

The door opened in front of Monica before she could say more, and Dr. Martin stepped into the room. There was enough blood on his surgical apron to take Monica's breath away. Realizing he had neglected to remove the apron before opening the door, the doctor wasted no time in doing so, apologizing for his thoughtlessness.

"Monica," Dr. Martin assured his niece, putting his arm around her shoulder, "the bullets are out. Robert will live. He's lost a lot of blood, and it will take time for full recovery, but he'll be completely healthy in a few weeks."

Dr. Martin removed his surgical hat and tossed it on the table nearest him while eyeing Cassidy. "Normally, I would advise that you wait until tomorrow to talk to him, but there is nothing normal about this situation, and he wishes to speak to you. I suggest you only ask the questions you desperately need answers to and then let him sleep." He turned to Monica. "You may sit beside him while he sleeps, but do not disturb him."

Cassidy was aware of Robert's labored breathing the second he stepped into the dimly lit surgery room. However, it wasn't until he stepped beside the bed and witnessed the pallor of Robert's face that he literally trembled. What if they hadn't found him when they did? What if Monica had missed the pencil arrangement? "I'm so sorry about this," he said softly as he sat in the chair beside Robert's bed.

"You have nothing to feel sorry about, young man. You saved my life." Robert's voice was weak and blurred. "Right now, I'm worried about Monica."

"She's outside that door even more worried about you," Cassidy assured him.

Though Robert's eyes failed to focus and his body felt limp and useless, he reached out his hand and touched Cassidy's arm. "Protect her, young man. Don't let anything happen to her."

"I promise you that nothing will happen to her, or to you. No one knows you're here, and the men who put the bullets in you think you're dead."

"Thank you." Robert's hand fell back on the bed. His breathing became sporadic gulps of air. "I need to . . . to tell you about the two men . . . who did this. They had their faces . . . covered when they . . . forced their way into my office."

A glaze fell over Robert's eyes. His mouth moved in slow

motion. His voice became a pained whisper. "They may have been able to disguise their faces . . . but they couldn't disguise their voices. They . . . they were the same two . . ." He rolled his eyes, fighting to keep them open. "The same two who . . ." His voice faded and his eyes closed.

"You rest," Cassidy soothed him. "Monica can fill in the blanks?"

"Mumm" was the only sound that crossed Robert's lips before he fell asleep.

Monica was waiting for Cassidy when he came out of the doctor's medical room. She stepped in front of him and placed her hands on his arms, looking into his face. "There's no way I can thank you enough, Cassidy," she said, her voice filled with deep respect.

"This mission took two people," Cassidy reminded her, reaching down and kissing the top of her forehead. "I think we both were in the right place in the right time—which reminds me, I need your help." Cassidy repeated his conversation with Robert. "However, before he could tell me the rest of the story, he fell asleep. Can you fill in the details?"

Monica described the two men, explaining their intrusion into Robert's office the morning Kelzi came with the deed. "It's probably best I not know everything you have up your sleeve. But be assured, when you need me, you'll know where to find me." She pulled Cassidy into a hug before handing him the keys to Robert's office. "Thank you, Cassidy. I'll never forget what you've done for Robert . . . and for me." She stepped back. "I love him, you know."

"Yes, and I'm glad you told him this morning," Cassidy sincerely replied. "Those words may have given him the incentive to fight for his life. Take good care of him, Monica."

Before Cassidy got to the door, Monica added one more point, "I can promise you that when Sally leads you to Robert's office, her eyes will be on you while unlocking the door; she'll make sure you don't see how the key fits in the lock. Then she'll step inside, insisting that you don't enter the room. You'll be forced to wait by the door while she retrieves the files you need. She won't be able to resist opening them just to see what it is you are working on for Robert. Once she's satisfied that it's nothing of interest to her, she'll hand you the files, insist you go out ahead of her, and then she'll secure the lock." A smirk appeared on Monica's face. "Believe me, she's that predictable."

SEVENTEEN

The Ghost

IT WAS 11:30 WHEN CASSIDY STEPPED INTO SALLY'S OFFICE. HE couldn't help but notice her immaculate office, her perfect hairstyle, the expensive, stylish green dress, and the dangling earrings and high heels that matched. He politely inquired if Monica had called.

Without looking up, Sally was abrupt in her response. "I'm busy right now. Take a seat and I'll be with you as soon as I can."

Thinking her voice rather frosty, Cassidy did as she directed, trying hard not to break out in a laugh. During the next ten minutes—his sentence for intrusion—he waited patiently, and it was worth the wait. Without deviation, Sally did exactly as Monica said she would do, making it difficult for Cassidy to hold a straight face. She reminded him of a pompous, puffed-up peacock, flaunting her superiority and giving instructions while her curiosity hungered for satisfaction. He was more than happy to play the part of the humble servant while she reached into the file and retrieved the folder he had asked for, studying it thoroughly before all but throwing it into his hand.

Sometimes in a crime investigation, things just seem to fall into place, making it possible to do what's needed while adding a bit of drama to the event. The plan was to ask Monica to tell Sally that she had an appointment that would take her away from the office for a few hours. Robert's disappearance had given Cassidy the opportunity to put Shannon's plan into reality. It wasn't what they had planned, but it had given them the needed time.

He left the office before Sally and then watched as she locked Monica's office door before ushering him down the hallway. He could actually feel her eyes on his back as he stepped into the elevator.

Cassidy was aware that Sally went to lunch at exactly noon and returned at precisely 1:00 p.m. When he parked behind the building, it was exactly 12:40 p.m. He climbed out of his car and slipped into the darkness beyond the door, flashlight in hand. By 12:45, he was inside Robert's office. He listened, watching the second hand on his watch move slowly around the circle.

He peeked through the office door. All was quiet. He went to his knees, crawling to Monica's desk, where he raised his head just high enough to see into Sally's office. He couldn't have timed it more perfectly. It was empty. Or at least it was until he saw Sally get off the elevator. He groaned, shaking his head. Why did the woman choose today to break her unbreakable routine?

Oh, to have a wizard's wand and an invisible cloak, he thought to himself. But being a mere mortal, he had to improvise. Scooting backwards, he squeezed himself through the door and into Robert's office, locking it as silently and quickly as possible. Then he put his ear to the door and listened, knowing that ears have their own eyes—when the ears have been trained to see. Less than a minute later, he heard Monica's office door open and close.

He heard someone moving about. Then a file drawer opened. A few minutes later, it closed. A total of three drawers were opened and closed, with enough time in-between for something to be removed or placed inside. Next, he heard the familiar tones of a smartphone—then Sally's voice.

"I found some documents with Robert's handwriting on them. I'll have a note written and placed on Monica's desk before she's back in the office." There was silence for a few seconds, then Sally's voice again. "I'm not sure, but she said she would be gone for a few days. She's not smart enough to make the connection. As long as she's out of the office, I wouldn't worry."

How often does a sleuth find himself in the right place at the right time to hear the right stuff? Cassidy gave himself a mental pat on the back.

Sally may have known about Robert. But she wasn't as clever as she thought. She underestimated Monica's intelligence. He waited, listening for the clicking sound that would tell him Sally had locked Monica's door—meaning the coast was clear.

Click! Then silence. It was time to set the stage.

He crawled into Monica's office, keeping his head low. He unlocked the door that Sally had just locked before crawling back into Robert's office, leaving that door unlocked as well. He stepped in front of the statue and pulled it forward. The wall slid open. He stepped through to the other side and pulled a lever to close the wall panel, after which he left the way he had come.

Once inside his car, Cassidy checked the time. It was 1:05. He pulled onto the dirt road. From there, onto the highway. From the highway, he took the side streets and quiet roads to throw the mole off his trail if, in fact, there was a mole. It wasn't that he was necessarily paranoid . . . then again, maybe he was. All he knew was that had to be extremely careful.

Thirty-five minutes later Cassidy was standing in front of Kelzi, telling her of Mehia's unconceivable invention that made it possible for him to listen in on an extremely private meeting being held inside the judge's chamber. "Though there was nothing said that I didn't already suspect, I now have proof." He was careful, however, not to mention Robert nor Monica. It wasn't the time yet to bring that subject up.

Kelzi smiled at Cassidy's enthusiasm. He had set in place all that was needed to accommodate Shannon's strategy—a strategy that demanded perfect orchestration. Her nerves tingled in anticipation of the moment.

She was just about to add her thoughts to Cassidy's when his smartphone rang. "Give me a minute," he said before he turned and walked a short distance away.

When the conversation ended, he turned back to her. "There's something else I need to tell you." He paused and drew in a deep breath. It was time to talk about Robert.

"And?" Kelzi inquired, noting the serious expression on Cassidy's face. When he finished telling her the story, she sat there as if she was still listening to something more than his voice—as if her eyes were focused on something not visible to Cassidy.

"It's not your fault, Kelzi," Cassidy insisted, interpreting her expression as a feeling of guilt.

"No it's not," she agreed. "It's all part of the plan to tie up any loose ends that might allow two thugs to get away without paying for their part in this fiasco. Robert knew the risk and he wasn't afraid to take it. He's safe. No one knows that he's alive. He's well hidden with Monica at his side."

Kelzi's last remark brought a smile to Cassidy's lips. "And because of all of this, Robert now knows that Monica loves him, and he can let her know that he is in love with her. Think of the years that would have been wasted if what happened hadn't happened."

One moment passed then another as the two contemplated the miracle that, in the beginning, seemed a tragedy. The words Mother Earth speaks in many ways touched Kelzi's heart, allowing her to grasp the full understanding in all that had preceded this moment—there was a purpose. Her parents' death was not in vain. Her years on the reservation had given her an education not found inside a schoolroom . . . an education that taught her deeper understanding of her own life and her purpose in protecting the land of her people.

"I'm prepared for whatever happens over the course of the next few days," Kelzi said. "And you will have a leading part."

"With Shannon as our captain, think of the adventure we have ahead of us." Cassidy grinned as he took a step back. "And I have to admit that you look attractively casual, but not without attitude, in your native costume."

Shannon announced his presence with the words, "The young man has a point there."

Kelzi turned to see Shannon standing just behind her. "So you think I have an attitude?"

"'Tis truly a blessing that ye do, lass. It'll be one that gives ye mind strength when weakness seeks ye out."

Thinking Kelzi's question was for him, Cassidy's voice only added an affirmative, "Yes, and it's one of your winning attributes."

A smile crossed Kelzi's face. She couldn't disagree with these two men who would stand by her and be her source of protection. She took a moment to assess the handsome man standing in front of her—causing her heart to flutter. "I'm afraid you resemble Shannon in more than just your looks."

"I'll be agreein' with ye, lass." Shannon grinned, running his fingers over his mustache. "An' I'll be havin' ye tell the lad we've lots ta talk aboot, knowin' he'll be willin' an' able ta carry out all that'll be asked of him. So listen close, lass, so all that goes thru yer ears comes out yer mouth."

"Understood." Kelzi turned to Cassidy and explained what was about to take place.

Cassidy couldn't help but felt a little giddy, considering the unbelievable circumstances he now found himself in. All the investigating he could do himself and all the clues he could find through his sleuthing would amount to very little compared to what he would be a part of under the guidance of an angel. With his hands in the pockets of his Levis, he watched Kelzi while she looked into thin air—nodding and making comments—before turning to him and repeating Shannon's instructions. They did a second walk-through for the purpose of making sure everything was completely understood.

Fifteen minutes later, Cassidy took Kelzi in his arms and held her close, just for a minute, before he got into his car and drove away, visualizing how the plan would play through.

Shannon studied Kelzi long enough to touch the stitches on her forehead. Next he opened the door to an old green 1940 Chevy pickup, assisting Kelzi into its antique interior before climbing into the passenger's side.

Kelzi curiously touched her forehead, feeling nothing but the smoothness of her skin. "Why didn't you just use your angel status to heal the cut on my forehead in the beginning?" she asked, once Shannon had settled himself on the passenger's side.

"An' nae let ye see me comely stitches?" Shannon chuckled. "There are some things that are ta be done fer a good reason at the time they are done. Do ye understand what I'm sayin', lass?"

Kelzi's gave her angel a thoughtful look as she considered his answer. "What you're saying is that I needed to see the wound and feel the stitches so that I would understand the truth."

Shannon nodded without adding more to the conversation.

Kelzi took a few minutes to put into perspective the miracle of her life as she sat on the old leather seat and brushed the dust off the black, round-handled gearshift. "You are very good at what you do, Shannon," she said at last, wrapping her fingers around the steering wheel.

"I thank ye fer the compliment, but 'tis a simple task. An' now the time has come ta redden the fire."

Kelzi turned the key and the truck started without complaint. A few minutes later they were driving down the highway, five minutes behind Cassidy.

As they drew closer to their destination, Kelzi's heart began to beat with anticipation as she reflected on the task ahead while her thoughts reached back into her past. In her mind, she outlined the lessons taught to her by her grandmother. Then she outlined the lessons she was learning from Shannon. When compared, they were much the same . . . faith, courage, trust, spirituality, and truthfulness. Her father reminded her to always carry the vision of truth in her heart when she was only five years old. She never forgot his advice, for it was meant for today.

Her law experience—so logical and arbitrated—had no meaning to her at this moment. There was no logic needed here. There was only belief in higher wisdom and knowledge and faith in an angel who had been sent to be her advocate.

"Thar'll be those 'oo know of ye, but'll nae know yer face." Shannon's voice broke through her thoughts, interrupting any further self-discussion. "Thar'll be those 'oo know nothin' at all. But they'll be glancin' at ye as ye walk by, fer the lovely face they'll be seein', an' yer ta smile kindly as ta nae be thought unfriendly."

"I think what you're trying to tell me is that by smiling, I'll come across as a tall woman with a pretty face, a friendly smile, and soon forgotten. To show no emotion, I'll be seen as an unfriendly woman with an attitude."

"Couldn't have said it better meself." Shannon gave her one of his angelic smiles.

"Understood. But right now I better concentrate on finding a place to park."

Shannon pointed to an empty parking space next to the law building of Franklin and Peterson. "Will that one do, lass?"

Kelzi glanced over at the mountain man. "I see you've planned everything right down to the parking place. Just tell me you know how to drive."

"Ye'll nae be frettin' aboot that," he assured her. "It'll be whar ye need it ta be ere' the time comes that ye'll be needin' it."

Kelzi pulled into the parking place, set the gearshift in park, turned the engine off, and stared at the building in front of her. "I sit here somewhat lacking the true vision of what I'm about to do. I only know that I have you beside me and I shouldn't be concerned about what is about to transpire; however, I find myself still trying to understand the miracle of it all."

Shannon patted her on the shoulder, letting a dramatic sigh

escape his lips. "Have ye nae witnessed one miracle given ye, only ta question another?"

Kelzi turned to meet the eyes of her angel. "Oh no! That's not what I mean to say. It's just that as a lawyer I rely on and understand logic. In my profession I have to look for tangible proof. That's what lawyers do." She paused, taking a deep breath. "To comprehend all that is happening to me . . . and for me—"

Shannon interrupted her. "The fact that only the two of us see, an' touch, an' sit inside somethin' that's invisible ta other eyes, 'tis a bother ta ye, lass?"

Kelzi attempted to shadow her doubt. "Perhaps."

Shannon smiled. "Nae ta fear fear, I'd be the same if I'd be sittin' whar yer sittin'. But ye cannae pit an auld heid on yung shouthers." He paused and winked. "'Tis an old Scottish sayin': Ye cannae give the youn' the wisdom of thar elders."

"Please try, Shannon. Share your wisdom with me," she begged.

"'Tis a simple thin' if one understands the universe. But man prefers ta make it complicated. He wants ta know an' understand what's a mystery ta him. He desires ta add up the mathematics, divide the theory by the known, an' multiply the numbers by the X, Y, an' Zs. He searches an' researches in his up-ta-date lab ta find the answers. He studies books written by man, leavin' God's books ta gath'r dust. He ne'er thinks ta ask the One 'oo knows." He lifted his eyes upward. "'Tis man's way ta want tangible proof fer the in-tangible—logical explanations fer the illogical. Scientific evidence fer what he wishes ta be scientific . . . nae natural . . . nae of God. He wants answers an' proof wher' thar are none in man's world. What I'm askin of ye is throw logic out of the way, lass, so ye can think with yer soul. Let science tend ta itself fer a day. Fer now, just know that Cassidy will be thar to unlock the doors."

Tears filled Kelzi's eyes. There would no longer be even an in-kling of doubt to tempt her to look away from the truth that needed no worldly logic.

Sally sat at her desk, her long fingernails tapping against the desktop in rhythm to the music playing on her iPad while attending to an open folder in front of her. Her phone rang, bringing a scowl to her face. She hated disruption. It wasn't until after the third ring that she finally picked up the receiver and placed it against her ear, letting her eyes gaze out into the hallway, as was her habit.

That's when she saw the tall, attractive woman dressed in an eye-catching Indian jacket and slacks walk past her office. The silver earrings the woman wore glistened against the long black hair that fell almost to her waist.

The woman turned her face toward Sally and their eyes met only for an instant, as the woman spoke just one word. At least Sally thought she heard her speak—her mouth moved and a strange, haunting word seemed to pierce the glass. Sally dropped the receiver. A tremor of shock trickled down her spine. She could literally feel the hairs on the back of her neck bristle. It was all she could do to keep her wits about her while keeping her eyes on the woman until she disappeared into Mr. Franklin's office.

Sally knew that door was locked. She locked it herself after that pesky young lawyer left. She hurried down the hall and into Monica's office, took a breath, and called out in a tone of authority. "Whoever you are, you're not supposed to be in here."

The reply was an eerie silence, causing her to hesitate before walking to the door that led into Mr. Franklin's office. With a feeling of uneasiness she placed her hand on the knob, turning it slowly. There was no sound when she opened the door to the empty room. With some reservation, she stepped inside, surveying every corner, trying to understand what she had seen— or thought she had seen. Finally, she reached into her sweater pocket and pulled out a set of keys. Her hands shook slightly as she searched for the key that would lock the doors she knew she had carefully locked earlier.

Once Sally was back in her office, she sat down at her desk and tried to calm her nerves. Was it possible? Could she have imagined the whole thing? The past few days had been a strain on her. What happened to Robert wasn't supposed to happen, but it wasn't her fault. Hadn't she warned Obadiah about hiring ex-cons?

When Mr. Peterson walked into the office that morning, she told him that Robert had to go away on business and had given Monica the time off as well. She asked if his wife enjoyed the surprise anniversary getaway. He answered in the affirmative, thanking her for taking care of things while he was gone, before he disappeared inside his office.

"If you had been standing at my desk just a few minutes longer, Mr. Peterson," she muttered under her breath, "I wouldn't be sitting here wondering if, or what, I saw." The word she didn't understand wouldn't leave her alone. It started with an A. As . . . something. It wasn't a word she recalled ever hearing before. It haunted her, nonetheless.

In an attempt to step back into reality, Sally focused on the folder's contents sitting on her desk while trying to forget the word she couldn't remember. She kept glancing up at the glass as a precaution. Everything seemed normal again. People were passing by on their way in and out of the building. The sound of their voices were reassuring.

With a sigh of relief, Sally became occupied with her work again, and—once again—the hall became strangely quiet. The hairs on the back of her neck began to bristle. She looked up, startled to see that same woman walking by her office again. The same eyes pierced her eyes. The same word escaped her lips: *Asgi'na.* Sally stared at the woman when she opened the door into Monica's office, following the same pattern as before.

This time Sally's reaction was anger more than fear. "Enough is enough!" she called out as she hurried to Monica's office, finding the door unlocked again. She walked through the secretary's office and into Robert's. "Whoever you are and whatever you are trying to do lacks humor, and just in case you didn't know, Halloween is over."

Silence greeted her—once again. The office was empty—once

again. Then she remembered the sliding panel on the back wall. She walked up to the statue and tried to pull it forward, but it refused to budge. "The stupid ex-cons must have broken it," she muttered. Anger swelled inside her for allowing herself to be a victim of a prank. Yet the anger refused to stop the chills that continued to run up and down her spine.

Her fingers were trembling to the point that she had difficulty hanging onto the keys. Once she was able to insert the key into the locks, she quickly locked the doors—for the second time in less than twenty minutes. When she was behind her desk, she crossed her arms, pressing them hard against her rib cage, and sank into her chair in an attempt to calm her nerves.

A thought stirred in her. "Could it be . . . ?" she uttered, feeling the anxiety that had sent unrelenting pain of an oncoming migraine through her head. "No," she scolded herself while massaging her temples. "The thought is ludicrous."

Still, she couldn't be sure. She had heard about ghosts who came back to haunt the people who caused their deaths, if the deaths were deliberate, and this woman certainly looked like the one who had walked down the hall that day. Both women were part Cherokee. Both had long black hair. But if this truly was the same woman, her death was not Sally's fault. She only told Obadiah what she knew when he asked. But even as Sally sat there trying to convince herself of her innocence, she recognized her guilt. The money offered in return for her help clouded her judgment, intentional or otherwise.

In an attempt to stop her mind from rambling, Sally needed to find something important to do. She turned to the screen on her computer and began to search her document file. Fighting to keep her mind on her work, she didn't allow her eyes to drift to the window in front of her desk. Hearing the voices of people passing each other in the hallway was all she needed. She pressed her finger to the screen on her iPad, letting her music calm her nerves.

The music was consoling enough for Sally to almost forget the noise coming from the hallway until the song she was listening to ended and a pause between songs alerted Sally that there was no noise coming from the hallway at the moment. She looked up only to be pulled back into the nightmare. The same woman with black hair and eyes that drilled deeply into hers passed in front of her—the word *Asgi'na* echoing from her lips.

Sally froze. She wanted to scream, but her voice was silent. She forced her eyes away from the glass. She stood and walked, setting one foot in front of the other until she stood in front of her boss's office door. Not bothering to knock, she grasped the door handle, opened the door, and hurried inside, slamming it shut behind her—pressing her back against it.

The noise brought her startled boss to his feet. "What on earth?" Lawrence Peterson exclaimed, mystified by the distorted expression on her face. "Sally? What is it?"

The sound of Lawrence's voice cut away at the numbness, and Sally started to cry uncontrollably. Words came tumbling out of her mouth between fearful sobs. "Her eyes were glaring at me. Her face looked . . ." Sally struggled to find the words, her hands flitting about in the air. "Three times she walked past. Three times she said the word . . ." Sally closed her eyes as if she was trying to remember. "Asgi . . . ," she whispered to herself. "Asgi . . . *Asgi'na.*"

"Ghost?" Lawrence asked.

Sally's eyes opened wide with fear and her hands flew to her mouth. "*Ghost!*" Her knees gave way and she slumped to the floor.

Lawrence was immediately at her side, kneeling beside her. "Calm down, Sally," he said.

Calm down? He wanted her to calm down? She could see the concern in his eyes and hear it in his voice, but his words were stupid. How could she calm down when she wasn't even able to think straight?

"I'm going to help you up and take you over to the sofa where you can lie down, okay?"

Sally nodded and allowed him to lead her the other side of the room. She felt the sofa beneath her, a pillow being placed under her head, and the warmth of a blanket as it was tucked around her.

"Just take deep breaths," Lawrence said, his voice echoing somewhere in the distance.

She nodded, grasping the blanket with both hands and holding on tight. "I've just had the most horrible experience." Her teeth were chattering between sobs and words.

"Tell me," Lawrence said gently.

"She looked just like that woman."

"What woman, Sally?"

"The ghost! Aren't you listening?" She wiped her tears with the handkerchief she found in her hand. "She looked just like the picture of that Tsali woman."

"You mean the one who died in the car accident up over the mountain? Lawrence's frown deepened into a look of confusion.

Sally nodded frantically. "Someone who looks exactly like her . . . or it was her ghost . . . her *Asgi'na*." She grabbed her head to keep it from spinning. "I don't know what I mean. I may not like what she is . . . or was . . . but I didn't . . ." She shut her mouth, rational enough to realize she was about to give away information not meant for her boss's ears. She took a deep breath, forcing air into her lungs in an attempt to clear her head.

"What I'm trying to say . . ." Sally rubbed her hand over her forehead. "What I'm trying to say is that the woman had been in a meeting with Robert earlier along with another lawyer. I saw them . . . I saw them walk into Robert's office. Later, I saw the man come out and leave the building alone . . . I never saw the woman leave." Sally pressed her hands against her eyes. "The next day her picture was in the paper saying that she had died when her car went over a cliff."

The words began to fall from Sally's mouth between hysterical sobs. "Today she walked by my office three times, that word coming out of her mouth . . . three times."

Lawrence handed her a glass of water. "I didn't think you believed in ghosts," he said soothingly. "Neither do I. There has to be a logical explanation. As soon as Robert gets back, I'll talk to him and we'll get to the bottom of this. But right now I'm taking you home."

Sally closed her eyes, knowing Robert wasn't coming back.

Cassidy's smartphone vibrated in his hand. A message came up on the screen.

Gs[G g\9z umdgjm. (The mouse smells the cheese.)

Cassidy had to allow himself to feel a touch of success as he slipped the smartphone into his pocket, while he watched Lawrence Peterson assist his secretary through the main doors of the building. The words of Sherlock came to his mind. "There are always some lunatics about. It would be a dull world without them."

Obadiah, the real estate agent and Sally's uncle, held the receiver to his ear, listening to the strained and almost unintelligible voice on the other end. He didn't interrupt—not that he didn't want to. What was being said was so broken up between sobs of panic that understanding the context was almost impossible.

"Sally . . . Sally, calm down," he finally shouted into the receiver. "You're not making sense." But even as he spoke the words, one thing did make sense to him. Sally, who was known for her nerves of steel, was in hysterics over something so frightening that it had melted the metal.

There was a pause on the other end—a stifled sob—and then the words came, composed and cold. "I have just seen the ghost of the Tsali woman, or what appeared to be her ghost, in front of my office." Another quick sob was followed by another intake of breath. "Now do something about it." The phone went dead. Sally had hung up on him, leaving him stunned with words that had come through crystal clear.

Obadiah had just finished showing some prize property to a man who was willing to pay the price he was asking. His feeling of elation over the sale was short lived with a few words from the "ice queen."

While he didn't believe in ghosts, he did believe in blackmail. But why would they use Sally as a setup? It made no sense. The one thing that did made sense at this moment was that someone was trying to interfere with the purchase of the land he and his partners had spent years in painstaking preparation to buy. It was time to give Judge Fowler a call.

The conversation was brief. After giving Judge Fowler a condensed version of his conversation with Sally, Obadiah submitted a question. "Is it possible this was nothing but a hoax to cause us to panic?"

"The Tsali woman is dead," Fowler reminded Obadiah, "and I don't believe in ghosts. However, someone apparently thinks they saw something or knows something that is blackmail-worthy. If so, all they've got to do is cause panic within the group and wait for us to crumble. We've got to keep it together for the next twenty-four hours."

Obadiah had to admit that the judge's words were tagged with logic. Still, he added a warning. "Nonetheless, I think it wise to be ready to act, just in case. I leave it in your hands."

EIGHTEEN

The Stage Is Set

LAWRENCE PETERSON'S FIRST PRIORITY ONCE HE RETURNED TO HIS office was to find out what was going on. Robert was his friend as well his law partner. Yet he had never mentioned the name Tsali in all their discussions.

He dialed Robert's phone number. When there was no answer, he had a strange feeling that something was wrong. Robert always kept his phone in the closest pocket to his ear. When he dialed Monica's number, all he got was her voice mail.

"Monica," he said after the beep, "this is Lawrence Peterson calling. I can't seem to find your boss. Call me."

Just as Lawrence pressed the off button, a text message alerted him. It read:

> It is vital that you call the State Attorney's office and insist that Judge Walker attend the hearing concerning the Cherokee land. Tell the judge that he needs to keep his visit confidential, and keep his presence unknown. Call Judge Walker now—for Robert's sake.

Lawrence dropped his phone to the desk. His shoulders slumped back against the back of his chair while his head fell against the headrest. "Oh, Robert," he sighed, closing his eyes. "What's going on here? First, something literally frightens Sally

156

out of her wits . . . then it's as if you've completely disappeared." He leaned forward, placing his elbows on the desk and his hands over his face—rubbing his eyes before reading the text message again, focusing on: Call Judge Walker now—for Robert's sake.

Wasting no more time, Lawrence pulled a small address book from inside the middle drawer of his desk. His fingers fumbled through the pages until he found the judge's name and phone number.

Returning to the place where he and Kelzi had become reacquainted, Cassidy read a coded message on his phone screen. "I don't know if you're anywhere near," he said aloud to Shannon, while putting the phone back in his pocket and feeling just a little uncomfortable, "but I thought maybe I'd let you know that a plan is developing."

"Are you talking to me?" he heard Kelzi say from behind him, her voice raspy with fatigue.

He turned and found himself staring into beautiful but weary eyes, lined with dark circles and a lovely face drained of color. "Are you okay?" he asked, immediately aware that the question was a stupid one. "Forgive me," he apologized. "Of course you're not okay." He took her in his arms, gently cradling her head against his shoulder. Why hadn't he considered the fact that the ghost walk might not have been a walk in the park for Kelzi? That it could have been physically demanding and emotionally draining?

The two stood there, holding each other in silence.

"I almost felt like a ghost," Kelzi whispered, breaking the silence. "Tremors of fearlessness surged through me each time I did the ghost walk." She quietly added, "And thank you for unlocking the doors for me."

Cassidy smiled. "It was my honor." Quietly he led her to a tree she could sit beneath, lean her head against its trunk, close her eyes, and allow her energy to regenerate itself.

Twenty minutes later, when Kelzi's eyes opened, she found Cassidy lying on the grass next to her, his eyes looking into hers.

She smiled. "Did everything go as planned for you, Sherlock?"

"It was all elementary, dear Kelzi. All I had to do was to crawl back and forth in Monica's office, making sure the doors were unlocked." He leaned in close, whispering in Kelzi's ear. "Tell me, is your guardian angel satisfied?"

"Tell the lad I'm as pleased as a frog's tongue in a spatter of flies," Shannon said. "Fer the battleground. 'Twas free of blood, yet worthy of the enemy's attention."

Kelzi repeated Shannon's words with a raise of an eyebrow and a playful glint in her eye, the expression on her face completely back to simply beautiful. "In all that we experienced, it was an amazing ghost walk, was it not, Cassidy?"

"Indeed it was," Cassidy answered, moving over to sit beside her, leaving no space between them. Not by accident, his lips touched her ear. "It was ingenious. I was so worried about you, Kelzi, even though I knew that an angel named Shannon was with you."

"And I worried about you because you were the one who had to take all the chances to make sure everything went exactly as planned," she replied, letting their lips meet. It was a tender kiss, but one where love separates itself from friendship.

It only took Cassidy a second to grasp the intent of the kiss. It made his heart flutter and his knees go weak. He stood, pulling her up beside him and drawing her into his arms. "Everything about this day has been unbelievably enthralling. It's like we're playing out one of our imaginary adventures—only this time we find we have real questions yet to be answered and real dangers yet to encounter. I only pray that when this is over we will, once again, be standing by this stream picking up where we left off. And when that happens, I'm going to ask you to marry me, Kelzi Tsali."

Cassidy stopped abruptly. "I didn't mean for that to slip out." He couldn't believe his own stupidity—not in saying the right words—but at the wrong time and wrong place. In fact, it would probably rank near the top of the list as one of the most unromantic, ill-timed proposals of all time.

Kelzi, on the other hand, was so touched by the enchantment of Cassidy's proposal, it left her speechless.

Cassidy turned away and was just about to suggest he get back to the city when he felt the pressure of Kelzi's hand in his.

"Can you imagine how incredible this day will read when I write about it in my journal?" Kelzi sighed. "First I'll date it. Then I'll write about the morning, which will take up about half a page. Next I'll write this: When we met back at the stream, and all the business of the adventure had been discussed, the man I have loved all my life proposed to me in the most original and romantic way. His words left me speechless. After that I will fill another page with soppy, romantic stuff like how I carried his heart in mine for eighteen years, while he carried mine, and how tender the night was when we met again. I'll write stuff that our daughters and granddaughters . . . and even great-granddaughters will read, and they will want to find a husband just like the one their mother, grandmother, and great-grandmother found."

Shannon removed a cloth from his pocket and wiped the tears from his face. "Couldn't of said it better meself."

Kelzi smiled. "Did I mention, in all that blabber, that my love for you deepens each time I look into your eyes?" She placed her hands on Cassidy's cheeks and kissed him.

Cassidy took Kelzi in his arms and replied to her kiss with one of his own—which was suddenly interrupted with a beeping sound coming from his pocket, warning him of an incoming message. "I've got to take this," he apologized, putting the smartphone between them.

Kelzi glanced down at the message on the screen. What she saw brought a bewildering frown to her face.

Hig Ewf Yn ow gZj. {n> \y armistZm awsd dg8> Ewf Genm.
Ay ka/k. ArmistZm. Fnl.

"I think we've stirred the pot," Cassidy commented just before he began to decode the strange-looking combination of letters. "Listen. 'Today Cherokee wolf comes to life. Tomorrow, bears come together against Cherokee wolf. Be ready.'"

"Who are your spies?" Kelzi asked, impressed with what she saw. "Who knows the Cherokee language and code as well as you do and is willing to do this for you?"

"A true sleuth never reveals his sources," Cassidy replied, the look in his eyes revealing that his secret was safe . . . even from her.

At that moment, Shannon caught her attention with a slight adjustment to the slant of his hat, a sign that it was time to tell Cassidy the plans of the next day. Kelzi raised her finger and gave Cassidy a nod. She turned to the tree at the right of her, and from the look on her face, Cassidy believed she was listening to some rather intriguing instructions.

He waited. He found himself captivated by the look on Kelzi's face—the serious intent of her eyes when she listened, nodded, whispered a question or a comment.

When at last Kelzi turned back to Cassidy and began explaining Shannon's plan, he was all ears. His reply, when she finished, was that it was brilliant. He closed his eyes, envisioning the plot that had been presented to him, wishing he could be a witness to the outcome.

Kelzi watched as Shannon walked toward Cassidy, disappearing behind him. "Tell the lad the outcome'll be fearsome. An' tell him he need nae concern himself with yer safety fer I'll nae be leavin' yer side till the work's done."

"Shannon says the outcome will be fearsome and . . ." Kelzi stopped, a frown clouding her eyes. "Why do I need to tell him the last part?" she whispered to Shannon.

"His mind be filled with fear fer ye, an' he cannae be troubled so." Shannon peeked out from behind Cassidy. "Tell him, lass."

She did as he asked, leaving Cassidy with a look of surprise that deepened as he asked the question, "Does this angel read minds as well?"

"Tell the lad his face is a book a child could read."

Before Kelzi could even get the words out of her mouth, Cassidy's eyebrows began twitching, his eyes darting to the left and then to the right as he turned in circles. "Where is he? Tell me where he is." There was more than just a touch of frustration in his voice.

"He's beside you."

"Which side?" Cassidy answered, spinning his head from the right to the left, and back again.

"To your right," Kelzi announced, amused by Cassidy's persistence.

Cassidy twitched slightly as he turned his face to his right. He reached out his arm, waving it slightly back and forth. "This is surreal . . . like reading a fantasy book while living the fantasy—wishing you could turn to the page where the angel becomes visible to more than just the main character." His eyes focused on the unseen. "I believe in angels, Shannon. There is no doubt in my mind that you are here. I wish I—"

Suddenly Cassidy felt something brush his shoulder and the emotion of the touch caught his breath. "Thank you," he heard himself say before he found himself speechless.

'Tis ye 'oo have the faith ta believe. The words flowed into Cassidy's thoughts while his ears heard only silence.

"Thank you for letting him feel your presence, Shannon," Kelzi said as she watched Cassidy drive away.

"I cannae keep it from one 'oo has so much faith," Shannon replied. "I'll be sayin' ta ye, lass, his faith will be his guide till all things needed ta be dun' will be dun'. *Ko-hi-i-ga te-hi asgi'na ka u-di-yu-li te-hi yo-na. Te-hi wa-ya ka a-tsu-s-ti a-se-quu-i ta a-la-s-di te-hi yo-na.*" [Today the ghost will shadow the bear. The wolf will run free to fight the bear.]

"*Ne-hi a-no?*" [You know?]

"*A-ya a-no.*" [I know.]

"*Ua-do.*"

"You're welcome."

NINETEEN

The Plot Thickens

TUESDAY MORNING AT ELEVEN O'CLOCK, KELZI DRESSED IN THE DEER-skin pants, tan shirt, and moccasins before placing the necklace Shannon had given her around her neck. She climbed into the driver's side of the old relic and turned the key in the ignition, realizing she hadn't discussed the ghostly walks with Shannon.

Once Shannon settled himself in the passenger's seat, however, he commenced to explain before Kelzi could even ask a question. "Thar's nae a need ta ask yer angel aboot yer ghost walk, lass. Ye have the answer inside ye. Ye walked with the fierceness of a Cherokee warrior. Ye wer' aware of the strength that lies within ye, strength given' ta ye from yer grandmother. Ye'll understand me words more in the adventures yet ta be had."

Kelzi put the relic in gear and proceeded to pull onto the narrow road near the cabin. "I think it's more than that, Shannon. I think I also get my strength from the angel who walks beside me."

"Thar may be a wee bit of truth in that," Shannon disclosed. "But I'll nae be takin' the glory."

Kelzi pulled out onto the main highway and shifted gears, noting that Shannon's eyes seemed drawn to the driving apparatus. "Do you know how to drive this relic?" she asked out of curiosity.

Shannon gave her a sly look. "Nae, lass, an' I'd be sayin' I care

nae ta learn. Safer it be ta have a horse 'neath me. Nae needs gaso-
line, only a bit of hay an' oats. Needs no road, only a wee trail or
nothin' at'll ta get ta whar he's goin'. So, if 'tis all the same ta ye, ye
will drive. Yer angel will navigate, an' nae a soul will see the relic,
as ye call it. Only the two of us."

Relieved that the relic would be completely invisible to the
human eye, Kelzi nodded in agreement to Shannon's assessment.
The modern world did have its problems. She pulled onto the road
leading to the highway feeling a quiet moment of peace, wishing
it would never end while wishing the day itself was over. Then
it struck her. When the land was safely back in the hands of the
Cherokee, this angel whom she had grown to love and admire—
who had all the answers—would return to Heaven. The revelation
gripped her heart and would not let go. "I'll miss you, you know."

"As will I miss ye, lass." He patted her gently on the shoulder.
"But we've a ways ta go afore the time comes, an' I'll nae be leavin'
yer side till then."

Kelzi sensed the gravity in his voice. She glanced over at him
just long enough to see the seriousness of his expression, which
contradicted the mischievous twinkle in his eyes.

"What are you trying to tell me . . . without telling me?" she
asked, raising an eyebrow.

It was as if Shannon's attention slowly drifted to another realm
of thought, taking Kelzi with him. She could feel his words more
than she could hear them as he prepared her for what would be
waiting ahead for her. "What ye'll see an' that which ye'll feel will
nae be natural ta ye. It cannae be explained ta ye wit' logic—only
wit' the spirit. There are some 'oo nae believe in ghosts. They'll
think that yer nae the real Kelzi Tsali, but an imposter—an' they'll
do ye nae favors but wish ta be done with ye. They'll have no power
over ye, Kelzi. 'Tis ye 'oo'll have the power."

Kelzi thought back to the morning in the hallway outside the
law offices. "I'm not afraid, Shannon. I have you beside me."

"Aye. 'Tis true. Ye'll be walkin' half the road an' half the mud,
an' I'll nae be leavin' yer side." Before Kelzi could question his

words, he continued, "Sometimes I'll be askin' ye ta walk outside yer path of logic, lass."

Kelzi sighed, wishing she could read Shannon's mind as easily as he could read hers.

"Yer visit ta the secretary is seen as a hoax ta those 'oo desire yer land." Shannon continued, pointing to the building just ahead and to the right of them. "Thar suspicious, unbridled fear rides in thar heads. What ye'll see afore ye, this day, will be suspicion backed up by guards an' silly witches craft.

"The one inside the buildin' we're comin' ta—Andrew Perkins is the name—an' the most fidgety an' cowardly of the lot. Carries a lot of weight, he does, but 'tis all in his belly. The bloke's chubby face'll be filled wit fear an' the fancy hairpiece on his head'll fall from its throne. Er ye ready, lass?"

Kelzi nodded. "I know the script. Just lead me to the stage."

Shannon motioned with his hand. "'Tis afore ye."

A guard, over six feet tall with muscles bulging against his official guard uniform, stood just outside the contractor Andrew Perkins's office. Another guard, looking much like the first, was walking the perimeter. Both had just been hired as Andrew's bodyguards the day before.

Their eyes were quick—their reflexes quicker. They were ready and waiting, though doubtful that Mr. Perkins's proposed evil spirit was something to concern themselves with. So, when Kelzi stepped out of the invisible relic, seeming to appear out of nowhere, they weren't prepared to handle the situation.

The first guard burst through Andrew Perkins's door. "Boss, we've got company!" he shouted, his eyes wide and unbelieving, his face pale. "She came out of nowhere."

Through the window, Perkins could see the second guard standing in front of Kelzi. He listened to the dialogue through an open window, behind the safety of his locked door.

"Give me your name, lady," the guard demanded.

Kelzi didn't respond. She simply walked out around him.

"Hey, lady! Can you hear me?" the guard shouted, turning on his heels. He reached for a stun gun attached to his belt. "I think it would be wise if you simply turn around and go back to where you came from." He hesitated, letting his eyes survey the spot where she had appeared as a chill crept down his spine. "Wherever that is."

Kelzi continued steady in her steps as if she hadn't heard him.

Next came the warning. "If you don't turn and walk away from Mr. Perkins's office, you'll feel the pain of my stunner."

Kelzi was almost to the steps that led into Andrew Perkins's office when the guard jumped in front of her again, the stun gun pointed directly at her. "I'm not kidding, lady," he growled.

"Please move out of my way," Kelzi replied, her eyes connecting with his.

"I'm not moving out of your way. You've been warned. Now I'm—" A strange look suddenly appeared on the guard's face as he found himself backing away from the woman, unable to stop himself. He could only watch her as she walked up the stairs. His stun gun fell to the ground. He could taste fear. Had his boss been correct in his belief that she was an evil spirit?

Andrew's window made it possible for his eyes to follow Kelzi up the steps as well. His ears heard the knock on his door, yet his body remained unresponsive. "Don't unlock it," he said, wiping sweat from his face.

The second guard nodded, stepped behind the door, and waited. Neither man had long to wait. They heard the click of the lock. They watched the doorknob turn and the door open. A tall, part-Cherokee woman walked into the room, her eyes fixed on Andrew, ignoring the guard standing behind her.

"I have come to tell you that what you have done will soon be undone. You cannot take the land from my people." Her voice seemed to echo through the room, causing both men to cringe.

"Grab her." Andrew's raspy voice was barely audible. The hair on his chubby arms and neck bristled.

When the guard reached out to grab Kelzi, he suddenly went flying backward. Andrew felt his skin crawl. The papers on his desk fluttered. His knees went weak. He fell into his chair. His hairpiece fell in front of his eyes. The work here was completed. Shannon had seen to the confusion. Kelzi turned and walked out of the room, closing the door behind her.

Slowly, the guard pulled himself up from the floor, his face attesting to his own fear. "What was that?" he whimpered, his heart pounding in his chest—his knees shaking so bad that he found it difficult to stand without hanging onto the wall.

"I told you what she was!" Andrew yelped with the dread that tugged at his overweight body. His hands shook and his breath was shallow as he punched the numbers on his smartphone.

When Judge Fowler picked up his phone, Andrew's hysterical voice alerted him of trouble. The words he could put together set Fowler's insides on fire. "Just calm down," he finally shouted into the receiver. "It's a staged prank with a few special effects."

"That's easy for you to say!" Andrew shouted back. "You weren't here to see it. If it's a prank, it's a ringer."

"I'm only asking that you keep your wits about you." Fowler lowered his voice. "It's a theatrical attempt—a simple magician's trick to try and scare us out of taking the land we've worked so hard to acquire."

"Answer me one question, judge," Andrew growled. "With the Tsali woman dead, who else cares enough about this to resort to theatrics to scare us off?"

Judge Fowler had to admit there was something to what Andrew had said. "Be in my office in an hour. There will be a meeting with the seven of us, and we'll get to the bottom of this before tomorrow."

"Gentlemen," Judge Fowler began when the men were settled in their chairs. "Andrew has had a rather strange experience to tell us about." He nodded to Andrew to take the floor.

The room fell strangely silent as Andrew's eyes swept over the group. "None of you have seen what I've seen, so listen carefully to what I have to tell you." When he finished, his face seemed to have a ghostly look of its own. His legs were so weak, he fell back into his chair. His hairpiece slid slightly to the left side in his attempt to wipe away the sweat that had formed on his forehead.

It was a scene that would have brought chuckles and grins from the men seated around the table had Andrew's words not already filled their minds with apprehension.

"And the hunters become the hunted," O'Connor sneered while brushing a piece of lint from his extremely expensive, light-brown suit jacket. "Let's look at reality here. Someone knows something they're not supposed to know and they're playing with our minds. That's all!"

"Then give us something to work with." Judge Fowler scowled. His fist slammed again his desk in frustration. "Could it be that someone else is after this property and they're rattling a few ghostly chains to scare us off?"

Something in the judge's suggestion caught Hatchett's attention. "If I may?" he exclaimed, lifting his small frame out of his chair. "Weren't the Rannys close friends of the Tsalis?"

All eyes turned to Hatchett as if he had brought light to the room and their heads began nodding in agreement.

"Consider the possibility that Cassidy Ranny, who happens to be a very snoopy, annoying lawyer, could have something to do with the ghost hunt," Hatchett continued. "I think it's a possibility we need to consider."

Judge Fowler's eyes narrowed as he tapped his fingers together. "The kid knows his way around every law firm in the country. However, the suggestion that he might be involved brings with it a few questions. Who is he using as a stand-in for the Tsali woman? What does he know about our plan and how did he get that information?"

"Everything has gone without a snag up to this point," Hatchett reminded everyone. "I stand with Obadiah. That rascal, Cassidy, has put a hitch in the wheel!"

The room became quiet while the men considered the possibility of Hatchett's remarks.

"I suggest," Chief Rawling proposed, "rather than brooding over the question, we find Mr. Ranny and make sure he stays out of town until all the papers are signed and delivered."

"Excellent idea," Judge Fowler replied, once again connecting his fist with the desk. "Are we in agreement?"

All heads nodded.

"One more thing," Chief Rawling said in no uncertain terms. "Before we close this meeting, I want to make sure we agree that no one else dies."

Voices rang out in the affirmative.

The chief stood and placed his cap on his head. "Leave Cassidy Ranny to me." The second he was outside the building, he had his smartphone against his ear, having a brief conversation with the officer on the other end, giving him orders to put an all-points bulletin out on Cassidy Ranny. "Once Mr. Ranny is found, I want him locked up," he ordered.

"What's the charge, sir?"

"Suspicion of giving false testimony, and don't stop looking until you find him." Feeling confident that if Cassidy Ranny was mixed up in the ghostly visits, he wouldn't be for long, the chief put his phone back in his pocket and went on about his duties.

After an official call from the police chief, Detective Kennedy Slader parked his police vehicle under a shady tree next to the city park and reached into his pocket for his phone. He punched in a number and waited. After three rings, a voice on the other end responded with, "Do we have a problem?"

"That's what I need to know," Kennedy replied. "There's an all-points bulletin out on you. Have you been poking your nose where it doesn't belong?"

"Yes."

"Excuse me!"

Ignoring Kennedy's reaction, Cassidy asked for details as to why the city cops were after him.

"I have no idea but they're pretty darn serious about putting you in jail. Care to tell me why?"

There was a slight pause before Cassidy answered, "I'll tell you when you come and arrest me."

"When I what?" Kennedy shouted into the phone.

"You heard me. Meet me at the west entrance to the city cemetery in twenty minutes."

Kennedy's smartphone was suddenly dead in his hand, and all he could do was stare at it, trying to make sense of one of the strangest conversations he had ever had.

Cassidy was waiting when Kennedy drove into the cemetery. Then Kennedy listened quietly as Cassidy told him the most incredible story. However, he was utterly stunned when Cassidy made a strange request of his best friend, who had no other option than to say yes.

"Now, put me in handcuffs," Cassidy insisted before they left the cemetery. "We've got to make it look legit."

Feeling like a traitor, Kennedy did as he was asked. Filling out the papers inside the station made him cringe. But handing Cassidy over to the jail warden was almost more than he could bear.

TWENTY

The Ghostly Visits

ANDREW'S STORY LEFT THE OTHER SIX MEN MORE THAN JUST A LITTLE bit edgy. When they returned to their places of work, real-estate magnate Obadiah Hatchet prepared to defend himself just in case the ghost was to appear before him. He had a stun gun concealed inside his jacket and a crucifix around his neck. He sat at his desk and waited, his fingers tapping nervously against his desk.

Judge Fowler rationalized that he had enough surveillance cameras and enough men with means to trap the woman should she step inside the courthouse.

Contractor Mitchell Oliver surrounded himself with his workers on a job away from the city.

Theodore Angers, CEO, tried to work, but he couldn't focus. He removed his glasses and pressed his fingers against his eyes, wishing he could simply disappear until this whole fiasco was over. He drew his slim, five-foot-eight-inch frame away from his desk while running his fingers over his mouth. He slowly walked to the office window, letting his eyes analyze the movement on the sidewalk two stories below. Though his work wasn't getting done, he knew exactly how many people walked past his office building. Fifty-three, counting the four dogs on leashes, five teenagers who looked like they should be on leashes, and eight strollers with babies basically leashed to them. Then it occurred to him. A leash, though not visible, kept him standing at the window . . . restraining him . . . almost choking him, and he couldn't get it off.

The lawyer, Brannon O'Connor, returned to his office thinking nothing could be as absurd as what he heard in the judge's office. He believed in neither God nor ghost. His philosophy was that we are what we are because we make ourselves superior or inferior. We are our own creators, our own destroyers. One man (or woman in this case) cannot control another man without that man's consent.

O'Connor wanted this woman to walk into his office. He wanted to expose her façade and get on with the preparation for the hearing without any further distractions.

He sat at his desk, his perfectly styled blond hair catching the rays of the sun. His expensive jacket hung on a hanger. His expensive shirt was without a wrinkle. Everything about this man was expensive, and he wanted nothing to uproot his financial situation.

Thinking himself worthy of a visit from whoever it was trying to thwart this business venture, he simply waited for it to occur. But when the afternoon faded away and nothing happened, he was offended. Did this woman actually think him unworthy of a visit? With his vanity bruised and his self-importance tainted, he growled, "Come on. I'm waiting, unafraid. My secretary has gone for the day. There's no one to block your way."

He had just leaned back in his chair when the blinds suddenly flapped against his window. He twitched. The papers on his desk fluttered. He jolted. His eyes darted about the room. Nothing else moved. He waited. All was quiet and still, except for the pounding of his heart and the blood pulsing through his veins.

Slowly, he raised from his chair and walked to the window, running his hands over the blinds, checking for some sort of theatrical device that would trigger the sudden motion. There was nothing. He walked back to his desk and gathered all the papers together, shaking them one at a time, his eyes searching for whatever could have caused the disturbance. There was nothing.

He waited, he watched, he listened. Everything was quiet. The minutes passed. His heart finally settled back to a steady beat just before his eyes caught movement—his office door was opening. He found himself totally unprepared for what he saw.

There she stood, tall and beautiful, with the markings of the Cherokee blood that ran through her veins. The hair on the back of his neck prickled when he heard the words, "I will not let you take what belongs to my people."

O'Connor closed his eyes, shaking his head while fighting to gather his wits about him. When his eyes opened, she was gone.

He blinked several times, trying to absorb what he had just witnessed, and, yes, he had to admit he tasted fear. His mind reeled in an attempt to explain with logical reasoning what his eyes had seen.

"They are playing with our minds," he said aloud, as if he were trying to convince himself. He put his shaking hand into his pocket and removed a handkerchief. He wiped the sweat from his forehead and the palms of his hands, assuring himself that it would make an entertaining story to tell in the hearing tomorrow, as well as give cadence to an already solid case in behalf of his clients. Still his proposed assurance lacked conviction, making it difficult to convince himself.

"Well, lass," Shannon said with a cheerful smile as Kelzi sat behind the wheel of the antique truck once again. "'Twas it nae exhilaratin'?"

"'Twas beyond that, Shannon. 'Twas beyond the imagination. Only Heaven knows and understands the miracle of what I've just experienced today. I only wish you could explain it to me in words that I could understand."

Shannon removed his hat and ran his fingers through his thick white hair. "'Tis a wise lass that kens her angel kirtle, fer the logic ain't thar, nae the words of man ta explain it."

"And this lawyer who doubts God exists. Did we cause him to reconsider?"

Shannon chuckled. "He'd rather be believin' we used the tricks of the amazin' technology that abides in yer world than believe in God or ghosts. But he'll be watchin' out of the corner of his eye on the morrow. An' in case ye nae noticed, he thinks rather highly of himself. A man of grand self-importance, he is. 'Twill be a splendor watchin' him inside the courtroom." Shannon replaced his hat. "I'm thinkin' the morrow's goin' ta be a glorious day."

"Today was a glorious day as well," Kelzi added, feeling the mind-sweeping effects of this last ghostly experience. She wanted to ask Shannon to explain a few things, but refrained. When the cabin came into view, Kelzi found herself preoccupied with what had already happened and what was yet to come. Shannon, on the other hand, already knew. It would only be a short time, nonetheless, before the lass would be asking about something that would cause a bit of explainin'.

"Okay, Shannon," Kelzi inquired suspiciously, her eyes searching for Cassidy's car as they pulled in next to the cabin. "Where is he?"

"Always a step ahead of us—watchin', listenin', an' waitin', while the ones he trusts become his eyes an' ears," Shannon replied, pretending innocence.

"If he's one step ahead of us, what's he watching? Who's he listening to and what's he waiting for?" Kelzi complained, her eyes searching the area around the cabin. A sudden wave of panic hit her, and she glared at the mountain man sitting next to her. "Where is he, Shannon?"

"Ah, ye would be askin' that, wouldn't ye?"

Kelzi noted that he seemed a bit uncomfortable in his silence. "Yes, and I need an answer . . . please."

"Well, ta be right truthful with ye, lass, he'd be sittin' inside a jail cell."

Kelzi's mouth dropped and her eyes bulged. "He's what?"

"Ye heard me right, lass." Shannon's voice was kind and his eyes were tender when he patted her hand as a father would when he's telling his child that her puppy will be happy in Heaven. Then he opened the door of the pickup and slid out.

She answered him as a child would when told such a thing as she watched him walk around to her door. "And you know because?"

"'Tis the place fer him ta be, fer now, though he'll nae be thar fer long. Only till the hearin'," Shannon assured Kelzi, opening her door and helping her out. "We'll go inside the cabin whar ye can rest an' I can explain it all ta ye."

Kelzi nodded, letting him take her by the arm, leading her to the comfortable, overstuffed settee in the small sitting room. She was shocked at how completely exhausted she felt. Though her mind and her spirit were prepared for the ghostly appearances, her body felt as if it had been trampled on. She looked up at Shannon, her eyes heavy with fatigue. "Explain it to me," she whispered, closing her eyes against the world.

Shannon wrapped a blanket around her. "'Tis a good thing ta happen, though it sounds nae ta be," he began. "It tells the lad that these men think he's part of this. It tells him that he cannae come back here, fer he'll be followed. 'Twas a warnin' ta him when the police picked him up fer nay a reason than ta do so."

Kelzi was beginning to understand. "They're not fools, are they? They've added two and two together and came up with the relationship between the Rannys and the Tsalis, correct?"

"Aye," Shannon replied. "An' they're thinkin' with him behind bars, nae more harm can come ta thar plan. Now, ye need ta get rested. The morrow'll be here soon enough."

"Can I just sleep right here?" Kelzi yawned.

Before Shannon could tell her she could, Kelzi was sound asleep.

While she slept, Shannon walked outside to breathe in the night air and listen to the sounds that echoed in the mountains and the streams. He raised his eyes toward Heaven. "'Tis a fine thin' ye've had me do, an' I'll be ever grateful ta ye fer it." His brows came together, and he thought for a moment before he continued.

"Though 'tis a happy man I'll be ta come home, I might want ta stay here a wee bit longer ta be sure all goes well fer the two of them—meanin' . . . Ye know what I'm meanin'. Thar's nae a need fer explainin'."

Shannon lay beside the stream as he had done so many years before and closed his eyes, letting sleep come. In his sleep, he would have a dream of his own, and oh, it was a glorious one.

It was 2:00 a.m., ten hours before the hearings and sleep would not come to Judge Fowler. His mind was spiraling with events of the past eighteen years while he stood at the window of his den, his robe concealing the nightclothes beneath it. His hair looked as if it had been tangled through his fingers.

Fowler stared into the emptiness of the night, catching something out of the corner of his eye. It was a face—lined and aged from moral decay and eyes that portrayed guilt.

Suddenly a wave of nausea flooded him. He forced himself away from the window and his reflection. "It wasn't supposed to be like this," he grumbled, reaching for the comfort of his padded chair before his knees buckled beneath him. Closing his eyes, Fowler leaned his head back against the cushions and waited for the nausea to subside. He wiped away the sweat that slid down his face with the sleeve of his robe.

"If that crazy old mountain man had stayed up in the mountain where he belonged, the land would have belonged to my ancestors. Then it would have been handed down from father to son until it belonged to me—and none of this would have happened."

Fowler doubled his fists and slammed them against the cushioned armrests in a tantrum, demanding that he be vindicated of the crimes—rationalizing that the people had to die because a man named Shannon Ranny acquired that land in the 1780s and then gave it back to the Cherokees.

But in all his raving, he was unable to wipe the guilt from his hands. Greed had been his motivation, and with all his rationalization, greed was still his motivation—and he couldn't rid himself of that knowledge.

Now, just hours before the deed would have his name on it, Fowler felt as if he was drowning in a nightmare filled with questions void of answers. Who was the woman pretending to be the ghost of Kelzi Tsali, and was Cassidy Ranny the one behind the ridiculous masquerade?"

He grabbed his phone and dialed a number. If he wasn't able to sleep, he'd make sure Chief Rawling wasn't sleeping either.

The police chief picked up on the second ring. "It seems we're both working overtime," he yawned into the receiver.

"Just tell me what you're doing to make sure this woman is not in the courtroom tomorrow."

"The night shift is searching the outlying areas of the city for signs of anything out of the ordinary. Men are stationed around the courthouse watching for anything suspicious. If there is a plan to disrupt the proceedings of the hearing, it will be nipped in the bud. I've taken every precaution and yet—just like you—I still can't sleep."

Chief Rawling's reply did nothing to ease Fowler's concerns.

Inside a dimly lit jail cell, Cassidy lay quietly on a rather lumpy cot, thinking of the events of the day. He couldn't remember when he had had so much fun. "Mr. Holmes," he said, as if the investigative genius was sitting beside him, "you would have been proud of me."

There was movement and a loud burp from the man who had been sleeping on the cot across from Cassidy.

"Ya talkin' to me?" he asked, his voice thick with the effects of alcohol.

"Scully, is that you sharing my cell?" Cassidy laughed, recognizing the voice. It belonged to one of his friends, an alcoholic who kept mostly to himself.

Scully rolled over, opening his bloodshot eyes. A loud burp

escaped his mouth while his brows furrowed and his eyes blinked several times before they focused on Cassidy's face. "Why, Mr. Lawyer Ranny, sir," he muttered. "Takin' up the liquor, are ya?"

"No." Cassidy laughed. "There's been a misunderstanding, is all. After all, am I not retained by the police to supply their deficiencies?"

"Tha's wat I keep sayin'," Scully slurred. "Maybe not in those purty words . . . but they don' listen ta me, nether." Burp! "But I'm glad ya ain't usin' the liquor—bein' a Mormon boy and all. It can destroy the senses and the mind, and everything else in yer life."

Cassidy smiled. "You just go back to sleep, and tomorrow we'll see about getting you out of here."

"Thank ya kindly, sir." A soft snoring sound coming from the cot told Cassidy that Scully was out for the night. As soon as tomorrow was off his mind, he would see about getting this kind but terribly disturbed man some help.

Cassidy's thoughts turned to the events of the day. Everything that had been set in motion had gone without a hitch, except maybe for the arrest. And even that may have been part of a better plan.

He was grateful to his friend Kennedy Slader, who had been where he needed to be, doing what needed to be done in order to make sure Cassidy could do what he needed to do. If Kennedy hadn't found him in time, Cassidy would have, in theory, avoided the police while in reality leading them to Kelzi. He would have made a terrible and deadly mistake. Wasn't there a scripture somewhere that said God puts adversity in our path to protect us from further harm? That's exactly what had happened. One night in a jail cell was a blessing in disguise.

TWENTY-ONE

The Beginning of the End

IT WASN'T UNTIL KENNEDY WOKE UP THE NEXT MORNING THAT HE FELT a mixture of excitement and uneasiness begin to churn inside. Luckily, his wife and son were visiting grandparents in another city, making his promise to Cassidy much easier to keep.

After a quick shower, he left his uniform hanging in the closet in exchange for a western shirt and Levis, cowboy boots, and hat.

He backed out of his driveway, keeping an eye on his rearview mirror, checking for a tag-along, just in case.

When he felt he was safe, Kennedy followed Cassidy's instructions and took a road that led him away from the city, entering and exiting certain side streets until he found the dirt road that led him to a burnt-out cabin and an old relic of a pickup. He parked, got out of his car, and leaned against it, nervously waiting for Kelzi to appear—not knowing what to expect when she did.

Everything around him was quiet except for the rustle of a warm breeze. The remains of the old cabin drew his attention for a few minutes before his eyes and ears became set on high alert. Surely the woman had seen him drive up. He called out her name. "Kelzi, I need to talk to you. Cass—"

Before he had a chance to finish his sentence, he felt his head connect with something harder than his skull. His knees buckled and he fell to the ground, barely conscious enough to see the outline of black hair and the features of a beautiful woman standing over him.

"Wait," he moaned through the throbbing pain. "Cassidy sent me."

Shannon leaned over Kennedy then glanced up at Kelzi. "'Twould have been wiser if ye had waited until ye had more evidence before using a limb against the lad's head."

Kelzi let the branch fall to the ground, saying nothing. She simply gazed down at the man on the ground, who was holding his head.

Shannon knelt down to conduct a medical assessment. "The lad'll live." He glanced up, giving Kelzi a rather stern glance.

Ignoring the mountain man's eyes, Kelzi knelt next to Kennedy, doing her own assessment of him. The dark glasses that should have been on his face were thankfully unbroken on the ground beside him. His Stetson, however, lay dusty and dented next to his head. His eyes were closed tight, and he was groaning.

"Where is Cassidy that he can't come himself?" Kelzi demanded.

Kennedy tried to open his eyes. "Why did you have to hit me so hard?" he moaned.

"You didn't answer the question."

"Okay . . . okay. He's in jail."

"Who put him there?"

"Me. To protect him . . . and you . . . who I didn't know about until I talked with him," Kennedy whimpered, touching the lump that had already begun to form. "You could have asked that question before clubbing me."

"Now that that's established, I apologize for hitting you on the head." Kelzi removed her jacket and rolled it into a pillow to cushion his head. "But I don't know you, and I ask you, what would you do if you were in my shoes and people wanted you dead? Would you wait until I introduced myself, taking a chance that I might be holding a weapon?"

"You were holding a weapon, but I get your point." Kennedy groaned. He blinked rapidly in an attempt to focus his eyes. "My name is Kennedy Slader. I'm here because I'm a good friend of Cassidy's. He sent me to tell you that he is in jail and there has been a slight change in plans." He looked into Kelzi's face. "I think I can sit up now."

Kelzi reached out, taking his arm. "Here, let me help you. It's the least I can do." She helped him into a sitting position. "Can I get you some water?"

"Thank you. That would be a nice peace offering."

By the time Kelzi returned with the water, Kennedy's pain appeared to have subsided. In his hand was a note. "From Cassidy," he explained, handing it to her while accepting the water.

Kelzi quickly unfolded it.

> *Kelzi, Kennedy will watch your back when you enter the courthouse. He doesn't know about Shannon, and I think it's better to keep it that way. Once you're inside the courtroom, Kennedy will bring me to sit at your table.*
>
> *—Cassidy*

"Do you trust me now?" Kennedy asked when she finished.

"I trusted the lad all along," Shannon muttered.

"So I made a mistake," Kelzi growled, her brows furrowed deep in a self-defensive frown. "It's not the first one nor will it be the last. It's just that I'm a little jumpy right now. A stranger driving up without warning, on a day that I'm supposed to appear in court with a deed that certain people don't want to see—and who will do everything in their power to see that it is not seen—gives me the right to be defensive in my opinion."

"I understand. Really, I do," Kennedy said, holding his hand against his head. A few drops of blood had stained his fingers and darkened his blond hair.

"It's not you I'm trying to . . ." Kelzi heaved a frustrating sigh and leaned over Kennedy, inspecting the wound.

Shannon handed her a paste of herbs and mud. "Pat it gentle-like on the wound. Ye'll be wantin' ta make it smooth so it'll nae be lookin' like a mit of little bugs lyin' around, enjoyin' thar stay."

Kelzi gave him an impatient frown. "I learned to do this at the age of ten, thank you."

"Excuse me. Did I miss something?" Kennedy asked, giving her a puzzled glance.

"I . . . I was simply talking to myself," Kelzi muttered, giving Shannon a frustrated stare while smoothing the paste over the wound. "How does it feel?"

Kennedy blinked his eyes and carefully moved his head back and forth. A smile slowly appeared on his face. "Like this is something you should patent. The pain seems to have subsided, and I feel almost human again . . . and I think I can get up now."

When Kennedy got back on his feet, he and Kelzi stood eye to eye, his muscular body still a little unsteady. Maybe she should have thought twice before clubbing him on the head. Had she waited, she would have seen his hazel eyes were friendly and honest—highlighting his rugged, handsome cowboy look and the dimple in his chin.

She apologized to him, once again, for doing him harm, then asked him to explain about Cassidy's predicament. From that point, she simply listened while Kennedy told her about Cassidy's phone call and all that it led to. Then he explained the situation they would be encountering once they got close to the city.

"There are seven rather concerned men who are not sure what to expect, and a few who, by the way, are a little afraid of ghosts. So, to make everyone feel better, the way to the courthouse is lined with police officers watching and waiting for something—or nothing—to happen. The outside of the courthouse is surrounded. Inside, there will be cops everywhere watching for a tall, beautiful, determined, part-Cherokee female. I think that description matches you."

"What you're saying is that the way will not be simple."

"Exactly."

Kelzi looked at her watch and suggested it might be wise if they eat something. "I know it's only ten forty-five but are you a little hungry?"

"I am rather hungry," Kennedy answered, studying Kelzi.

"I have some flatbread and berries in a basket by the stream. It's not much, but it'll fill you up. Then I can rid myself of guilt and you can be on your way."

"But how will you get to the courthouse?" Kennedy asked, seeing no other vehicle nearby except the rusty old pickup.

"It's best you not know," Kelzi assured him, handing him his dark glasses and doing the best she could to dust off and smooth out the Stetson. "Sorry about the hat. I'll make sure you get a new one."

"Don't feel too bad." Kennedy laughed, brushing the dust and leaves from his Levis and shirt. "I've been thinking of getting a new one for quite some time. Now I have a legitimate excuse—and I'll get my own, though it was kind of you to offer."

Kelzi opened the old-fashioned picnic basket, placing the flatbread in Kennedy's right hand, before spreading a handful of blackberries on top. "I'm curious as to your relationship with Cassidy that he would trust you with this information.

Kennedy rolled the flatbread around the blackberries. "He saved my life once. He taught me what this world is all about. My wife thinks he walks on water. My son thinks he's more fun than riding the roller coaster. And I will be forever grateful to him." He paused. "Am I giving you too much information here?"

"No, I think you've given me just what I asked for." Kelzi smiled, filling a tin cup with water from the stream and placing it beside him.

"Cassidy gave me a sketchy, condensed version of this situation we find ourselves in. Then he added that it would be best if I not know any more or I might run the other way."

Kelzi laughed, and Kennedy took a bite of his meal before explaining the promise he made to Cassidy. "You can rely on me, Kelzi," he promised, licking the berry juice from his fingers and draining his cup. He washed his hands in the stream and stood. "I think it's time. Are you ready?"

Kelzi smiled and nodded. "Thank you, Kennedy Slader, for

what you are about to do for me, for Cassidy, and for the Cherokee Nation."

"It will be my pleasure, Kelzi Tsali."

As soon as Kennedy's car disappeared into the distance, Shannon stepped back from Kelzi. "Let me see ta yer appearance afore we leave," he said, holding a beautiful, beaded buckskin jacket over his arm.

Kelzi watched him rub his chin as he gave her a critical eye and asked if she passed inspection.

"Aye, but 'tis nae the inspection I'm concerned aboot, but the look ye carry with ye inside the courtroom."

"Excuse me?"

"Made these fer ye, lass." Shannon handed her a brown leather skirt and a beige blouse. "I'll be askin' ye ta step inside the cabin an' put these on, an' then ye'll understand."

"As ye wish, dear angel," Kelzi teased, stepping inside the cabin. When she returned, Shannon presented her with the jacket that took her breath away. "It's beautiful," she beamed, touching it. "No, it's more than beautiful—and why are tears running down my cheeks?"

"'Cause ye feel the spirits of all 'oo will stand with ye this day," Shannon explained, taking the jacket from her and holding it so she could slip her arms into the sleeves. He stepped back. "Ye are a true beauty, an' yer beauty speaks fer yer people."

Shannon handed her the deed, telling her to hide it in the pocket inside her jacket.

"The truth cannae lie, an' lies tell themselves. Only man can strip the truth of its honor. Only man can steal an' murder. But they forget that God is watchin' while they betray him in thar deceitful hearts."

Kelzi carefully rolled the deed inside the leather and hid it inside her jacket. Then she picked up the metal box before reaching up and kissing Shannon's cheek. "I'm ready," she said with a gentle smile.

Shannon, knowing it was going to be a very remarkable day for the both of them, pulled the strap of an interesting pouch over his head, resting it on his left shoulder. "An' I be ready."

Kelzi frowned, looking at the pouch. "What do you have in there?"

"Aw the wit I the world's no in ae pow." He grinned.

"Meaning?"

"I'd be sayin' that all the wit in the world is nae in one head. Will ye be needin' more?"

"I think I got the message. I'm just glad you're on my side."

"Aye, as ye should be, lass, as ye should be."

TWENTY-TWO

The Courtroom

As they neared the courthouse, the traffic became more congested. "I'd be thinkin' there'll nae be an empty seat," Shannon surmised. "An' on the morrow they 'oo fill the paper with thar words will be writin' the tales an' the truth all mixed up into a muddy soup."

Kelzi gave the mountain man a sideways glance and noticed the sparkle in his eyes. "I think you'll have quite a story to tell yourself when you retur . . ." The word caught in her throat, held there by the realization that this might be the last day she would have this remarkable angel at her side.

Shannon reached over and patted her shoulder gently. "'Twill be a sweet memory we'll both be carryin' with us, lass."

Kelzi took a deep breath and smiled through the mist of tears that, once again, unwittingly surfaced. "Why can't I stop the blubbering? I'm not the weepy kind."

Shannon smiled. "Aye, perhaps ye are just becomin' acquainted with yer tender spirit."

"A man with all the answers," Kelzi chuckled. "Now I know I'll miss you."

The courthouse was finally in their sight, along with the media and the people who had come to watch the show. Not a soul noticed a rusty, green, antique pickup driving toward the courthouse. Shannon's heavenly powers seemed to accommodate everything needed in this earthly adventure.

"We'll be drivin' ta the back. Thar'll be a door ye'll enter," Shannon instructed, "once I've cleared the way." He patted the pouch at his side.

Kelzi turned onto a narrow side road, following his directions. Within minutes, they were parked behind the courthouse. At least twenty policemen stood guard from end-to-end along the length of the building, their guns ready. One stood directly in front of the door, none the wiser that an old pickup was now parked next to him.

"Ye'll be stayin' right whar ye are till I motion fer ye ta come," Shannon instructed as he climbed out of the pickup, holding the pouch protectively against him. "Do nothin' till then. Ye understand?"

"I'll nae be taken me eyes off ye," Kelzi replied.

Her Scottish inflection brought a tender smile to her angel's face as he turned from her and approached the officer closest to the door. He reached inside his pouch and pulled out two skunks and a bottle of bees. He set the two skunks down next to the door then opened the bottle of bees, letting them escape low to the ground.

The bees fussed about the skunks just long enough to arouse the skunks' tempers, sending them in both directions. Their tails flipped high in the air, releasing their choking odor of defense. All of the policemen began to gag from the odor while swatting at the bees.

Shannon removed two more skunks and sent them on their way, harassed by one more jar of bees. In the confusion of skunk odor and bee stings, no one had time to guard the door.

Kelzi found herself amazed and amused at the same time as she watched Shannon work his magic, forcing herself not to think of what it was going to be like when he was no longer with her.

Instead, she concentrated on what she had to do once inside the courtroom. She moved quickly when he motioned to her. Plugging her nose, she rushed into a dark, musty, unused hallway. A few minutes later, Shannon stepped through the door, suggesting they be on their way.

"I'll have to say I'm impressed with your choice of weapons," she whispered as he led her down the hallway. "However, I worry that the scent of the skunks has found more than my nostrils to cling to."

"As ye should be," he said contentedly. "Thar nay be a hint of skunk odor on ye, lass. Nay ta fear. But thar'll be a few more weapons waitin' in the bin."

"Promise me there'll be no more skunks." Kelzi gave him a look of sheer panic.

"Nae skunks at all, lass." He narrowed his eyes. "Only what be needed fer the next encounter."

Shannon led Kelzi to a walnut-stained wooden door. "Stay here till I come fer ye," he cautioned. Then he disappeared.

Kelzi's wait was less than a minute before Shannon stood beside her again. He gave her a decisive look before smoothing her hair where it was slightly out of place, straightening her jacket, and adjusting the necklace. When he had finished with the makeover, he stood back, pleased with her appearance. "Neither look ta yer left er ta yer right, but straight ahead, as if thar's nae fear or concern inside ye," he advised. "Kennedy's waitin' fer ye. He'll see ye soon enough, an' I'll nae leave yer side."

Kelzi could feel the tingling that ran up and down her spine, the knotted nerves in her stomach, and the thrill that left her spellbound. "Tell me, Shannon, what am I to expect?"

"Ye'll expect me ta run shotgun. Nae a soul'll be able ta restrain ye from enterin' the courtroom."

When Kelzi opened the door and stepped into the foyer, she could see Kennedy. She moved forward through the crowded hall, which was bustling with reporters, news cameras, and onlookers.

The room suddenly became quiet, people staring at her as she walked past, keeping her eyes straight ahead. In the background she could hear a female commentator's hushed voice, most likely speaking into a small recorder.

"She walks with classic beauty. Her long black hair flows behind her. There's no expression on her beautiful face. Her eyes are focused on nothing but the door of the courtroom she is about to enter. She's wearing a beautifully tailored brown leather skirt, a light beige blouse, and a remarkably designed, beaded buckskin jacket—its sleeves fringed. Around her neck is a delicate necklace of silver and jade. On her feet are fringed leather moccasin boots. She stands approximately six feet tall. What I see before me is as beautiful as a Rembrandt." There was a silent moment before the reporter continued. "Yet there is something that distracts from the picture I've just described. In her left arm, she holds an old metal box."

Kelzi felt the eyes of all those in the hallway, assessing her as the commentator described her. She could feel the approval of some and the disdain of others.

She kept her eyes on the door she was about to enter when a man stepped in front of her to block her way. She looked into his face and, suddenly, she was transported back in time to her childhood home and the man who had just removed the hood from his head—the man who had stood by while another man murdered her mother. She looked into his face, keeping her anger hidden beneath a calm façade, a bit of Ahyoka's wisdom tucked within her heart. Let no one control your emotions. When anger reaches inside you and takes control, it reaps its own reward, one that takes away your liberty.

Kelzi took a deep breath and stared into Chief Rawling's eyes, feeling somewhat vindicated when he was unable to hide his shocked surprise. She could understand his disbelief. She and Shannon had passed through a net of roadblocks and countless cops outside the building before she could get near the courthouse.

The chief, trying to hide his astonishment, threw back his shoulders in an attempt to regain command of the situation. However, his height didn't equal hers, and he felt the intimidation of having to look up in order to see into her face. "It seems rumors have spread and now we have a crowd on our hands," he said with authority, loud enough for all to hear. "But no matter. I cannot allow you inside the courtroom."

Kennedy stepped in front of Kelzi, facing the police chief. "Sir, this woman is the lawyer for the defense. You can't keep her out of the courtroom."

Chief Rawling eyes were like ice as they pierced Kennedy's. "This hearing needs no defense."

"Oh, but I'm afraid it does, sir." Kennedy didn't move, his eyes as cold as Chief Rawling's.

"Are you out of your mind, Kennedy?" Rawling was livid.

"No, sir."

"Then tell me, whose side are you on?"

"The side of justice, sir. It's that simple." Kennedy's answer caused the chief to take a step backward. "Now, if you will let Miss Tsali pass, it's almost time for the hearing to start."

The look in Rawling's eyes revealed not only the anger but also the fear that stirred inside him, while the veins in his neck protruded with frustration. His voice was a growl when he whispered, "You'll pay for this, Kennedy!"

"I'm sure I will," Kennedy replied, turning his attention to the two policemen standing guard at the door to the courtroom. "Let Miss Tsali pass."

"The doors will remain closed," the police chief shouted.

The two policemen pulled their weapons and stood firm.

Shannon patted Kelzi's hand. "'Twill only take a wee tick of the clock, lass, if ye'll be excusin' me." He left her side, and she watched as he approached the two officers. Suddenly the guns they held disappeared. Shannon slipped them in his pouch while the two officers stood speechless, staring at their empty hands. Then, as swiftly as the guns had disappeared, the two stumbled over each other, falling to the floor, and the door to the courtroom opened.

The scene brought a shocked response to an unexplainable incident. Everyone took a few steps backwards out of caution, remembering the rumors of ghosts. Chief Rawling stood frozen, his eyes glazed, his mouth moving with no words forthcoming.

Without further incidence, Kennedy guided Kelzi around the police chief and into the courtroom. As he led her up the aisle, silence penetrated the room, the audience seemingly electrified by the appearance of a supposedly dead woman. Hushed comments filtered through the room concerning Kelzi's beauty and the aged metal box she carried in her arm.

Once they reached the defense table, Kennedy stepped aside, letting Kelzi take her seat. He waited until the box was in its place before he leaned down and asked, "Did I see what I thought I saw?"

She smiled up at him, giving him a look of sympathy, and nodded. "Just know that we're not alone in this battle."

"I think I'm just beginning to recognize that." He seemed as if he wanted to ask another question. Instead, he excused himself and walked through the door to the left of the defense table, closing the door behind him.

"'Tis a good thing ye didn't leave him lyin' on the ground," Shannon remarked, sitting down beside her. "Though, if ye had, I'd been quite capable of gettin' ye here myself. But 'tis a joy ta have his assistance."

When Kelzi didn't reply, he looked at her closely. "Are ye all right, Kelzi Tsali?"

"I am," she replied, her eyes scanning the courtroom as much as she dared. In her scan, she caught O'Connor glaring at her in disbelief, the look on his face almost comical in its astonishment. It was clear that she had not been expected. She gave him a nod before turning away from him. It was wise to ignore him—for now.

The door to her left opened again. This time Kennedy was escorting Cassidy into the courtroom. Kelzi had never seen Cassidy in a suit and tie. He looked remarkably handsome . . . and brilliant . . . and sophisticated . . . And maybe it's wise to cease with the adjectives for the time being, she decided, giving him a quick smile when he took the seat beside her.

Cassidy reached over and took Kelzi's hand. "Ready?" he asked.

Kelzi's reply was a simple nod and a confident smile.

The side door opened and a man wearing the uniform of the court walked into the room, taking his place near the door of the judge's chamber. The clock on the wall ticked away the last thirty seconds before the hearing would begin.

"All arise," the officer of the court's voice rang out when the second hand of the clock pointed to the top of the hour.

The second Judge Fowler entered the room, Kelzi flashbacked to a younger version of the man. He was removing a white hood from his head while her father and mother lay on the floor, covered in blood. Now, he stood in front of her as a judge. She watched him adjust his robe with a quick movement of his left hand before taking his seat. Her emotions remained without feeling.

"Be seated," Judge Fowler called out to the audience. He organized the papers in front of him before looking up at those occupying the chairs in front of him. When his eyes met Kelzi's, his face went from pallid to scarlet.

She watched him turn to O'Connor with questioning eyes. She saw O'Connor cross his fingers and nod his head. She smiled. Why? Because she knew something neither the judge nor the lawyer knew. She sat back in her seat, letting her eyes drop to the box, touching the lid with her fingers.

Judge Fowler took a pair of reading glasses from inside his robe. He put them on and made a slight adjustment so they lay straight across his nose. His voice seemed defensive as he began to read from a document in his hand. "In or about 1770, a man by the name of Shannon Ranny owned prime land in the Carolinas. Before he died, he deeded this land to the Cherokee people.

"For many years the Cherokee people lived and farmed the land. Then, as the years passed, fewer and fewer stayed until finally the land became uninhabited. It was at this point in time that one man—a Cherokee, who lived at the edge of the land—held the deed, though he did not maintain the land. The man's name was Amedohi Tsali.

"Fourteen years ago, Mr. Tsali and his wife died, leaving behind no reference to a deed in his legal documents. Other evidence determined that Tsali's eight-year-old daughter also died in that fire."

He paused and glanced up at Kelzi, giving her a frosty glare. He returned to the document in front of him, adjusted his glasses, and continued. "It was when going through the process of rendering the deed no longer valid that a copy was found in the State Attorney's archives with a stipulation attached. The wording on the stipulation stated that the deed could not be deemed invalid for twenty years after the signature of Amedohi Tsali had been placed below that of his father."

He paused again and took a drink of water from the glass beside him. Then he elaborated the lies and exaggerated the truth as he continued. "For fifteen years, this land has lain untouched, its condition an embarrassment to our community. That twenty-year stipulation has now reached its expiration date. Therefore, it is the right and the proper decision of this court that the land be sold to a group of investors desiring to beautify and develop it. The investment will not only be an asset but will strengthen the economy of this county as well."

Once again he glared at Kelzi, knowing he had to acknowledge her presence in the courtroom as well as her intention, since she was acting as a lawyer for the defense, though, as far as he could see, there was no need for a defense. Still, he followed procedure. "I understand that we have in the courtroom a woman who claims to be the daughter of Amedohi as well as a lawyer herself. She is here in defense of what I assume to be the original deed, which no one has yet seen."

Brannon O'Connor stood. "Your Honor, I would like to see some identification proving that this woman is indeed who she claims to be." He held up a piece of paper. "I have in my hand a copy of a birth certificate in the name of Kelzi Tsali, born to Amedohi and Kate Tsali, on July 5, 1989. I also have a death certificate claiming she died in a fire in 1997. There are no grade school records past the second grade. No high school records. No college records. In my research, I've found no Kelzi Tsali anywhere on the graduating list of any of the schools of law."

While O'Connor was speaking, someone from behind Kelzi touched her shoulder. She turned to see Yona standing behind her. He handed her an envelope. "Open it," he whispered.

Inside, she found three documents. The first document was her Cherokee document of birth. The name on the certificate was Ahyoka Kelzi Tsali. It listed her date of birth and the name of her father and mother. The second document was her graduation certificate from the Abedabun High School on the Cherokee Indian Reservation. The third document was her certificate of graduation from Harvard School of Law in 2011, under the name of Ahyoka K. Tsali.

"Your Honor," Kelzi stood. "In my hand, I hold three documents." As she held each one up, she explained its purpose. "I am Ahyoka Kelzi Tsali. I hold a law degree from Harvard Law School, and I am here to represent the Cherokee land mentioned in your oratory. Now, may I ask the names of those who have requested to buy the land that I hold the deed to?"

The room became silent except for the whisperings of reporters connecting with their contacts. Brannon O'Connor rubbed his hands together, looking a little peaked. The judge looked even more so when O'Connor avoided his eyes and stood, prepared to debate.

"This woman already knows the names of the men who have petitioned for this land," he exclaimed. "She has made herself known to a few of them in an attempt to frighten them into backing away from their offer by pretending to be the ghost of a woman who was killed in a car accident several days ago. She claims she has documents verifying her identity. But I ask you, whose identity? Who was the woman that died when her car went over a cliff and burst into flames, consuming not only her body, but her identity as well?"

He pointed to Kelzi. "Your Honor! This woman is a phony. She tries to frighten a few people with childish pranks of make-believe ghosts, hoping they will run and hide, giving up that which they have worked so hard to acquire. I would ask why? Does she have plans for this property? Is she involved in a scheme to acquire it for nothing? The documents she holds in her hand could belong to the real Kelzi Tsali. But the real Kelzi Tsali is dead."

"And you are sure of that?" Cassidy asked.

"I am," O'Connor retorted.

"Would you like to tell the state court judge how you know?"

From the back of the courtroom, a man stood. He was slim, of medium height. His brown hair showed signs of gray. His face wasn't handsome, per se, yet his eyes illuminated total honesty, which gave him a rather fine-looking appearance. His suit exhibited good taste without being expensive, revealing the fact that he didn't care to impress anyone.

Kelzi noted that when Judge Fowler recognized the man, his nerves began to fray. She could see the prestige of his office crumbling around him.

Cassidy turned to address the man he had just introduced to the court. "Judge Walker, because Judge Fowler is one of the men whose names are on the list of those who wish to purchase said property, I would ask that he be excused from the bench and that you sit in his place."

Judge Walker took the necessary steps down the aisle and stopped just behind the gate that separated the official from the onlooker. "I received a telephone call yesterday from Mr. Lawrence Peterson—a well-known lawyer you will recognize," he explained to Judge Fowler. "In our conversation he told me of the situation we have here today. Because of certain information we discussed, I felt it imperative that I be here at this time."

Kelzi watched Judge Walker step through the small gate and stand directly in front of Judge Fowler. His words were quiet, yet she could hear Judge Walker explain to Judge Fowler that he could not, in all honesty, make a judgment in this case that would be fair and impartial. He then handed a legal document to Judge Fowler that stated, "Judge Walker will relieve Judge Fowler of his duty and sit as judge."

Lines of perspiration trickled down Judge Fowler's face, soaking the collar of his robe. He stood, called for a ten-minute recess, and then escorted Judge Walker into his chambers.

Cassidy flipped open his smartphone and began texting.

"Bored already," Kennedy scoffed.

"I've been given an assignment from Monica and Robert," Cassidy grinned. "I'm to text them as the trial proceeds." He took a snapshot of Kelzi and pressed "send."

Mitchell Oliver, Theodore Angers, and Andrew Perkins, seated near the back of the courtroom, stood and quietly slipped out the first convenient door they could find. Obadiah wasn't far behind. When they were far enough away from the building to talk without being overheard, Andrew opened the dialogue, his voice strained with fear.

"This was supposed to be an open and shut case. Now it's unraveling before our eyes." He began pacing back and forth, running his fingers through his hair. "I'm telling you, there's something strange about that woman. It's like she's one step ahead of us, knowing what's going to happen next before we've even thought about it. It's creepy." He stopped pacing and turned to face the other three men. "I'm telling you. It's not natural."

Theodore stood with his back against the trunk of a tree. His arms were folded across his chest in an attempt to keep from shaking, while a chill continued to creep up and down his spine. "That woman sitting in there impersonating the dead, or dead herself, comes back to life to punish us for our evil deeds. It's as simple as that."

"Okay, okay. Let's not do anything foolish," Obadiah said, trying to keep his wits about him as his eyes caught Chief Rawling coming toward them. When the chief stood in from of them, Obadiah gave him a scowl. "I'm curious to know how that woman got through all the nets you had hanging out there."

The chief shook his head and shrugged his shoulders. "This is what I know." He tried to make sense of it all while explaining about the skunks and the bees that somehow appeared behind the courthouse, leaving several officers sick from the smell and swollen with bee stings. "I can only assume that this trick was her ploy to get inside the building. How she got as far as the courthouse is still a mystery."

"Like I said," Mitchell snarled, his trembling hands wiping the perspiration from his face, "Maybe she has come back from the dead. Think about it. There's one of her and seven of us, and she's always one step ahead of us—ready to take away everything we've worked for."

Chief Rawling studied Mitchell, concerned over the man's frame of mind. "Mitch," he said, "why don't you take a walk and get control of yourself before you go back into the courtroom."

Mitchell glared at the chief. "Good idea." He turned and walked toward the parking lot.

"I think I'll take a walk, as well." Theodore muttered as he turned away, following Mitchell.

"Hope they don't do anything stupid," Obadiah scowled. The others nodded in agreement and returned to the courtroom, just as the doors were closing and the door to the judge's chambers was opening.

The words "All arise" brought everyone to their feet as Judge Walker stepped through the door of the judge's chambers. He acknowledged the lawyers before making himself comfortable in the padded chair. "Please be seated," he said, before opening the folder he held in his hand and studying it for a brief moment.

"This is a rare occasion when one judge replaces another in the middle of a hearing of this kind," he said, looking at the audience. "Judge Fowler has graciously accepted the decision and now

sits with Mr. O'Connor. We shall continue with the proceedings."
He turned to Kelzi. "It is my understanding that you claim to be
Ahyoka Kelzi Tsali, am I correct?"

"Yes, Your Honor."

"May I see your documentation?"

Kelzi handed her documents to the officer of the court, who
presented them to Judge Walker.

"Your Honor," O'Connor belted out, "Documents can be al-
tered, especially if the person they belong to is dead." He turned
to Kelzi, giving her a dark look filled with hatred. But beneath the
hatred, Kelzi spotted fear.

The judge glanced at O'Connor before turning his attention
to Kelzi. "Do you have someone here who can identify you as the
owner of these documents?"

From the back of the courtroom, a voice was heard. "Your
Honor, I can identify my granddaughter."

Everyone turned in their seats to see the Cherokee Shaman
step forward. No one there could doubt that she was, indeed, Kelzi's grandmother. The resemblance was enough to convince the
judge and the audience.

"Will you identify yourself?" the judge asked, giving her the
floor.

"My name is Ahyoka Tsali, the grandmother of Ahyoka Kelzi
Tsali, who sits at the desk to your right, in defense of our Cherokee land."

Judge Walker gave Ahyoka a friendly nod, inviting her to come
forward. "Would you be willing to take the stand and testify under
oath to that which you claim?"

"I will," Ahyoka replied, making her way to the chair inside
the square box.

After taking the oath, Ahyoka was asked by Judge Walker to give
testimony to prove her claim. She explained all that had happened in
Kelzi's life. "I can produce witnesses if I need to," she said at the end.

The judge then acknowledged O'Connor. "Do you wish to
question the witness, Mr. O'Connor?"

The lawyer pulled a handkerchief from his pocket and wiped his sweaty palms before standing. "I have no questions for this witness, Your Honor." O'Connor looked down at his notes as if he needed to look at something. It was all an act. He knew exactly what he was going to say next. "I have one question that I would like to ask the court."

Judge Walker excused Ahyoka from the stand, suggesting that she sit behind Kelzi. "Go ahead, Mr. O'Connor."

O'Connor felt like he was losing control. Everything that had transpired up to this point had turned what was supposed to be a simple hearing into a charade, putting him and his clients on the defense with everything he had prepared no longer relevant. The only way out of this nightmare was to ask what should have been asked in the beginning. Anger flared in his eyes, and though he wanted to shout out the words, he forced his voice to maintain professionalism. "We have yet to establish the fact that there is a valid deed to the property, Your Honor."

"You're correct," Judge Walker replied, removing a copy of the deed from the folder in front of him. "Curiosity sent me to the archives, where I found a copy of the deed, therefore verifying that a deed did exist at one time."

"Then I ask you, can a copy of a deed prove that the deed itself is still valid if the court cannot examine it?" O'Connor questioned. "And, if the deed no longer exists, can the copy take its place as a valid deed?"

There was complete silence among the spectators, who waited in anticipation for the judge's answer.

"Anyone can make a copy of a deed, Mr. O'Connor, as you already know," Judge Walker cited. "A copy does not entitle anyone to own the land. Only the one holding the original deed has that right."

"And if that deed has a stipulation attached that requires the deed holder to sign his name every twenty years, in order for it to remain valid, and twenty years elapsed without a signature, is that deed then legally invalid?" O'Connor argued.

Judge Walker had also obtained a statement explaining the circumstances surrounding the twenty-year stipulation. "It is, Mr. O'Connor."

O'Connor gave Kelzi a hard look. "Now if Miss Tsali is indeed Miss Tsali, I demand that she produce that deed."

Judge Walker turned his attention to Kelzi. "Miss Tsali, if there is a deed, I think now is the time to let the court view it."

Kelzi nodded and reached into an inner pocket of her jacket, removing the document. Leaving it wrapped in the buckskin, she handed it to the court officer, who in turn handed it to the judge.

After taking the time to study the bloodstains, Judge Walker carefully untied the leather strings and unrolled the buckskin to find a weathered piece of parchment on which the deed was written. He found himself speechless as he stared down at it, studying it, almost afraid to touch. He marveled at the appearance and the durability of the parchment. He noted the X beside two of the signatures written in Cherokee.

"This deed is at least two hundred years old," he exclaimed. "The parchment is made from animal hide." He looked up. "The deed is authentic."

TWENTY-THREE

The Decision

ANDREW GLANCED OVER AT OBADIAH. HE COULD SEE THE MEN WERE thinking the same thing he was. Maybe it was time to leave before things got any more bizarre. Without being noticed, he vacated his seat and walked out into the hallway. It wasn't long before Obadiah joined him. They quickly made their way to the parking lot, looking for Theodore and Mitchell's vehicles. They were nowhere to be seen.

Obadiah's insides were beginning to feel the pressure of intense anger mixed with fear. "Looks like they are one step ahead of us,"

Andrew agreed, offering a bit of advice. "I'll just go my way and you go yours. That way neither of us will know where the other is hiding." With nothing more said, they parted.

O'Connor requested that he be allowed to see the deed, his arrogance having evaporated somewhat under the circumstances.

The judge carefully wrapped the deed back inside the buckskin and handed it to the court officer, who handed it to O'Connor.

The lawyer removed a thick magnifying glass from his briefcase and took his time examining not only the deed but also the parchment it was written on.

Kelzi watched the expression on O'Connor's face. She knew it would be stupid for him to request it be examined by a professional. Anyone could see its authenticity.

Judge Fowler simply sat in his chair, asking no questions, demanding no answers. It was as if he had fallen into a trance.

"Open the box, lass," Shannon said to Kelzi.

Kelzi slid the box in front of her and removed the lid.

"Take out the corn."

She removed the corn and placed it on the table.

O'Connor set the magnifying glass down and stifled a laugh when he saw the huge, ugly, tattered thing. "What do we have here?" he said sarcastically. "Lunch?"

"That will be enough, Mr. O'Connor," Judge Walker reprimanded him before turning his full attention to the ear of corn.

The spectators became instantly attentive. The box had been an item of conversation from the moment it was seen in Kelzi's hand, the moment she walked into the courtroom. Now that its contents were revealed, the mystery deepened.

"Peel away the shucks, an' lay em next ta each other in the order they come off the corn," Shannon instructed.

Heads turned. People stood, and all eyes were on the giant ear of corn as Kelzi began to carefully peel the shucks away, each shuck revealing three symbols. Cassidy watched in amazement as the symbols began to reveal their purpose to him.

By this time, Judge Walker's intense curiosity brought him to the table. "No pictures," he ordered when three reporters edged their way to the front. Begrudgingly, the cameras were put away, but the reporters stayed where they were—with recorders in their hands.

When Kelzi removed the last shuck and placed it alongside the others, she noticed something edged into the cob. She looked closer to see the piece of silver. "What is it?" she whispered, glancing sideways at Shannon's smiling face.

"Break the cob apart, lass."

Placing her hands on either side of the silver, Kelzi broke the cob in half. A thin, four-inch, round, flat plate made of silver fell onto the table. On it were impressions of what appeared to be a form of writing.

"Thar are five more concealed," Shannon said. "Keep breakin' it till they fall in yer hand. Lay 'em in order below the shucks an' remove the necklace. Place it below the plates. 'Twill take all three in the tellin' of the story."

Kelzi continued to break the cob until six plates lay on the table. She arranged them in the order Shannon instructed.

For the first time in his life, O'Connor was speechless, his fascination as intense as anyone else's in the room. He still held the high-powered magnifying glass in his hand, but the deed was forgotten.

"What are they?" Judge Walker asked, looking closely without touching them.

"They tell the story of the journey of the Cherokee people," Cassidy explained.

The judge looked at Cassidy. "Can you read the language?"

Cassidy reached up for the magnifying glass. O'Connor handed it to him without protest.

Cassidy laid the magnifying glass next to the silver plates and began reading from the first shuck. The room was so quiet that his voice was heard throughout. "What these symbols tell us," he said, touching the first shuck, "is that in ancient times, the Cherokee were called *Aniyunwiya*, meaning 'The Principal People.'"

Cassidy moved from one shuck to the other as he talked. "Their story is written on these silver plates. The plates are preserved for their people in this day, so they will remember their heritage and the sacrifices of their ancestors."

He laid one shuck on top of the other as he read the symbols, interpreting their meaning. He continued. "The plates are hidden inside the heart of the corn, which will preserve them until the day comes for them to be discovered long into the future."

When the last one was read, Cassidy spread them out once more. He picked up the magnifying glass, and handed it to Kelzi, who held it over the first plate and began to translate the symbols. As Kelzi read the history of the Cherokee people, the courtroom became silent.

> *I led my people through the narrow neck of land northward into a country unknown to us, our lives hanging on that of which we had no knowledge. We had no meal. No corn. No means to survive. We did not wish to battle. We only wanted peace and to be left to ourselves.*
>
> *In a dream, I saw the buffalo and the deer in the North Country. I saw rivers filled with fish and fertile ground with tall stalks of corn.*

Kelzi touched the second plate with her fingers, captivated by the story that had begun to unfold.

> *The Great Spirit guided us, and we walked for many days until we came to the place of my dream. Here we made our clan strong with all the earth had to offer, with all the sky had to give, and we were a happy people.*
>
> *The Great Spirit gave us a promise of a good life if we lived in harmony with each other, and a promise of the Spirit World when it was time for us to die, and our lives were content.*

Moving the magnifying glass to the third plate, Kelzi continued:

> *But happiness did not last for my people. Others followed, greedy for what did not belong to them, and my people began to suffer because of their greed. Still, the Great Spirit promised me that no one would take from us that which we did not freely give, as long as there remained one righteous brave among us. But the children of my children became war-like, making many bows and arrows and spears for battle against other tribes. It was what we had to do for the survival of our clan. We had to fight for what belonged to us, and our happiness and peace fell away from us.*

The fourth plate:

I asked the Great Spirit why this was happening. He did not answer me. I fasted for three days and lifted my spirit to him. Still he did not listen. I walked to the hills where I would not be disturbed and lay upon the grass so I could see beyond the sky. I did not move until night came and the stars shone around me. Still the Great Spirit was silent. The next morning, just before the sun came over the hill, sleep overcame me, and a vision took me. It was a vision of great sadness, and tears fell from my eyes. I knew what the future of my people would be.

The fifth plate:

They were to suffer great sufferings and become separated from each other. To preserve our language, thin silver plates were to be made, much like those of ancient days. They were to be large enough on which to write many words and symbols, yet small enough to hide, and we were to keep them hidden. In the vision, I was guided to another place, far from where we had our village. There I saw our people who had become separated, many years before.

Before my vision ended, the Great Spirit showed me what would bring me happiness until the day I returned to the spirit world where I lived before I came to this earth.

The final plate:

In the last of days, my people would blossom like a rose and would once again become a strong people—a people of great knowledge—a delightsome people in the midst of a great nation. There, my vision ended, and I awoke a happy man.

I am too old to make the journey eastward, but I

will send what is left of my people to this place. They will take the plates of silver, protected in the belly of the corn. Many years from now the corn will be given to one who will read this story of my people to many who will listen.

Kelzi took a deep breath. Her mouth felt dry. Her eyes were blurry. Her heart felt strangely quiet. She silently reread the last two sentences. She shivered with emotion as she felt the pride, humility, and honor in the knowledge that she was the one the ancient warrior was talking about.

All who listened to her words sat quietly, feeling the sheer emotion of what had just been revealed. Many shed tears in the acceptance of all they had heard them.

"Now 'tis time ta explain the meanin' of the necklace," Shannon whispered.

Kelzi stood and took the necklace in her hand, holding it up so Judge Walker could see it. "It's important that I explain the design of this necklace so you will truly understand my people. This necklace was made by the Indian chieftain Sogwili. It tells the story of the Phoenix, symbolic even in the ancient days of the earth. Here, the Phoenix burns up in flames and then rises from its own ashes to live again. What you see here is symbolic of life, death, and the resurrection. I want you to see this so that you will know beyond doubt that my people were—and still are—a believing people."

She reached down and picked up one of the small silver plates. "What I read to you from these plates is the truth written by a believing man." She laid the necklace and silver plate beside each other on the table and sat down.

The courtroom was silent. Even the air was still. From somewhere in the back of the room, a whisper rang out. "It's as if I can sense their spirits all around me. It's amazing." A soft murmur followed as the audience nodded their heads in agreement.

At that point, Judge Walker retrieved the deed from O'Connor's table, then returned to his seat. He tapped the gavel softly on its base as a signal that the court was still in session. "I think all who are sitting in this room have been taught a truth not found in history books."

He laid the gavel down and clasped his hands in front of him. "After hearing and seeing the evidence before me, there is only one conclusion this court can come to. That is to accept the deed in the possession of Kelzi Tsali as authentic. The land will continue to be protected as Cherokee land and the twenty-year stipulation will be removed. The Cherokee people can live in peace, building up their own communities and businesses as they see fit." He raised the gavel and let it fall on the wooden post. Instead of loud shouts or applause, there was simple reverent nodding of heads.

As the judge prepared to leave the bench, Cassidy signaled to Kennedy. Kennedy stood and walked out of the room through the side door.

Cassidy stood. "Your Honor, there is one more item of business that needs to be addressed before we end this hearing."

"And that is, Mr. Ranny?" Judge Walker inquired, giving Cassidy a thoughtful frown.

"I had the good fortune of spending the night in jail with a man who told me a very interesting story," Cassidy began. "A story that caused him so much guilt that he has spent the past eighteen years trying to wipe it out of his memory by drinking himself into a stupor. I would like this court to hear his story, for it gives light to much of the purpose of this hearing."

Judge Fowler had had enough. He jumped to his feet and demanded that this hearing had nothing to do with anything but the authenticity of a deed.

Judge Walker chewed on his lip, letting his mind sort out the strange order of events that brought him here, as well as the even stranger order of events that had occurred from the moment he walked into the courtroom. "A hearing is a way to retrieve information, to determine if a trial is necessary, Judge Fowler, as you already know. The proceedings so far have been some of the most unusual and informative I have ever encountered in all the years I have served on the bench. I think I would like to hear what this man has to say."

"Your Honor!" O'Connor slammed his fist on the table and stood with so much force that his chair flew out from under him. "This has turned into a fiasco. Who is this man? Should I not be given a chance to review his statement?"

"I think you should, Mr. O'Connor. Bailiff, escort . . ." He looked at Cassidy for a name.

"Scully Straton, Your Honor."

Judge Walker nodded to the bailiff. "Escort Scully Straton into the courtroom so Mr. O'Connor can review his statement." Then he leaned back in his chair to observe the faces of two men sitting at the lawyer's table, noting the drained look on their faces. This had to be the most compelling court case he had ever been a part of. A very wise young woman had prepared for and set everything in order as it needed to be so there would be no questions asked, no page unturned, no doubts when these men would be tried in court for their crimes.

The door opened and Kennedy walked through with Scully at his side. The bailiff motioned for Scully to follow him to the stand.

Cassidy was surprised and impressed with his appearance. His hair had been washed and trimmed. A shower had removed the grime and odor. A razor had removed the unnecessary facial hair. The new suit of clothes fit nicely over his gaunt body. The transformation was a miracle itself.

Kennedy twitched his eyebrows and grinned, taking his seat next to Cassidy. "The man cleaned up good, didn't he?"

To which Cassidy replied, "Indeed he did."

The judge nodded to the officer of the court.

The officer stepped in front of Scully and asked him to raise his right hand. "Do you swear to tell the whole truth and nothing but the truth, so help you God?"

"I ain't going to lie to nobody," Scully said, looking a little offended.

"Nor did I think you would," Judge Walker assured him. "It's just a necessary procedure that anyone who sits in that chair to testify must take the oath."

"Then I'm okay with it," Scully uttered after a moment of thought.

"Mr. Straton, do you know why you are here?" Judge Walter asked once the man was seated.

"Yes, sir."

Would you tell the court what you told Mr. Ranny while occupying the same jail cell?"

"Yes, sir." Scully cleared his throat. "Then the weight of guilt will be off my chest." He looked at Cassidy. Cassidy gave him a supportive smile and nodded for him to continue. "It's like this, sir. I had gone there that day to repair a plumbing leak . . ."

"Excuse me, Scully, but where had you gone?" Cassidy interrupted apologetically.

"To the home of Mr. Tsali, sir," Scully replied.

"Thank you," Cassidy reassured him. "Please go on."

Scully shifted in his seat, wiping his clammy hands against his suit pants. "Like I said, I was to fix a plumbing leak. But when I got there, the door was open, so I stepped inside and was about to call out, but the house felt kind of creepy-like. Ya know, like something weird was going on. Then I could see smoke coming from the front part of the house—the living room, I decided. And sure enough, when I got there flames were shooting everywhere."

Scully wiped the back of his hand over his mouth. "That's when . . . when I saw their bodies." His eyes moistened and he looked at Cassidy.

Cassidy gave Scully a nod and asked, "Whose bodies did you see, Scully?"

"I saw Mr. and Mrs. Tsali's bodies . . . lying on the floor in the front room . . . with blood on their clothes."

"What did you do then?" Cassidy prompted.

"I covered my nose and mouth with my shirt, and I hurried inside the room. I knelt down to see if they were still breathing, but they weren't, and I could see a bullet hole right through their hearts."

Scully squirmed in his seat and covered his face with his hands. "Then the fire started getting too close, and I couldn't do nothing for them so I ran away . . . but I can still see them lying there. Every day I can see them lying there with fire everywhere."

Cassidy stood and walked to where Scully was sitting. "It's okay, Scully. I'll stand here by you."

Scully let his hands drop and tears began to fall from his face. Cassidy handed him a handkerchief. Scully wiped at the tears and blew his nose. "It's like I said," he continued, his eyes on the floor in front of him. "I see them lying there every day, and I live in this cowardly body, every day trying to forget. The liquor helps until I'm sober again, and the memory returns. So I drink again—to forget."

"I understand," Judge Walker sympathized. "Please go on with your story."

"I heard a voice coming from outside. I hurried back the way I'd come because if someone saw me, they'd think I'd done the killing. I hid in the bushes and stayed there until I heard the fire truck sirens. Then I ran."

"I'm curious," Judge Walker asked. "Why didn't you go to the police with this information?"

Scully fidgeted with his tie, revealing his sudden apprehension. He glanced at the judge before dropping his eyes again—the shame growing inside of him. "I'd have to say, sir, that that's when I started using the liquor to forget that I didn't have the guts to tell the police because I was afraid of Officer Rawling."

Chief Rawling almost fell out of his chair in shock. *What has that stupid old man seen that could destroy all we have worked for?*

"Why were you afraid of Officer Rawling, Scully?" the chief heard Cassidy ask the skinny alcoholic, who was about to ruin Rawling's life, and there was nothing he could do to stop it. He could only sit and listen to what he knew to be the truth as it fell from Scully's mouth

Scully looked at Cassidy, swallowing hard. "Because his voice was the one I heard outside the house, and the things he said made me know that he was one of the men who set the house on fire."

"This whole thing is ludicrous!" shouted Judge Fowler above the noise that had erupted in the courtroom.

"Silence in the courtroom!" Judge Walker demanded, using the gavel to underline his words. When the room was quiet, he turned to Fowler. "You were saying, Mr. Fowler?"

The veins in Fowler's neck were visibly protruding. His shoulders were stiff, and his voice was almost shrill in his anger. "This man is a drunk," he hissed. "Can't you see the possibility of someone offering him all the liquor he could ever want, if he would sit here and tell a story so full of lies that it stinks with slander?" He turned to Cassidy, his jaw set, his eyes filled with fury. "Most likely someone like Cassidy, who already admitted to sharing the same cell with this idiot for over twelve hours."

Judge Walker raised his hand to silence Fowler before turning back to the witness. "Mr. Straton, did Mr. Ranny offer you money or liquor if you would say the things you said in this courtroom?"

"No, sir. It was me that told him the story. He didn't ask to hear it."

"And how did you get inside the house without the men seeing you?"

"Probably because I went through the kitchen door, and nobody was in the back of the house."

Judge Walker nodded. "But wouldn't they have seen your truck?"

"Not that day 'cause I had to walk. My pickup had a flat tire and I didn't have a spare. But I was never late for an appointment no matter the excuse—and I wasn't late that day either." He paused. "Many a time I have wished I had been late so I wouldn't have seen what I saw. But sometimes I wish that I would have been early and maybe . . . maybe they would still be alive . . . or I would be dead and out of my misery."

The spectators seemed all but hypnotized by Scully's words. There was no purpose in doubting them. The fear in his voice and the tears in his eyes revealed the truth.

"Tell the court what you saw several hours later, Scully," Cassidy said, urging Scully to continue.

"I went back to where the house used to be," Scully replied, attempting to keep his hands from shaking.

"Why did you go back?" Cassidy asked, wanting to leave no stones unturned that would allow O'Connor to step on.

Scully cleared his throat. "I was curious, I guess." He wiped the handkerchief over his upper lip. "I didn't mean no disrespect, mind you. I just wanted to see what was happening.

"I didn't want to get close because there was still a lot of cops and firemen hanging around. But I got close enough to hide behind some crumpled brick and watch Officer Rawling digging in the ashes like he was looking for something." Scully took a deep breath and ran his hand over his mouth once again.

"Did he find what he was looking for?"

"I think so, because twice I saw him pull out something and put it in his pocket. I was too far away to see what it was he put in his pocket, though."

Rawling's face lost it color and he felt like he was going to throw up. His lungs seemed to deflate, leaving him without enough air to speak or move. The feeling in his body slowly evolved into numbness.

O'Connor stood once again and slammed his hand against the table top. "Judge, are you going to believe this deception?" he shouted, his face flushed with anger.

"Is it a deception, Mr. O'Connor?" the judge responded, his voice stern.

Before O'Connor could reply, Kelzi stood. "Your Honor, may I say at this time that I also saw the men who murdered my parents? Mr. Straton is correct in his testimony."

Judge Walker glanced at Kelzi before turning his attention back to Scully. "Thank you, Mr. Straton. You may step down."

Kennedy escorted Scully to a chair just behind Cassidy then returned to his seat, giving Judge Walker the floor again.

Watching Scully, Cassidy had to believe they had witnessed another miracle when he was placed in the jail cell with Scully so he could hear his story.

"Miss Tsali," the judge said, now focusing his full attention on her. "I'm going to ask you to turn your responsibility as the defense lawyer over to Cassidy Ranny, allowing him to call you as a witness."

The agreement was made and Kelzi took the stand and the oath before sitting down in the witness chair. When asked to tell her story, she did so with pain and pride. "My father hid me inside a two-foot square vent. They couldn't see me, but I could see the men who murdered my parents. When they removed their masks, I saw their faces. They were supposed to be my father's friends. Judge Fowler—he was a simple lawyer then. Police Chief Rawling—at that time, a cop. Obadiah Hatchett—who my father financially helped get his business going."

Kelzi turned so her eyes met Judge Walker's. "That day, and the faces of these men, are forever burned in my memory."

The audience was once again attentive, compassionate, and believing. When Kelzi finished, the emotion that filled the courtroom was wrapped in silence—and in the silence, she could feel the presence of her father and mother beside her. She could see her uncle now sitting beside her grandmother. The four had given her the courage that guided her and the strength that made her stand unafraid.

Her thoughts were interrupted by Judge Walker thanking her for her testimony. He complimented her for having taken it upon herself to protect the land of her people.

Next he turned his attention to O'Connor. "Do you have any questions for Miss Tsali?" he asked, though he suspected nothing would be forthcoming from the lawyer, who looked as if he had just drowned in deceit.

Chief Rawling sat silently in the background. Scully's testimony had wrapped the noose around his neck. The words of the Tsali woman only clinched the hanging. Why hadn't she stayed dead like she was supposed to?

The chief contemplated his next move. He searched the room for Andrew, Obadiah, and Theodore without success. Everything was beginning to fall apart. One thing he did know was that he needed to keep a cool head for now.

Maybe the story written on those stupid little plates had some merit after all. The Great Spirit's promise outranked all their efforts to have the land belonging to another people. The police chief gave a heavy sigh and sat silently waiting for the judge's decision. He didn't have to wait long. He watched Kelzi Tsali hand a piece of paper to the judge. It had to be the list of names Robert had given to her.

Judge Walker studied the paper then turned his attention back to the courtroom. "I have before me a list of names written down by Mr. Robert Franklin, a colleague of Mr. Peterson. Until an investigation can be conducted, the men whose names I am about to read will be taken into custody for questioning."

He turned to O'Connor. "I see your name on a list that ties you to this association of men. I don't know how deeply you're involved or if you're just a lawyer doing his job. But until this investigation is over, your license will be suspended."

O'Connor tossed his pen on the table and sank back into his chair, feeling the weight of defeat.

Judge Walker looked around the courtroom. "Mr. Ranny, I'm going to assume that the man sitting beside you is an officer of the law. Am I correct?"

Cassidy nodded. "He is, Your Honor. His name is Kennedy Slader."

The judge turned his attention to Kennedy. "Officer Slader, if you will please approach the bench."

"I don't know the faces of many of the men whose names are written on the piece of paper handed me," Judge Walker said quietly when Kennedy stood in front of him. "I will leave it to you to make sure they are taken into custody."

Kennedy nodded that he understood and assured the judge he would see that the men were soon rounded up. When Kennedy returned to his seat, he patted Cassidy's back and smiled at Kelzi. "Thanks for trusting me, both of you. It's been an incredible journey."

At this point, Judge Walker tapped the gavel against the base, explaining that Kelzi Tsali held the deed and had signed said deed as the chieftain of her Cherokee Clan. The twenty-year stipulation was removed. He glanced at Kelzi, giving her an obvious show of respect, and then once again tapped the gavel against the base.

The hearing concerning the Cherokee land and the deed to prove ownership thereof was now closed. Judge Walker's brain was literally wheeling with all that he had heard and seen. He listened as the officer of the court stepped forward, instructing all to arise.

The audience stood and waited until the judge disappeared from the courtroom. Cameras flashed and reporters flocked to watch and report as two men were handcuffed and escorted from the room.

Brannon O'Connor closed his briefcase, hoping to slip away unnoticed, thinking he was lucky to have escaped arrest. His plan was to simply disappear before a thorough investigation could get underway and the wagging tongues of the others put him right alongside them in a prison cell.

The idea was short-lived, however, when he saw Kennedy walking toward him with electronic device disguised as an ankle bracelet. He was going nowhere without the whole police department chasing after him. He allowed the bracelet to be locked around his ankle and walked from the room.

"I hope you're enjoying this as much as I am," Kelzi whispered to Shannon without looking in his direction. When he didn't answer, she turned to find him only to see he was nowhere in sight. Shannon, she cried out in her heart. Don't leave me yet. However, she could already feel the emptiness stirring inside her, and her heart felt as if it was going to break.

"He's no longer with me," she cried to Cassidy, fighting back the tears. "And I feel as if a piece of my heart has been cut away."

"I know," Cassidy replied, taking Kelzi's hand and pressing it against his lips. "But right now your grandmother is waiting for you."

Kelzi quickly wiped away the tears that had managed to escape.

"I feel your sorrow for Shannon," Ahyoka whispered as she put her arms around Kelzi. "You will miss him and that is good. But he has completed his mission and has returned to his family. Yet he is not far away."

Kelzi took a step back and looked into Ahyoka's eyes. "You know about Shannon?"

"I do. He is a true man of the mountain whose love for the Cherokee people transforms him into one of great influence." She placed her hands on Kelzi's cheeks. "You followed the path that has made you equal to Shannon in many ways. He is very proud of you, and he will always be your angel."

Kelzi embraced Ahyoka, tears streaming down her cheeks. "You are my angel too, Grandmother. You have taught me many things."

Ahyoka placed a kiss on Kelzi's cheek before reaching for Cassidy's hand, drawing him into their circle. "I will always be here for you when you need me. But, for now, I think this handsome young man standing next to you is the one you need."

"Thank you." Cassidy smiled, reaching out to take Ahyoka's hand. "I feel honored to have met you, and I want to thank you for all you've done for Kelzi—for all you've given her." Then, in a tender moment, he put his arms around Ahyoka and whispered, "And I hope Kelzi takes your last bit of advice very seriously."

Ahyoka gave Cassidy a gentle smile as they parted and the three gathered together the small silver plates, broken pieces of corn cob, and shucks and returned them to the metal box. Just to touch them brought tears to Kelzi's eyes and peace to her soul. They were gifts from her ancestors—gifts that held the truth, the truth that, at last, brought life back to the Cherokee land. Truth that would protect the beautiful burial grounds high in the mountains.

Kelzi turned to Ahyoka. "Do I give these to you, Grandmother?"

Ahyoka closed the lid and handed the box to Kelzi. "They are yours. They are meant for you so you will always remember all that you have done for your people. I wish you well, Granddaughter, and remember the reservation will always be your home. Visit it often."

At that moment, Kelzi heard her parrot calling out to her. "Kelzi, Kelzi, Kelzi." She turned to see Yona coming toward her. Perched on his finger was her parrot.

"Chekee!" Kelzi cried, holding her finger out as an invitation.

The parrot needed no coaxing. "Kelzi," he chimed, fluffing his feathers and spreading his wings. Instead of landing on her finger, however, he found his place on her shoulder, where he snuggled against her neck.

"Thank you, thank you, thank you, Uncle Yona." Kelzi laughed, allowing Chekee's feathers to whip her hair.

TWENTY-FOUR

The Confession

CASSIDY GLANCED AROUND THE COURTROOM. HE THOUGHT HE heard someone call his name. From the back of the courtroom he noticed Robert's partner, Lawrence Peterson, coming toward him, his face weary and his eyes rimmed with apprehension.

As soon as Lawrence was close enough to Cassidy, words tumbled out of his mouth. "Robert and Monica are both missing. I've tried their phones but I get no answer. No answering machine . . . no nothing. I've pounded on their doors. No one answers. Now, after sitting in this courtroom listening to everything that has transpired, I get the feeling you know things you haven't revealed to anyone." He stopped long enough to take a breath. "Where are they, Cassidy? Are they alive?"

"I promise you they're safe." Cassidy ushered Lawrence to a bench in the back of the courtroom. "Please sit down and let's talk." Once Cassidy relayed all the facts, he handed Lawrence a piece of paper on which a phone number had been written. "Robert is waiting for you to call."

Lawrence pulled his smartphone out of his jacket pocket and began punching in the numbers Cassidy had given him. "Thank you," he mouthed while waiting for the phone to ring through.

"I should be thanking you, Mr. Peterson," Cassidy replied.

At that moment, Lawrence knew who had insisted he call Judge Walker. Before he could comment, however, he heard Robert's voice in his ear. He gave Cassidy a thankful nod and a look of deep respect before leaving the courtroom.

Cassidy's attention turned back to Kelzi. He walked up to her and smiled, brushing her cheek with his fingers. "It's been quite a journey, hasn't it."

Kelzi nodded with a sigh. "I feel almost hollow inside without Shannon beside me." Picking up the box and holding it close to her, she continued, "What I have inside this box, Cassidy, is my purpose of life, and I can hardly contain my emotions." After a moment of thought, she reached out her hand to Cassidy. "Take my hand so I can feel your love."

Cassidy took Kelzi's hand and kissed it. "It is you who gives me love, Kelzi," he whispered.

Just as the two stepped away from the courthouse, they heard a voice call out, "Kelzi Tsali, I need to talk to you!"

Cassidy and Kelzi turned their heads in unison, fixing their eyes on the man wearing casual clothes and a baseball cap. Something about his looks seemed vaguely familiar to Kelzi.

"Are you talking to us?" Cassidy asked, outwardly suspicious of the man—noting his uneasy stance and his twitching fingers—two factors that revealed the possibility of criminal intent.

"I am." The man stepped closer, focusing his attention on Kelzi. Cassidy cautiously stepped in front of Kelzi in case the man had intentions of harming her.

"My name is Timothy Price. Do you remember me, Kelzi?"

Kelzi studied the man's face for a moment. He had the same deep-set eyes and curly brown hair as someone she knew long ago. "I remember you, Timothy Price. Your father was our gardener, and you used to tease me when you weren't helping him."

Timothy nodded, feeling ever so much the traitor he had become. "I need to tell you why I did it."

"Why you teased me?" Kelzi asked with a frown.

"No," Timothy replied, his face etched with emotional pain. "Something much worse than that, and I can't hold it in any longer." He looked around him. "Can we find some place where we can talk in private?"

Cassidy suggested they go around the courthouse where a bench rested beneath a shade tree. When they were seated, Kelzi and Cassidy waited for Timothy to start the conversation.

"I saw everything that happened that day eighteen years ago." Timothy's voice resonated with guilt. "I was fourteen, and I was so scared when I heard the gunshots that I hid in the woods for fear the men might see me." He ran his trembling fingers over his mouth in an attempt to control his emotions. "Then I saw you outside the house, Kelzi, and it scared me even more . . . 'cause who I'd seen going in your house. I was really scared because of what might happen to me if they found me."

"You saw me?" Kelzi questioned.

"I only saw you for a second or two, just before the sun got in my eyes. Then I couldn't find you. When they said you had died in the fire, I thought maybe I had seen a ghost, but, for some reason, I knew I hadn't.

"For almost eighteen years, I kept your secret just as I kept their secret until three months ago when . . ." Timothy began to feel the pain of his next words even before he could say them, and tears fell down his cheeks. "When the doctors found a tumor inside my four-year-old son's brain."

He looked at Kelzi, his eyes pleading for her to understand. "I don't have the kind of insurance needed to cover the costs for treatments. I was desperate . . . so desperate that I let myself believe what I was doing was right. But it wasn't right. I was a stupid coward and I hate myself for doing what I've done."

There was a pause as Timothy wiped the tears from his cheeks. "I have to tell you that I approached the judge and told him I had a proposition that would be to both of our advantage. At first, Judge Fowler was furious when I told him that I knew who set the Tsali home on fire. He threatened my life, telling me I could die as easily as you and your parents had.

"Once the judge understood, however, that a written account of that day would be sent to the State Attorney's Office if anything happened to me, he caved. We made a contract. I told him you were still alive and he gave me what I needed—money.

"An agreement was drawn up that stated my son would receive the best medical treatment, paid for by undisclosed contributors to a fund in his name for certain information given. You know the rest. I sold my soul and put my child's life above yours, Kelzi. It was a stupid thing to do, and I realized the fact, too late.

"I was told no harm would come to you. I was a fool to believe them, and though I was desperate, there is no excuse for what I've done . . . nor is there forgiveness."

Kelzi put her hand on Timothy's arm. "Have you ever wondered why you saw what happened that morning? Have you considered that maybe your son had to get that sick before you would expose the information you kept secret for so many years? I believe there was a purpose for everything to happen the way it did."

Timothy wiped his hands over his eyes. "I wish I could believe that."

"The years I lived on the reservation," Kelzi said, "my grandmother taught me many things about the earth and the sky, the sun and the moon, the placement of the stars. 'All things have a purpose,' she told me. Then she would add, 'All things happen for a reason.'"

Timothy looked from Kelzi to Cassidy and then back to Kelzi. "Are you saying that maybe I was supposed to . . . ?" He couldn't finish.

"Yes," Kelzi answered. "All things are as they should be."

Timothy took a handkerchief from his pocket and wiped the tears from his face. "Thank you, Kelzi." He paused before continuing. "I missed you when you were gone. I know that sounds crazy after what I did, but it's true. I meant no harm to come to you."

"And no harm came to me," Kelzi replied, giving him a nod of assurance.

Cassidy shook Timothy's hand. "We'll pray that all goes well for your son."

Timothy looked stunned. "You would pray for my son after everything I've done?"

Kelzi reached out and embraced him. "You are a good man, Timothy. Never forget that."

After a quiet dinner, Kelzi and Cassidy decided it was time to pay Monica, Robert, and Dr. Martin a visit.

Robert was still physically weak, which was to be expected, as close as he had come to death. However, his face was retrieving its color and his emotional state was uplifting.

Robert and Monica had already received a play-by-play account of the hearing from Dr. Martin, who had sat on the back row inside the courtroom. "It was an unbelievable undertaking for the both of you," Dr. Martin said. "I admire your courage and your complete honesty." He placed his hand on Kelzi's shoulder. "You, young lady, were an inspiration to everyone inside that courtroom."

"That she was," Cassidy agreed. "And believe me when I say there was a purpose for all that happened over the past several days. That purpose was to bring the truth out of hiding and bring to justice those who had buried it."

Monica wrapped her arms around Kelzi and held her close while tears fell down both their cheeks. Then she turned to Cassidy and placed her hands on his arms. "I'll never be able to thank you enough for what you did for Robert. You are truly a man of courage."

"I can say the same of you, Monica. It took two of us to save Robert," Cassidy assured her, giving her a gentle embrace.

TWENTY-FIVE

Shannon's Farewell

CASSIDY HELD KELZI'S HAND WHILE CHEKEE PERCHED HIMSELF UPON Cassidy's shoulder. Together, they viewed the remains of a once-beautiful cabin and the old, rusty relic of a pickup. "It's hard to imagine that these were real to me," Kelzi said, touching the seared and rotted logs. "It was all so real, Cassidy. Walking inside the cabin and sitting at the table, eating flatbread with a magnificent old mountain man named Shannon."

Cassidy kissed her forehead while Chekee observed patiently. "I have a feeling he'll never be too far away."

Chekee fluttered around, making his own inspection of the ruins while Cassidy and Kelzi discussed restoring the cabin to its original state, adding a touch of modern technology now that Cassidy's name was on the deed.

"'Tis a beautiful lass, she is. I'd be givin' her a kiss if I wer' the one standin' here adorin' her, an' I've been known ta give a wee bit of timely advice—from time ta time."

A deep frown crossed Cassidy's face. He glanced first to the right, then to the left, before turning around to see a man who looked exactly like the drawing in his mother's album. "Shannon?" he said under his breath while staring at the angel—now in front of him.

"Aye, lad" was all Shannon said while giving Cassidy a wink and a broad smile.

Cassidy chuckled. "I couldn't agree with you more."

"What did you say?" Kelzi asked, turning to Cassidy.

"Ah," he stuttered, taking a few seconds to appreciate his miracle before replying. "That I couldn't agree with you more." Then, without wasting any more time, he kissed her just as Shannon advised him to do. However, he added something delicate and romantic to the moment—a beautiful engagement ring.

"And they lived happily ever after." Shannon smiled from somewhere above them. "Ah, 'tis a blessed thin'."

The sun beamed down upon the ashes and the ashes stirred in the breeze.

> *"May the warm winds of Heaven blow softly upon your house. May the Great Spirit bless all who enter there. May your moccasins make happy tracks in many snows, and may the rainbow always touch your shoulder."*
>
> —*A Cherokee blessing*
> *Shannon's gift to Kelzi and Cassidy*

CONCLUSION

Lawrence Peterson's secretary, Sally, pleaded "insanity" at her hearing, which kept her from going to prison.

Judge R. P. Fowler, Contractor Mitchell Oliver, CEO Theodore Agners, Police Chief Cecil Rawling, Contractor Andrew Perkins, and Real Estate Executive Obadiah Hatchett sit in jail, awaiting arraignment for crimes that would send them to prison for several years to life.

Through police communication, the two ex-cons were located at a nearby emergency room, where they were being treated for arrow wounds. They were arrested and await arraignment for the attempted murder of Robert Franklin.

The man who forced Kelzi over the cliff was arrested while waiting in his van for the two ex-cons.

Timothy's son received the medical attention he needed thanks to Cherokee Nation donations.

Robert and Monica were married in the fall. Kelzi and Cassidy stood in as best man and maid of honor.

Shannon's cabin was restored to its original stately beauty just as Kelzi and Cassidy planned. They spent their honeymoon there. A journal lies on a lovely restored table, in which have been written the miracles brought to Earth by a man named Shannon.

Because the rusty old pickup played such a vital part in the events that brought success to the mission, it's now in the shop in the process of being restored.

Shannon and all of his incredible and spiritual miracles would always be remembered in the hearts of those who were part of this amazing journey.

CHEROKEE WISDOM

ONE EVENING AS THEY SAT BY THE FIRE, AN OLD CHEROKEE TOLD HIS grandson about the battle that goes on inside all people. He said, "My son, the battle is between two wolves.

"One is Evil. It is anger, envy, jealousy, sorrow, regret, greed, arrogance, self-pity, guilt, resentment, inferiority, lies, false pride, superiority, and ego.

"The other is Good. It is joy, peace, love, hope, serenity, humility, kindness, benevolence, empathy, generosity, truth, compassion, and faith."

The grandson thought about it for a minute and then asked his grandfather, "Which wolf wins?"

The old Cherokee simply replied, "The one you feed."

CHEROKEE PRAYER

O H, GREAT SPIRIT, HELP ME ALWAYS TO LISTEN TO THE TRUTH quietly with an open mind when others speak and to remember the peace that may be found in silence.